NIGHT SNARE

The dark broke with a lightning swift strike of light, so intense my sight was seared and a new dark enclosed me. I hung, I felt, in empty air, unsupported over a vast gulf into which I would drop—to fall on and on forever and ever! Fear tasted bitter in my mouth, I swayed back and forth in the midst of a vast whirlpool of force that struggled within itself—with me as the prize.

I was helpless, at the mercy of whichever portion of those battled, intertwined powers won. In the meantime, I endured such terror as I had never known. For if I hurtled into that gulf I knew well that all that I, Kerovan, was would be gone, without hope—an extinction worse than physical death.

Andre NORTON

GRYPHON IN GLORY

A Del Rey Book

BALLANTINE BOOKS • NEW YORK

A Del Rey Book
Published by Ballantine Books

Library of Congress Catalog Card Number: 80-24835

ISBN 0-345-30950-2

This edition published by arrangement with Atheneum

Manufactured in the United States of America

First Ballantine Books Edition: May 1983

Cover art by Laurence Schwinger

For Susan, Anne, Marion, Cynthia, Carolyn
and Lisa, all of whom weave
their own enchantments at many looms

Joisan

ABOUT ME THERE WAS ONLY THE GRAY LIGHT OF PREDAWN, WHICH left the ridges black and harsh against the sky. Like all who deal secretly, I used this cover of shadows as I prepared to ride forth. Though I believed I was well armed in spirit for what I must do, still I shivered under my mail and leather as if I needed the cloak now rolled behind my saddle.

"Lady Joisan—"

That voice out of the dark, deep-set Abbey gate gave me a start. I swung around, my hand going without bid of conscious thought to the hilt of the sword swinging heavy at my belt.

"Lady . . ."

It was Nalda, who had been my right hand, and sometimes the left also, when the invaders drove us out of Ithdale and we wandered guideless westward across unknown lands. Last night I had given her, not my orders, but my confidence.

She had listened as I pointed out that those who were left of our people were now safe in Norsdale, that they would continue to be given shelter and work by the Dames, even as were the other refugees who had come this far, there being no near fear to trouble their future.

"But you," she said, shrewdly seizing upon what must have colored my voice, "you speak as if you will not be here."

1

"I will not—for a space. None of us can know what lies ahead from one day's dawning to the next. I have been your lady, and, in a manner, also your lord, during our wanderings. Now I must consider my own affairs."

"My lady, do you go to seek him, then—my Lord Amber?"

"Not Amber!" My answer had been sharp. That was the name we had given him when he first found us and we had thought him one of the Old Ones aiding us because of some whim. "You know that he is my wedded lord—Kerovan. Yes, I must go to him—or at least seek him. I *must*, Nalda."

I had hesitated then, shy of revealing my feelings to anyone, even to Nalda, true of heart though she had always been. But she had nodded. "When my lord rode forth these five days past—I knew you would follow, my lady. There is the bond between you, which cannot be denied. Nor are you one to abide behind safe walls to wait there in patience for tidings. You must be a-doing—even as you were in Ithdale when we strove to defend it." Her voice faltered. I knew that she remembered what ties of her own had been broken on that raw, red day when we had run from death, our escape so hard bought.

I had become brusque, for memory is sometimes a burden one must throw away lest it weigh too heavily, the past against what must be done in the present.

"To you I would give my keys, if those still hung from my girdle. I set you in charge of my people, knowing that you will see to their good—"

She had interrupted me quickly. "Lady, you have kin here. I am not of the keep household nor kin to the House. What will my Lady Islaugha say to this? She has recovered and no longer wanders in her wits—and she is a proud woman—"

"She may be my aunt but she is not of Ithdale," I had pointed out decisively. "This is our own matter, none of hers. I have told the Lady Abbess that you are to be my deputy. No"—I shook my head at the open question on her broad, sun-browned face—"the Abbess does not know my intentions. I have only said that this shall be so should accident or illness strike at me. Your authority will stand."

There was only one under that roof besides Nalda who knew what lay in my head or heart—and it was by her contrivance (that of the much revered Past-Abbess Malwinna) that I rode forth wearing unfamiliar steel and leather, mounted on a tough mountain mare, in the dim light of morning. Or would ride when I had done with Nalda.

She came closer, her voice a husky whisper. It would seem that she, no more than I, wanted to arouse any notice. Now her hand, pale in this dim light, raised as if to catch at the reins I had gathered up when I swung into the saddle.

"Lady, you must not go alone!" she said urgently. "I have been burdened with worry since you told me of what you would do. Outside this dale the country may be a trap—danger crawls there."

"All the more reason that I ride alone, Nalda. One only, who goes with caution, can slip between shadows." My hand rose to cup over that which hung about my neck—the globe of crystal with its imprisoned silver gryphon, my lord's own gift to me, and one that was—was what? I did not truly know; this might be the time for me to discover the power of that which I wore, carried, and had once used, without understanding what it could or would do.

"I have seen things, Nalda. Yes, and been a part of them also, that would make those raving Hounds of Alizon turn and run, their tails clapped between their legs, their jaws foaming with fear. I ride alone and when I return, then my lord shall be with me—that, or I shall not come at all!"

She stood, her shoulder brushing against my saddlebag, looking up at me with searching intensity. Then she nodded briskly as I had seen her do many times on the trail when we had come to the solution of some problem.

"So be it, my lady. Be sure when you come for an accounting all shall be as you wish. May Our Lady of the Harvest Shrine guide your way—for she is ever mindful of those who love true!"

I made my own farewell, but Nalda's invocation of Gunnora, the lady who is mindful of the pains and pleasures of womankind, was a warm thing to carry. In my heart I blessed her for such an invocation—though she gave it in the very shadow of the House of the Flames, where Gunnora holds no rule or place.

Or was there one behind the walls who would also give me a blessing strange to the learning of the Dames? As I headed out into the first thin light of day I thought of that other—the

Past-Abbess Malwinna, her ancient body so well tended by her "daughters," who perhaps did not even guess what her thoughts might be or where they might roam.

I had sought her out in misery, coming into her small walled garden, which was a place of infinite peace, though there was no peace for *me*, nor could there be now. Within me battled feelings that were hot and high. I had thought her perhaps too old to understand what I felt. She was so near the Dames' idea of perfection—how could she find sympathy for me?

Then my eyes had met hers and I knew that there was full awareness there. She did not weigh me in that long moment we sat so, eyes linked to eyes, or rebuke my savage impatience. All she took from me was that hampering self-pity, my sense of outrage, and so cleared my thoughts to positive ends.

"I will not let it end so!" I had cried out of my hurt and anger, which fed each other into a mighty storm.

Still our gaze had locked. She gave me nothing—I was young, uncertain. I wanted some one to say now, "Do this, or that, Joisan, and all will come right." Except there was no one left to so order my life. I stood alone.

That loneliness was the very core of what ate at me.

"I am his wife—not only by ceremony, but by my heart's wish!" I said that with defiance. To speak of such emotions here might well be a sin. The Dames of Norstead put aside all the desires of the flesh when they take their vows. "Two ways I can claim him—still we are not one!"

She did not answer—my words tumbled on, growing shriller as I thought upon my loss.

"We stood against evil, and after that, I thought our true marriage must come. He—I knew he was exhausted by the struggle, that he would turn to me soon—perhaps that he must learn a little to be himself after that ill fortune had passed.

"So I was patient." Now, remembering my words, my clasp on the reins tightened, I stared ahead not seeing the road before me. "I tried to let him know by word and act that in him I found all that any woman might desire. Marriage between House and House is not rooted in liking of maid for man, man for maid. We wed, or are wed, for the advantage of our kin. But I believe, yes, I *must* believe that sometimes a richer life comes from such couplings. I thought it would be mine!

"You know the marks he bears," I had continued, "the sign of the Old Ones. When his enemies seized and would have used me for their foul purposes he alone came. Then I understood that such marks meant nothing, he was not one to hold in awe, but one to love.

"His hurts were mine, his way my road. I know this will be so as long as that Flame Eternal burns upon any altar. But—what I had to give him was not enough . . ."

So I had poured out my hurt, and my hands had been tight upon the englobed gryphon which was all he had left me, even as I held it now, left-handedly, for comfort. The gryphon was the badge of my lord's house, but this talisman was far older, a thing out of the Waste where the Old Ones had gone.

I looked down at it. Even in this half light its tiny gemmed eyes glittered, I could almost believe that its half-furled wings had moved, that it longed to break free of the confinement of the crystal. It was a thing of Power, though neither my Lord or I knew how to use it. Also it was a Key—

I remember the words of that strange man who had come at the end of my lord's battle. Neevor, he had called himself. It was he who said that I held a key.

What I had was not enough! My pain caught at me, it had burned away pride. Pride of that kind I did not want. I shifted in the saddle, I was beyond the outermost farm, soon I must turn into the southern way-path. Still I could not control my backward-looking thoughts.

When I had made that same cry to the Past-Abbess she had answered me with what I had not expected—agreement.

"No, what you have is not enough."

"Kerovan." She had said his name in her soft voice, as if she blessed him. "He has been ever made poor. His father—to him a son was needed for his own pride, that one of his blood follow him in the great seat of his hall. Kerovan knew this with his heart before he could understand.

"Darkness feeds and grows stout on unhappiness, draws also thoughts which are misshapen and hurtful. We all have such thoughts—some held so secretly we do not know with our full minds that they exist. Yet, in spite of such a fashioning, Kerovan was not wrought into what they term him—monster. Rather he is stronger within than he believes.

"I have met your lord."

That startled me, for I knew that no man entered the inner part of the Abbey. I must have made some sound, for the Past-Abbess had smiled at me.

"Great age brings its own privileges, my child. Yes, when I heard your story I wished to learn more of him. He came and—in spite of his inner wall against the world—he talked. What he said was less, of course, than what he did not, but he revealed more than he knew.

"He now stands in a place from which run many roads—he must choose and that choosing shall make of him, for good or ill, a different man. Child, we know so little of the Old Ones. Though, in spite of prudence telling us to walk with care, we are drawn to the unknown—those wonders and perils beyond our understanding. Kerovan has their heritage; he is now like a child who faces a pile of glittering toys. But the caution born of his strange birthing makes him ever suspicious. He fears giving way to anything that he senses will make him feel instead of think. Most of all he fears himself, thus he will not be drawn to any he loves—"

"Loves?" I had been bitter then.

"Loves," she repeated firmly. "Though he knows it not, nor, even if he did, would he allow himself to be moved now. He feels safe within those walls of his—not only safe for himself, but for others. He will not come again to you, Joisan—though he does not admit this even to himself. He will not come because he cares—because he fears that the strange blood in him shall, in some manner, threaten you."

"But that is not true!" I had cried then. My hold upon the crystal gryphon became so tight that I might have crushed it.

"To him it is. Unless he can break his inner wall—"

"Or have another break it for him!"

She had nodded then. And again, when I had added, "I am not free, nor shall he be! Let him ride south at Lord Imgry's bidding as he has done. They will try to use him—even as they make wardsigns for evil behind his back. He shall find no friends there. Oh, why did he go?"

"You know why, child."

"Yes! He thought he had nothing else, that he might as well spend his life thus. So he tells his wife that she is free—and he

goes! Well, I care! I have no false pride. If Kerovan rides to the
bidding of those who would make him a tool—then I shall ride
also!''

"You shall. For this is a meant thing, and, perhaps, of greater
importance than you can guess now. Go with the Will of the
Flame. That shall be your cloak and shelter, dear child. May It
lighten your path and kindle joy in your heart at last.''

So she had not only given me her full blessing, but, by her
orders, the storehouse of the Abbey had been opened to me.
There I had chosen weapons and gear from that brought by
refugees, keeping my own council until all was readied. Then I
held my meeting with Nalda and so had come to this lonely ride
into the unknown.

My mare, an ugly beast if compared to the larger horses of the
plain, was mountain bred. I called her ''Bural'' which is a
landsman's name for a tough root it is hard to pull free. She
turned now under my urging into the trail southward that my lord
and his escort had taken earlier.

I had little hope of catching up with him; there were too many
days gone. Also, though this road must be my guide, I was wary
of riding openly.

The land was now a roaming place for more than one kind of
enemy. Before the war the Waste, which lay not too far distant,
had been a haunt for outlaws and masterless men, raiders. I also
had heard that there were small bands of the enemy quartering
the land to the eastward—though those had grown fewer of late.
Perhaps their scouts had found *this* trail, visited it to spy upon
any traffic there.

Once this had been a merchants' path. The abbey dales were
notably good for trade and several sponsored yearly fairs. However, there had been no attempt to keep this road open since the
invasion began and now it was overgrown; winter slides had cut
away slices of the way where it climbed the ridges.

I was glad of the coming of better light, for several times I had
to dismount and lead Bural over loose footing. Still I was not too
delayed until the second day of travel when a thick mist became
a threat. It was so complete a cloaking of the ground that I could
see less than a sword's length before me. Moisture gathered on
my helm, trickling down to wet my face, and my hands were
clammy on the reins as I led the mare on.

To continue so blindly was folly. I began to look for shelter. There were rocks and heaps of stone in plenty, but nothing in the way of a cave or even a half-roofed crevice. I had no mind to squat on wet stones in the open while waiting for better weather.

Then, before us reared a sudden barrier of rock. Bural jerked at the reins, turned her head stubbornly to the left, though whether that was north, south, east, or west, I could not have said. We had left the road earlier, as it lay straight and open for a space and I had no mind to be seen.

Since the mare was so stubborn, and the footing seemed less loose in that direction, I allowed her her will. Thus we skirted along the wall so closely that now and then the saddlebag brushed the stone. I do not know when I first noticed that it was not just an escarpment of natural rock, but in truth a wall made to some purpose.

The stones, though rough and very large, had been laid with such skill that I do not believe I could have forced the point of my belt knife into the cracks. Though on other rocks one could see the ash-green or rusty-red of lichen in growth, this wall was clear except for runnels of moisture condensed from the fog.

I was certain we had come upon another ruin of the Old Ones and I paused, holding out the gryphon as a test. The crystal was, as ever, warm, while the glittering eyes of the imprisoned beast were bright, but there came no real glow. Not all the remains scattered about the Dales were imbued with unknown Power. There were many no different from the new-made ruins of our own where war had swept. I judged this to be one of the dead places where I had nothing to fear.

Bural plodded steadily on. There was no break in the wall. Then, suddenly, the mountain mare snorted, her head came up higher as if she had scented something through the mist. She hastened pace, pulling determinedly when I would have held her back.

I drew the dart gun for which I had but little ammunition, took Bural's reins into my left hand. Swordplay I would trust to only as a last resort.

Now I smelled it also, hanging heavily entrapped in the mist, wood smoke! We could not be too far from a fire.

Before I could silence her, Bural uttered a loud whinny—and was answered! There was no holding her wiry strength, though my tight grasp on the reins brought her head around. She bucked and kicked out. Our struggle carried us into an open space where the wall came to an abrupt end.

In the murk there was a ruddy glow which must mark a fire. I saw a shape, well-veiled by the mist, coming from it toward me. As I brought up the dart gun, Bural broke away and went trotting straight to the fog-muted flames.

I dared not be set afoot in the wilderness, so must get the mare back, though that fire, in this place, was likely tended by enemies rather than friends. No refugees would have willingly chosen these barren heights as their road.

The one coming toward me swung aside to let Bural pass, making no attempt to catch at her dangling reins. Tall—plainly a man. Now I could see he carried bared steel. I must hold my own fire until I had a better target, for he probably went mailed.

I had seen death and had been ready to kill. But then my actions had been in defense, for myself or the lives of others. To shoot coolly thus, I discovered, was a difficult thing.

"Jervon!" A hollow call came from the ruddy blotch of flames behind the advancing man. He did not turn his head, but he stopped and stood, his sword still in his hand. All I could see of his face beneath the rim of his helm was a whitish blur, for as he halted, so did I, still and waiting.

Another came out of the fog, near to the height of the man but more slender. The newcomer held out both hands, shoulder high, palm out, in the age old sign for truce. Passing the man, that second stranger approached me confidently as if we were kin meeting.

The mail this warrior wore had a strange bluish hue, as if fashioned of a different metal. I slowly lowered the dart thrower, yet did not slide it back into the loop on my belt. Now the mist ceased to mask all so completely and I was looking into a face browned by the sun, yet of delicately cut feature. I was fronting not another man but a woman going armed like myself.

Her hands dropped, but not to draw a weapon, rather so her forefingers sketched in the damp air a sign. I saw that symbol gleam sharp and clear for a space of three or four breaths and then fade. It was blue—yet partly green—and I knew it for a manifestation of Power.

An Old One?

I drew a deep breath, put the dart gun away, knowing well that no man-made weapon could be used against such. Also I knew that any of the Power that was without harm for my kind was of that pure color. Just as places of safety in the Dales glowed the same shade by night.

She smiled, this woman of the Old Ones. Then she nodded as if the answer to some riddle had become clear. Now she held out her right hand to me.

"Come." That was neither order nor invitation, but lay between. Her fingers closed on mine as I unconsciously reached out. They held fast as if she half-expected me to jerk away.

Her flesh was as damp and chill from the mist as mine, but no different, that I could see, from humankind. I was sure she meant me no harm. Rather she looked on me with a smile as if I were one she had been awaiting for a long time.

She drew me on to the fire, and I went willingly enough. As we passed the man, he fell in on my other side, his sword now sheathed. He had a strong, comely face, though there were lines laid deep about his eyes and lips. Yet now he also smiled in welcome, as if he were brother-kin.

I sensed almost from the beginning that there was a deep bond between these two. They did not speak to each other or to me, but the three of us came companionably to a pocket where the fire had pushed back most of the mist.

Beyond the flames were two of the larger horses of the lower Dales, now rough of coat, such as my uncle had once prized in his stables before he rode south to die. There was also a pack pony, by which Bural stood, stretching out her head so that they might rub noses. All three of the horses had been stripped of gear, which was piled, saddles and packs together, behind the fire. At the side of that were spits whittled from wood impaling the fat, dripping bodies of three hill hens. The scent of the roasting meat made my mouth water.

The woman laughed, pointing to the hens.

"See even Gunnora has prepared for your coming. There is plenty for all of us. Sit, rest, and eat. But first—" She turned to her companion who, without a word, fetched a small saddle cask, drew the stopper from it with his teeth, while in his other hand he held a horn cup into which he then poured liquid from the cask.

The woman took the cup and pressed it into my hands, serving me in the manner that the lady of a Dale keep does an honored guest—the welcome cup to wash trail dust from a wayfarer's throat before he announces himself and his business.

Old formal manners—I remembered to bow instead of curtsy, and the proper words came to me without trying. "To the givers of the feast, thanks, fair thanks. For the welcome of the gate, gratitude. To the rulers of this house, fair fortune and bright sun on the morrow."

As I drank, the lady's nose wrinkled and she chuckled.

"For that last wish, we may all petition whatever Powers aid travelers here. Unless"—she raised a long finger, as she had used it pen fashion in the air earlier, and nibbled at it—"unless all this has been the work of some Plan."

I saw her companion frown slightly, as if a memory he did not like touched him. Studying them both in this better light I thought that he was just such a man as one might find in any Dale force, though one of rank to seat at the high table. Yet at the fore of his tarnished helm (for his armor had none of the brightness of hers) there was no longer any house badge. I found his face frank, open, strong of mouth and jaw as a man's should be, with an air of confident purpose about him.

The lady—I was sure she was not of Dale blood, which here in High Hallack, could only mean strange kin, Old. Though she also wore a helm, a small wisp of hair (as if she had assumed that head covering hurriedly at my coming) lay loose on her cheek. The color was very dark, also her features were thinner, sharper, and her eyes very large. I had never seen her kind in any Dale holding.

While I drank the welcome cup, they both sat at ease, cross-legged, on either side of me. I wondered what to say beyond the courtesy of my name. They could well wonder why I wandered alone among the hills, but to entrust strangers with the nature of my mission was folly.

Kerovan

IN A LAND SUCH AS OURS A MAN IS WARY OF DREAMS. WE OF THE Dales carry old fears, not the least being that perhaps, when we dream, our innermost selves receive warnings, orders . . . Save that we carry into waking only broken shards, to be haunted by them. Can a man dream himself into madness? I have sometimes feared so. For I was haunted . . . Yet with the coming of each morning I hoped again to wake from the shadow which new deep dreams had laid upon me and which I never could remember.

In a way I was captive—to whom or what I could not name.

When I last went into the Waste it was in search of Joisan to whom I owe duty. Yes, I *will* have it so—duty only. She must not be more to me. No matter what boy's hopes I once held, I recognize that they are not for my kind—half man, half—what? At least I now have the courage to know myself for what I am and show it. I need only look at my bootless feet, bare after all those years when I tried to conceal my otherness, to see the hooves upon which I walk . . .

I went then into the Waste, still, in part, Kerovan of Ulmsdale. What did I come out as? I do not know. Perhaps I will never learn—maybe for my own good. Yet I was driven by restless loneliness, sharp as any sword point against my flesh.

Joisan—no, I will not think of Joisan. I will harness my

determination to keep her out of my mind. I need only remember how they looked at me in Norsdale when I brought her there—safe, still her own woman. Then I broke our wedding bonds, I evoked wife-right for her, since she would not for herself.

That woman—the Past-Abbess . . . No, I will not think of her either. Their world is not mine. In truth, I felt no tie with the Dales, even though Lord Imgry had summoned me again. Because nothing, any longer, has meaning for me, I have answered his order.

Yet the dreams come and I cannot tear them out of my aching head as a man tears away the badge of a lord he no longer serves. I hate to sleep—unless it be to drop into darkness without another awakening.

My escort sit and talk around the fire well beyond me. Men, as I once was, or seemed to be. They avoid me and I know it is only Imgry's will that has kept them in my company.

Once I was fascinated by the Old One's secrets. I had gone exploring in the Waste with the Wiseman Riwal. Together we rode the Road of Exile. No—I am not going to remember!

Hair—like the polished leaves of autumn, her quick steps, her voice . . . Too strong a memory, a hurting which will never heal. I will not remember! I am not the Kerovan that was . . .

To tramp about the camp at night is a way to keep awake. My body aches with fatigue. The men watch me from the corners of their eyes, whisper. I do not allow myself to think of them—or . . .

However, one cannot fight sleep forever. I dream again . . .

There was one of the Old Ones—Neevor—I remember his name. Who he was or what I do not know. Once—twice—he has given me aid. A friend? No, those such as I have no friends. When I am awake I try to think of Imgry and what he wants of me. A cold man, strong with a pride that feeds on accomplishment, on strength of will and purpose.

We of the Dales (once I *was* of the Dales) have never given oaths to any one overlord. That was our great weakness when the invaders, having tested us with their spies, struck our land. Each lord fought for himself to defend his own holdings, so was speedily overrun.

Painfully we learned our lesson. The sea coast by then lay in their hands, while those among us who had the grace and largeness of spirit to attract others to serve under them were dead—either slain in fruitless battle, or by assassination. Only then we drew together under three of the southern lords who were far-seeing and strong enough to make a kingdom of sorts out of a loose confederation of holdings.

Of these Imgry is the least liked. However, no man who has served with him can deny that he has the iron will to gather support. A man does not have to be loved to be well served. He, most of all, drew together our broken forces, hammered them mercilessly into an army where old feuds were unallowable—an army knowing only one enemy, the Hounds of Alizon.

Only that army was so battered and weary they could make no real stand. They raided, like the snarling outlaws of the Waste, fighting like wolves even as those canny beasts hold to pack-kin.

Still the invaders poured into the port they had taken. The only advantage we had was that they brought no more of those strange weapons from overseas which had given us such blows—rolling over strongholds as a man steps upon a hill of ants. Those, we were told by the few prisoners we took, were not of Alizon but a new magic known to allies of our enemies.

The fact that these land-crawlers were broken, or helpless, for some reason we did not understand, meant little for they still had men and weapons in plenty. Though our smiths labored in the far western Dales, we could not make one dart do the work of two, and we must at times raid for the very supplies we needed.

I had been one of the scouts seeking out such supplies. My childhood in the far Dales, where I had been fostered with a hunter, gave me skills for such work. I had been content to serve so, for among my own kind I was suspect even before my physical differences were known—monster—half-man—rumor had always played with me.

Imgry had sent me north months ago because my father ailed. Also, there was always the chance that the Hounds, nosing along the coast, might strike inland there. I had visited Ulmsdale in secret, learning then that I had enemies of my own blood, my closest blood. My mother had hated me from birth, not altogether because of my misshapen body but because (as I learned) I failed to be the weapon she had sought, with her limited learning of ancient Power, to forge.

Too proud she had been of that learning; I was not her only

failure: When she and her companions sought to summon the sea to blast Alizon's men, they instead flooded the Dale itself and there remained no lordship for anyone. When I then would have returned to my duty with the army, I discovered the enemy between me and the Dale forces. Striking westward I had found— my lady . . .

No, I would not think of her as that—even though, by all the laws of the Dale, we were securely wed and had been since childhood, long before we ever saw each other. Joisan . . .

I cannot master my thoughts any more than I can master my dreams. I see her with her people, I see her with my cousin Rogear, who came to her under my name—she believing me to be an Old One; I see her in the Waste, under Rogear's control, being used by him and my mother as a tool because in her hands was that thing of true Power which I had found and given to her—the ball with its imprisoned gryphon.

Yes, I cannot flee her in mind as I have in body. I see her always, proud, full of courage, kind of heart, all things a man wishes for. A *man*—I was not a man, yet still I want her.

Why does she linger so in my mind—I have released her? There are good men in plenty in the Dales to give her all she deserves. I am not to be numbered among them.

I rode away more to free myself from her than because Imgry summoned me, let me face the truth of that. And I am so tired—yet when I sleep I dream . . . Still I must sleep—though there is a pride in me which will not let me show fatigue or weakness to those who ride with me. Yet at last I must give way . . .

The hall was so vast that its walls lay beyond my sight. Great pillars formed aisles along which drifted wisps of sweet-smelling mist, which coiled and wove patterns in the air as if invisible hands played with their ribbon lengths. There were no torches, no wall lamps, but there was light.

I moved between two lines of the pillars, seeing as I passed that runes were graven over their surfaces. These runes, also, held light of their own, some gray as early dawn, some faintly blue.

The runes bothered me. I should be able to read them—the messages they carried were or had once been of vast import— perhaps the history of a people or a nation long since vanished.

For this place was very old—the feeling of age lay so strong that it was a weight to press upon any venturing here.

Age—and knowledge. Our own keeps had their record rooms. There is something in a man which makes him wish to leave some remembrance of his life and deeds. However, the records of my people were as meaningless scrawls made with a twig in river sand compared to all this. Also it was a place of Power. Power that could be felt, tasted, filled this place throughout.

Still, I was awed, but not fear-ridden. All here seemed so far removed from the being I was that I could not be touched by it. The being that I was . . .

I was Kerovan. I clutched tightly at that scrap of identity. Where I was I did not know, but who I was—that I could not forget. My decision held defiance.

The pillars became only shadows I passed at a swift, steady pace. Though I heard nothing audible I was aware of a kind of whispering inside my head—small bodiless things pushed and plucked at some protective covering over my thoughts, striving to win an entrance.

Ahead was an intensifying of the light. The radiance, centered at that spot, began to change color, deepening to blue—then fading to a silver that was like a fire for brilliance.

Though I had no sense of my feet pressing any pavement, I sped along as might a runner intent upon his goal. There was a rising excitement in me as if I were indeed engaged in a race and that the end of it, for good or ill, lay just ahead.

That which was so alight was a dais, a point of which extended toward me. I guessed from what I could see that its full shape was that of a star. On that stood what might be an altar wrought of crystal—an altar—or a tomb—for a form rested within.

I reached the point of the star, there to sway dizzily for a moment—forward with the impulse that had borne me here, back when I encountered resistance from the air itself. Perhaps this formed a protection for the sleeper.

He was neither man nor bird; still a part of both species seemed fused in him. Though, as I looked upon him, this unnatural coupling seemed natural and right. His face was avian—provided with a bill-like extension, which was both nose and mouth; wide, if now closed, bird eyes. On his head rose a crest of feathers, which extended, growing smaller, down to his shoulders, then along the upper parts of his arms. However, his feet were not birdlike—rather broad paws showing the tips of mighty talons, which must have been withdrawn into sheaths. On the contrary, however, his hands were a bird's claws, laced together about the hilt of a sword, unsheathed, unblemished by time, the blade appearing not steel but a rod of light.

All this and yet he was no monster. Rather the same awe that had filled me since I came here intensified. There, surely, lay one who in his own time had been far greater than any of those who call themselves "men."

Why I had been summoned to this place I did not know, for summoned I was sure I had been. Those whispers in my head grew stronger, battered harder, with an almost frantic intensity as if they had but a little time in which to deliver some message and feared their mission was in vain.

Still I gazed upon the sleeper. More and more it seemed to me that there was something about him that was of the gryphon— that symbol of my House, which also hung imprisoned in crystal in the ball that Joisan wore. He lacked the beast body, the wings—yet his avian face—crested head—paw feet—claw hands— yes, there was a likeness.

That thought opened the door for an instant to the whisperers, for they became audible at last.

"Landisl, Landisl!"

I turned my head back and forth as one does to dislodge buzzing woodsflies, trying to escape that shrilling. Once before I had heard that name—for name it was—but where and when?

Memory opened—*I* had called it when I had faced the black sorcery of my mother's and Rogear's raving, though then it had been so alien that I had not understood.

"Landisl." My own lips shaped that once . . .

There followed a moment of dark, a twisting and wrenching, as if my body had been seized and jerked out of one life into another. I opened eyes upon light. But it was not the brilliance of the star dais. I blinked and blinked again, stupidly, be- mused . . . There was a fire, born of wood, real, of this world . . .

Standing over me was the chief of those sent by Imgry. Behind him the other men stirred in the early morning light. I felt a surge of rage—I had been so close to knowing—learn-

ing . . . This dolt had broken the dream—the first dream that had
meant something, from which I might have learned!

I still found difficulty in seeing trees instead of pillars—
fire . . . This time I did not lose the details I dreamed. Rather I
carried with me, as we got to horse and rode on through the
morning mists, a vivid memory of that other place.

In fact, I became more and more sure that that had been no
ordinary dream. Instead, part of me, which thought and could
remember, had been drawn into another time—or world—where
there still did lie the body of the gryphon-man, sleeping or dead.

"Landisl." I tried to shape that name waking and found that
now it was distorted, sounded so unlike, that I caught my tongue
between my teeth. Nor did I exchange any words with my
companions. I did not even note when they forged ahead, leaving a gap between us.

Finally I summoned resolution and shut the vision or dream
back into memory. I had an odd feeling that if I allowed myself
to dwell upon it too long, or too often, I might be lost somewhere, between the world in which I now moved and that other
place.

I concentrated with determination on what lay about me—the
morning's warmth of sun, the track along which we rode, even
the men of our company. My old scouting instinct returned and I
was as alert as if I moved on a foray.

Now I wanted to talk, though heretofore I had held aloof from
the others, speaking only when spoken to, which was seldom.
That the war in the south was in stalemate I gathered from
comments I had heard. Our own fighting had become a smatter-
ing of raids made by small squads of men. Imgry and his two
fellow-leaders were busied about the foraging of weapons, the
rebuilding or building of a closer knit army, under tight leadership.

The invaders, also, appeared less aggressive, willing to hold
to what they had seized, but making few attempts to enlarge that
territory. Two of the men I traveled with had been talking
eagerly of a Sulcar ship, which had made a landing to the far
south and been met by a scouting party.

Those hardy merchant adventurers had brought news of a
second war overseas, one that hampered the plans of Alizon. The
Sulcars, always fighters, had taken with them an invitation to
come coast raiding if they could, taking toll of the invaders'

captured seaports. Whether anything might come of this loosely discussed alliance no man knew, but the possibility was heartening.

However, we all knew that the Hounds must be defeated in the Dales, and that we alone must face the struggle for freedom. That was dictated, not only by stiff Dale pride, but the fact that we could claim no other allies—having always been a lone people living much to ourselves.

Or were we alone? I looked to the west as that thought stirred in my mind. In the beginning, generations ago, the Dalesmen had come up from the south. We are a legend-loving people with our songsmiths ever ready to blow up a small encounter into an epic battle. Oddly enough, though, we had no tales of our race that reached farther back than our coming into High Hallack. That our fathers then built well-fortified keeps here suggested they had left behind turmoil and trouble.

What they had fled from we do not know. We are not nomads by nature. Each lord kept his fort-keep snug, trained his sons to war as a matter of course. Yet we had faced no threat, until the coming of Alizon, that was more than a brush with outlaws, a kin feud between one Dale and the next.

Our people had come, however, into a haunted land. The Old Ones (and how many races and kingdoms there had been of them we shall never know) had already withdrawn. They left behind them numerous traces of their own, alien to humankind. There are places where no man dares venture, not only for his life's sake, but also because of a threat to his spirit. Other places are known to welcome, bring peace and healing. Some of our blood sought out what small secrets they could uncover, but that lore was often baffling.

However, though the Old Ones had left coast and Dales for some compelling reason, we are all certain they had not altogether withdrawn from our world. There was the Waste to the west, a vast buffer between us and even more unknown land, full of signs of Power, potent places. We knew well that there was life there—besides the outlaws—perhaps left to spy upon us, perhaps utterly uncaring, since their affairs and desires might be so far removed from those we understood.

There were fighters among the Old Ones—we have found traces of ancient and terrible wars. Metal seekers have brought out of the Waste masses so congealed and melted that it proved such had been the targets of vast forces.

If the Dalesmen had first believed that they only lived in High Hallack on sufferance, long, undisturbed years had lulled us into thinking that we had nothing to fear from those others. Still— suppose that the invaders, who knew nothing of this land, the things that trod the Waste, were to overrun us? Where next would they strike? Would they be stopped by legends and shadows?

We were not even sure why those of Alizon were unleashed upon us, traveling overseas to expend such fury upon a country, which, by all accounts, was far less rich and useful than their own. I had heard one story that a high-ranking prisoner, taken when one of their mighty earth-crawlers had broken down, reported that those who had lent them those alien weapons had said the secret of vast power was to be found here—enough to make them masters of the world. So their ruler lusted for that.

The only place where such a Power could be found might be the Waste, or in a land that might lie beyond that. If that belief was what had brought the Hounds upon us . . . Then—could those of the Waste be made to see that they had a part in our war?

No thinking man doubted that if Alizon invaded there they would come up against potent forces. But could the wielders of those be persuaded *now* to lend aid to the Dales?

I chewed upon that, finding it held a flavor I liked. To meddle with Power on our own, as my mother and Rogear had sought to do, was fatal folly. However, to enlist on our side those who had tamed it was another thing. Had *this* lain somewhere in Lord Imgry's mind?

I sent my horse forward with a click of tongue, suddenly eager to reach the journey's end—as we did by nightfall.

My last meeting with the southern leader had been in a forester's hut, no trappings of state had backed that tall man with the cold greenish eyes. Now I sat on a stool in a small keep's great hall.

Imgry occupied a high-backed chair which had been taken from the dining dais, yet still raising him above those who came to him. The man's authority was like an unseen armor, though the latter in truth he did not wear at present, only the plain leather of a lord home from a day's hunting. The hunt he spoke of, though, lay before and not behind him.

I had waited for some change of countenance when he sighted my bared hooves—they had been boot-hidden at our last meeting. Only I came to believe that indeed I could have been as inhuman as the gryphon-man of my night vision and he would not have noted the difference since I was there to serve a purpose.

For Imgry, only his own ambition and aims had importance. Everything he said, thought, acted upon, was for one purpose alone—to achieve plans that burned in him, to the extinction of all else.

He had laid out on the bench between us a much creased and spotted leaf of parchment. There were marks on it that my own past scouting had added, but much was blank, and, upon that blank surface, his hand lay now, palm flat.

"The answer lies here." That he was so frank with me was enough to make me wary. It was not in his nature to share even the thin edge of his plans with another. Neither was it in him to be conciliatory, to ask instead of order.

"Be a little more plain with me my lord!" During the time since I had at last accepted this man's orders I had gained freedom of a sort—at high price. He could not overawe me any longer.

"We have accomplished much." That was not boast, but a matter of fact. "Our smiths have worked the metals that came out of the Waste—in spite of the danger. We have now many weapons better than any of us have ever seen. We gather men—but also we have lost." Now the palm lying on the map clenched into a fist. "Still the invader ships land fresh troops. Oh, it is true that they have not advanced against us in force for a time. But that is not because we have held them. We can as yet only worry their flanks, strike a small blow here, another there. Though"—there was a faint satisfaction in his tone now—"they have at last learned the folly of pursuing us too far into land we know far better than they. Now"—he leaned forward a fraction—"*we* have learned for certain something new—"

When he paused I dared to strike in with a question. "Is it true they seek some mysterious power?"

He shot me a glance so sharp and piercing he might have used the dart thrower on his belt.

"So men talk openly of that?"

I shrugged. "It was a story told even before I rode north. There must be some sane reason why Alizon harries us, when, if we are to believe the word of traders, there is nothing in this land to match theirs. *We* possess no treasure."

There was no deference in what I said. I spoke as equal to equal. Imgry was a force, yes, and those of the Dales might be very glad it was wielded for them. However, he no longer impressed me. I was, in a way, inner-walled against him now.

He studied me with narrowed eyes. I think I had suddenly become a person, not a weapon ready to his hand. That impatience that lay ever close beneath the surface of his manner retreated a little. He considered me in a new way for I was not the boy who had gone to Ulmsdale—but a new factor to be fitted into the game.

"Your hand," I continued, "lies there upon the representation of the Waste. Is it there you believe your goal to be? No treasure in truth—but Power . . ."

His expression did not change, but I had a sensation of fronting pure cold. Heat of anger was not for such a man, his rage would ape the icy breath of the Winter Dragon. I had prodded him then as I sat there, unmoved, drawing on my self-confidence. Why should I care that this Lord was ridden by ambition—to carry on great things if fate allowed? I was not of his kin.

"Yes, it is the Waste—or what it can hold." He had decided to accept me as I was. "We do not know what it may be. This much we have learned from more than one prisoner—the Hounds want something they must find or control. In their own land they face an ancient enemy—one they would devour as they have much of the Dales. This enemy—by their accounts—may be kin to our Old Ones. They were armed in turn by others who have some way of divining what they seek but not the manpower necessary to take it. The knowledge lies here!" His fingers turned inward, his nails scraped across the map as the talons of a hawk might grasp jealously held prey.

Joisan

THE MIST HUNG LIKE TAPESTRIES IN SOME GREAT HALL, SHUTTING IN the fire those two whose warmth and life it served. Now I was there also and oddly content in a way I had not been since that hour when Kerovan had turned his back upon me and ridden forth from Norsdale. I watching him go dry of eye, though weeping in my heart. That sorrow and fear had been my own and I would not allow any to see the signs of it. But here—it was like—like being with kinblood. I marveled a little that I felt so.

"I am Elys," the woman said, adding no House or Dale to mark rank. Yet manifestly she was one who would sit at the high table in any hall.

"And this"—her hand reached forward a little as if, were there no space between them, she would lay fingers on his arm (again I felt the bond between them, and I hungered for its like)—"is Jervon."

"I am Joisan." Because they made no claim of land or kin, neither did I.

"Joisan," she repeated, her head a fraction to one side, almost as if she expected some echo from the mist.

That thought made me uneasy once again, broke through the dreamlike content which had held me for a fraction of time. I turned my head quickly. Only our four horses stood there.

"But you are also . . ." Elys's fingers twitched, as if, against her will, they sought to summon some trick of Power. Then her tone changed as she added the same warning Nalda had given me.

"This is a dangerous land in which to ride alone, Joisan."

I made the same reply that I had in Norsdale: "For one alone and careful, it may be less dangerous than in company."

To my surprise Jervon gave a low laugh. "She is right." He spoke across me to Elys. "Have we not proven the truth of that ourselves? As long as one stays away from certain—places." To that last word he gave emphasis.

For a moment I thought that his companion might take his words amiss, though I knew nothing of what lay behind it all. I saw her teeth close for an instant upon her lip. Then she nodded.

"There are dangers and dangers. Only . . ." She turned her head to catch my eyes in as direct a gaze as the Past-Abbess had bent upon me when I had informed her of my plans. I did not know whether I held this woman in awe or not, but I knew she was more than she seemed, and somehow she knew more about me than I had told or wanted a stranger to discover.

"You carry," she said abruptly, "such protection as will serve you well. How else could I have felt your coming hither so strongly? But you are not of those who by blood have the use of such."

My hands flew to the gryphon. Any chance to conceal it now was too late. That Elys guessed, or knew, something of its value I had no doubts now.

She shook her head quickly. My alarm must have been very transparent and easy to read.

"No, Joisan, I do not know the nature of what you wear or to what use that may be put. Only that it is a thing of Power. That you wear it so openly means that that Power is ready to your hand—"

"No!" Least of all did I make any claim of strange talents before one who was of the Old Blood. "This is a thing of Power, yes. But I do not know how to summon what it may control. Perhaps my lord can riddle some of it, for this is his gift—that is my wedded lord. I have seen it act—but not by my

will." Or had some of its strength gone forth that time I feared
for Kerovan's life *because* I had willed it? Who could tell me
that?

"And your lord is?" Jervon asked that.

My chin came up defiantly. Did he know of Kerovan? By his
gear he must have served or did serve now with the Dale forces;
he was clearly no outlaw. Perhaps he had heard those vile
whispers, rumors of "monster," "half-man," which had poi-
soned my lord's life, walked him away from me.

"My wedded lord is Kerovan of Ulmsdale," I answered and
brought pride strong into my reply. "He rides now to answer the
summons of Lord Imgry."

"Kerovan?" Elys made a question of the name as she spoke
to Jervon. He shook his head.

"There are many lords with Imgry—those who still live. Of
him I have not heard."

I was sure he spoke the truth, but Elys, it was plain, was not
satisfied. She turned that probing gaze now upon the gryphon
itself.

"He who made a gift of such a thing," she commented,
"must be no common man and of no common heritage."

I knew I must make a choice. After all Elys was one who
might well share Kerovan's burden, though she appeared to
accept it as a part of her life, not a curse. As Jervon also did.
That he did and their bond was the stronger for his acceptance
(as any, looking upon them as I did with eyes made wise by my
own hurt, could see) brought weariness upon me. These two
were strong because they had each other, were thus forged into a
more formidable whole. That was what I longed for with Kerovan.
Perhaps I lacked wit, or strength, to bring such coupling about;
perhaps I was too young, too poorly schooled in things of any
heart save my own. Envy arose in me like a black and bitter taste
in my mouth, a shadow on the spirit. But I gave them truth
because they held what I wanted, and perhaps some small crumbs
of knowledge of how they had gained that oneness might fall
within my reach.

"Lord Kerovan is partly of the Old Blood. He is—different."

I did not know what to expect, aversion, disbelief . . . What
followed made me gasp in surprise. Elys caught the hand which

lay upon my knee. When I dropped my other, in surprise, Jervon's strong fingers closed about it, linking us three together. From each of them flowed warmly into me a feeling of peace and comfort. That envy withered, leaving only wonder and a vast longing, a birth of hope.

The mist did not lift from this refuge between the ancient walls. We feasted on the fat-dripping birds, watched the shifting billows of the feather-soft cloud about us. The original purpose of the wall, which enclosed this space on three sides, we did not know—there was no sign that anything had been erected within.

Under us the bare rock had been smoothed to a pavement on which the mist left damp drops. From time to time Jervon disappeared into the mist, with an uneasiness about him that touched me quickly.

"This is a dangerous place?" I had felt none of that warning which the gryphon should have given. Elys shook her head.

"Not openly. Still, when one rides the Dales these days, there is ever a need for caution. Jervon is a man of war. His band was beaten into death, only he survived. It is not his way to accept any refuge he does not prove many times over."

"You—" I hesitated and then dared because of my deep need. If I only knew how these two had come together I might better be able to confront my lord. "You are not of the Dales—but he is . . ."

She caught my meaning I am certain, the one I could not quite put into bald and open words.

"I do not know of what blood I am," she answered me. "Those who gave me birth were washed ashore on the coast here after a great storm—seemingly they fled some danger, but what I was never told. My mother was one who had strange knowledge, she was *Wise*. Only, because she wished to give her lord children, she had to strike a dire bargain with certain Powers. When my brother and I were born at one birth, she paid for us with her life. My brother—" She hesitated. "He had none of her heritage. He distrusts such knowledge—it may be true that men cannot control the Moon Strength.

"The invaders came, my father went to war, later my brother. I gave what help I could to those coast people who had been our friends. Some things I learned from their Wisewoman—I was very young and had not much teaching. Our people fled inland and Jervon found us. He was sore wounded in both body and spirit. Later I had a message that my brother was in danger. So I rode, and Jervon with me, because his lord was dead and he had no kin left. We—''

Again she hesitated, then continued, her voice coming in a tumble of words as if she would quickly be done with the rest of the story. ''We did what was to be done for my brother's sake. With him there was no place for me. I am what I was born and few men—very few—can accept me so. Perhaps, in truth, only one . . .'' She looked now at Jervon as he came back to us through the fringes of the mist. There was that in her eyes which made me once more know envy. So, I was sure, I looked upon Kerovan—but all that *I* had to offer had not been enough!

''Now,'' Elys spoke more briskly, ''we ride together as blank shields, lending our sword strength to those who need it most. Yes, I am war-trained. It was my father who willed it so. We are kinless, landless, but never without what we need most.''

Kinless and landless they might be, Woman of Power, Man of Sword—but they were one.

''Where do you ride now?'' I asked. Though I had determined to make this quest alone, now I longed, suddenly and fiercely, for her to say south. Surely if they were blank shields the gathering of forces under Lord Imgry would attract them.

Rather to my surprise Elys shook her head. ''I do not yet know. There is . . .'' She looked troubled. ''Joisan, would you fear if I made a scry pattern for you?''

I remembered once I had seen that done—and also for me—in the bowl of the Past-Abbess. Then I had seen my lord but had known it not.

''You can do this?''

''Only for others, not for Jervon—not for me. It is like all Power—it does not work for the direct advantage of the summoner. Still I feel it should be tried now—for you.''

''Once it was done for me—only I did not understand then what was meant by what I saw.''

Elys nodded. ''Many times such foreshadows can be obscure. They can even deceive—always remember that. You must not confidently expect that this or that will come to pass. We make many decisions, turn right on some path when we might have turned left, enter into a hall wherein it chances that we meet with one to alter our future. There are ways beyond counting in which fate can be so changed. All we learn from the bowl is one single path. Do you wish me to do this for you?''

Jervon was now standing at her back, his face sober. When he spoke quickly, before I could answer, it was to Elys not me.

"This is needful?''

"I think so.'' Her words came slowly. "If Joisan agrees—this may be a part of why we were led here.''

He knelt to open one of the saddlebags, bringing forth something bundled in a heavy swathing of cloth. This he passed to Elys as if he handled bare steel, uncertain that it might not turn its cutting edge against him.

The wrapping was in two parts, the outer being a length that might have been cut from an old cloak. Underneath that was a fair piece of linen with across it, not in stitchery, but as if one had applied a scorching hot brand to its surface, brownish runes and symbols. All Elys's attention centered on what she did. I saw her lips move, though she spoke no words aloud. Yet it seemed that now the mist, held at bay by our fire, had a life of its own and began to encircle us, pushing against an unseen barrier.

What lay within the inner cloth was a cup of moon-bright silver, into the waiting hollow of which Elys poured liquid from a small vial she took from her belt pouch, measuring it drop by drop. Now I heard the murmur of her voice as she repeated in cadence what could only be the spell words of a Wisewoman.

Carefully she set the cup on the rock between us, holding both hands about it. Her eyes were closed, her head upheld as if she looked far beyond.

Then, she jerked her hands away—some mighty heat might have blasted outward—and looked directly to me.

"Watch then!'' I could not have disobeyed that order even if I wished.

I leaned forward, my hands on the rock, my arms braced on either side of the cup, my head bent so I might see clearly within.

At first there was nothing, only that thin film of oddly dark liquid. I could not see through it to the silver beneath. Then the liquid began to swirl about and about, rising in the hollow.

I felt dizzy, my head giddy, I could not turn away my eyes. Slowly the liquid stopped, now it filled the cup to its very brim, still dark . . . A mirror's surface but one that reflected nothing.

Nothing? No, there was movement there, not caused by the liquid itself. A shadow arose to the surface, changing, becoming clearer. Now I saw, not my own face reflected therein, but a sharp picture.

"Kerovan!"

He was there, armored, helmed, but still bare of foot—or hoof. The mail he wore was strange, holding the same blue sheen as that which clothed Elys. He sat with a bared sword stuck point deep in gravelly earth as if he must keep a weapon close to hand. Behind him grazed three horses, and there was a stream, coarse grass, some stunted bushes. There was a strangeness about that land as if it were not Dale country.

His face was that of a carven figure like unto those I had seen in the Waste—nothing remaining in it of the Kerovan I wished to see. In a way he was as walled in crystal as the gryphon—beyond my reach.

I dared not look too long directly upon him lest my longing draw from me the strength I needed. So I busied myself studying the place about him, trying to locate some landmark, some way of telling where he so rested.

How long that picture held I did not know. Then it began to fade, was gone. While, as a bubble is pricked and becomes nothing, that which filled the cup fell back to the bottom of the hollow.

"I think"—Elys spoke first, breaking through my frustration and despair—"that is the Waste."

I settled back, aware now of the ache in my shoulders, the pain of my hands, as if I had tried to dig into the unyielding rock with my fingers.

"The Waste?" I echoed. Why should Kerovan head back into that piece of ill omen? He had gone to Lord Imgry. Had the sight of his hooves, the knowledge that he was of what would seem to a Dalesman tainted blood, made him an exile after all?

Jervon shifted a little where he sat beside Elys. "So—" His

brows drew together in a frown. "Well, it was well within the realm of possibilities that sooner or later Imgry would be moved to try that." His eyes were on the cup around which Elys was once more enfolding the cloth, having thrown the liquid it contained into the fire, only to have her act followed by a burst of brilliant flame.

"Try what, my Lord?" Instinctively I gave him the honor title.

"Imgry"—with one hand he caressed his chin where an old scar made a half-discernible seam—"has always been one to plan—to dare—if another bears the burden of the action. I would say that it is now in his mind to meet with some of those in the Waste—and not the outlaws or scavengers—to perhaps propose an alliance."

Anger burned in me. "Using my lord," I burst out, "because he is of mixed blood and perhaps, that being so, some of those who wander or abide there might then feel kinship? He uses men hardly, does this Imgry!"

"It is because he does," Jervon replied, "that perhaps, in the end, he will impose peace in this land. He is not loved, but he is obeyed, and that obedience draws together men who might not otherwise be held to any strong purpose."

"But the Waste . . ." Lord Imgry's qualities of leadership meant nothing to me. "Kerovan has been there—he barely lived when he went up against one Power. And he has no longer access to this." My hand covered the gryphon. "He is not trained or armored against what prowls there. May Imgry be everlastingly cursed!" My hands curled talon-wise. I wished that I were a hawk to tear at the face of that cold and devious lord.

"Your lord must have chosen to do this. Imgry could not have forced him so." Elys still held the now shrouded cup. "There is that in him"—she spoke as if Kerovan were before her, or else that she indeed knew him well—"which would not yield if he wished it not. He is"—she shook her head slowly—"he is unlike any I have met before. A man of two natures, each held at bay lest they lead him to destruction. Within him is locked Power he does not want. He might even ride his present road because he seeks the peace of death."

How could she know him thus? Unless there was in her the gift of what the Wisewomen call the True Sight.

"No!" I was on my feet, looking around as if I could seize a weapon to destroy her words. I fought to master my fear as I said then, "If he is in the Waste, there, too, I go!"

"The Waste"—Jervon might have been speaking to an impatient child—"is very large. You have no guide—"

"But I do!" I did not know whence came my conviction as my hand was tight on the gryphon. "There is this—and I shall learn how to use it!"

"Perhaps that is possible," Elys said slowly. "But are there the seeds of Power in you?" She arose and began studying my face. "No, you do not know what you can do—not yet. However, this is the road you will follow—" Jervon started to speak. She stopped him with a gesture. "This is a choice she has already made, for good or ill. What remains . . ." Now she looked at him instead. "The Waste and a man who may or may not be found, a task which may or may not be beyond the doing. We have been only drifting, you and I, do we now make a choice also?"

His frown grew darker but he said at once, "If so be your will."

She shook her head vigorously. "Not *my* will. The day is past when I choose to ride and you follow. We go as of one mind or not at all."

I looked eagerly from one to the other. This Elys might not be one of the Old Ones, but she controlled a fraction of Power learning and through that might be able to claim kin-right with the Waste roamers. I had spoken of a guide, but I knew not how to make use of it. This was no venture of theirs, save I wanted to ride in their company. Their closeness of spirit was warm to my heart, so I clung to the fancy that being with them longer I could learn the secret of that—enough of it to smooth my way with Kerovan.

Jervon hitched at his swordbelt. "Might as well ride one way as another," he commented. "Also I think that your Kerovan"—now he spoke to me—"since he was dispatched by Imgry, would head directly westward from the headquarters. Thus we go south if we would pick up his trail."

"I have heard that Lord Imgry buys much of the salvaged Waste metal for the forging of arms," I said. "Therefore there

must be a going and coming of those who deal in that. Perhaps
Kerovan would follow their trails.''

"Well enough. Let morning come and this mist rise—then we
ride south and west. If there lies any trace of such a trail we can
cut it so in time.''

The mist that imprisoned us did not rise during the rest of that
day, still clinging heavy as night came. I watched it uneasily as
the darkness grew, for I kept thinking that, from the corners of
my eyes, I now and then caught a hint of movement within it
which was not the billows of the fog itself, but rather as if
something more tangible hovered there, using it as a cloak from
which to spy on us.

Jervon ventured out from time to time coming back with
armloads of dead wood, which he piled close to hand. Only
when the dark really deepened Elys put an end to that. She
confirmed my own suspicions when she produced from her belt
purse a slender stick of blue.

With this in her right hand and her left raised so that her
slender fingers were free to move in complex patterns, she
proceeded to draw lines on the pavement, fencing in our campsite, including the mounts, which Jervon had hobbled and brought
closer to the fire. What Elys finished at last was a star of five
points, setting the lines true with skillful accuracy, though the
labor wore away her strange pen.

In each of the outflung points she proceeded to add an intricate
symbol, thus locking us in. The horses had been restless for
some time past, throwing up their heads, snorting, staring into
the mist with signs for growing uneasiness. However, once her
work was complete, they quieted.

Nor, I discovered, did I myself now have that sense of being
watched by the unseen.

I shared journey food from my own store with my new
companions as we settled down in the warmth of the fire,
agreeing upon taking watches turn about to feed the flames.
Elys, by lot, was the first sentry. Wrapped in my cloak, not
laying aside my mail, I strove to sleep, crossing my hands over
the gryphon on my breast.

Jervon awakened me at the proper time and I watched the
paling of the stars as morning drew near. For the mist had

withdrawn, save for a ragged wisp or two. The star drawn for our protection held a faint light of its own. I studied it and wondered how one learned such lore. The Dalesfolk believed that only one born with the Talent could be taught, though we had Wisewomen, healers, gatherers of herb lore, and the like. Yet there had been the Lady Math—my aunt.

She had taken the lesser vows of the Dames, and to all such this kind of learning was a sin. Still, in the last hour of her life, she had brought forth a curiously carven wand—before sending me forth from our threatened keep—saying she would have her own kind of vengeance against the despoilers and murderers besetting us. The keep had burst apart in flame and flying stones, taking to their deaths most of those who had dared invade its inner walls.

That the destruction had come by her will I had never doubted, though I do not know what Power she had called upon in that hour or how she had summoned it.

Might it be that some of full Dales-blood, wary as they were of the brooding past, did indeed share a ghost of Old talent. Perhaps children born and nurtured in this haunted land were really apart from the parent stock. I had never considered that before.

It was our custom to look askance on anything that smacked of such learning. Those proven of half-blood were avoided, looked upon by most as . . . In the name of my dear lord, I refused to use, even in my mind, that ugly name. What of the rest of us who bore no outward stigmata? Did we also carry traits of strangeness that were not as obvious as my lord's cloven feet, his eyes of amber yellow, but that could, if known, exile us quickly?

Was this an argument I could use with Kerovan? If I could but display a little of the talent, prove to him that I was not as pure blooded as he believed . . . I moved restlessly around the fire, longing for the coming of true morning. Had I found an ally in Elys, one who would train me if I had that which would be fertile ground for learning?

It took many years to make a Wisewoman, it was said. I had no such time to spend. I remembered once again that meeting with Neevor, that stranger of the Waste who had said the crystal gryphon was a key, which I only could use when the time came. If so—surely his words argued I had some command of Power.

I wanted to shake Elys awake, demand that she aid me. But I fought against impatience, kept my desires in check for the proper time. This was not a matter that could be rushed, my mind told my heart—but oh, how my heart raged for action!

Kerovan

IMGRY MAY HAVE THOUGHT HIMSELF PERSUASIVE; THE FINAL DECISION was my own. I had listened to his summing up of what he believed the enemy wanted—and of what might be done in return by making contact with some authority within the Waste, to give a warning—and make an offer. The latter, to be sure, was an arrogant gesture on his part, for what had we to offer that could match those forces the Old Ones commanded? I did not have the ambition that drove Imgry. On the other hand, if by some fluke of fortune, I might succeed, I would have achieved something that the Dalesman must admit only a despised half-blood would dare to attempt.

He offered me a command, but I refused it. He did not like that. I think he wanted no ambassador to have too much freedom.

"One man," he had said, "to go alone is too high a risk."

"One *man*, Lord Imgry? Look at me. Ask any in this hall if I am in their eyes a man. You have made me your envoy because of my heritage. Then let me go as if I am truly of the blood you deem me. I shall ride openly and wait to see what fortune will send. What I can do, I shall. I promise nothing."

Reluctant as he was, he knew I spoke the truth. Nor was he niggardly with equipment. I was offered, and accepted, mail, sword, and helm, new-fashioned of the salvaged metal from the

35

Waste. All men knew that this was the best, an alloy we had no equal for in the making of fine armament.

I chose horses, three of them, from the lines. The mounts from the eastern Dales (there were all too few of those left now) were of little use in the west. Nor did I want hill-bred stock, for, hardy and tough as those were, the Waste was partly desert. A mount used to the plentiful waters of mountain springs could not stand the heat and lack of forage and drink.

What I took were such beasts as were used by the Waste scavengers. Luckily, in that sweep Imgry had ordered to gather all available mounts, these had appeared. Slightly larger than mountain-bred ponies, they were gaunt, with long necks out of proportion to their bodies. Their eyes were unusually large and heavily lidded, well lashed to screen out glare of sun and wind-borne grit. Their hooves were broader than normal, meant for the traversing of shifting sand. They had a reputation for being vicious, and it was always necessary to hobble or tether them at night.

Two I would ride turn and turn about, and the third would serve as a pack animal. It took me four days of careful prepara-tion, of selecting supplies. And I did not dream again on those nights between.

I refused the map Imgry had played with during our interview. Such sites as were marked on it had come by word of mouth from scavengers, who were not to be trusted, being always jealous of their sources of supply.

When Riwal and I had traveled the Road of Exile, that had been well to the north. The road that had led me to the place where Rogear and my mother had wrought their black incanta-tions was also in that direction—barren and desolate. If there was any life now to be found in the Waste I felt I would discover it elsewhere—though the Old Ones could not be judged by our standards. Still they must need water, sustenance of some kind, shelters more than a jumble of ruins.

Thus I decided to strike straight west, following for the first part of my journey the faint trail left by the scavengers bringing in metal for Imgry's forges.

I rode out in the early morning saying no farewells. The night before I had met with Imgry for the last time. He spoke again of the urgency for carrying my warning of invasion to any of authority I might find—of his complete certainty that somewhere in the unknown west lay whatever it was that the invaders really sought. He did not come to watch me out of sight—I was merely a dart he had launched. If I struck true, that was good; if I failed . . . Well, all he could do had been done.

My mount fought control, but when I was well away from the camp and headed west he settled down, while the two on lead ropes came easily enough. All of them from time to time held high their narrow heads, expanding red-lined nostrils as if they searched for some scent that was of importance.

We were four days along, the last three well into a scrub wilderness, before the one I rode cried out, making a sound like an eerie scream. The other two answered him, their weird cries echoing back from jagged-topped heights, which overhung the path so darkly we moved through shadows as thick as twilight. The walls of that cut grew increasingly high, drawing together overhead. Then the two cliffs actually met, forming an arch into an even darker day.

My mount broke into a fast trot I did not try to restrain. The others quickened stride in turn. We passed through a rough-walled tunnel to come out into a brighter light than I had seen for hours.

Here was the Waste. No remnant of any path remained, only bare rock as footing, though that was crossed here and there by a runnel of coarse sand. The land itself was a rolling plain. In the far distance were shadows against the sky, which I thought must mark highlands. For want of a better guide I fastened on those as my goal.

The led horses were no longer content to trail behind, but moved up, one on either side of my mount, matching their pace to his, as if they also had riders and we were readying for a charge. I thought that they were at home in this country and perhaps they could, by their attitude, give me warning of other life forms we might encounter though who, or what, could live in such a land as this I found hard to guess.

I made camp while the sun was still up in the afternoon sky, for my horses had come directly to a dip in the land, at the bottom of which there was a sluggish stream pushing out of the ground, running for a space, only to be swallowed once more by the greedy earth. However, along its banks grew grass and

several stunted bushes. Out of the nearest of those clumps burst
winged creatures. They moved with speed, but I saw that they
were black of feather and their heads, hanging downward on
oddly crooked necks, were rawly red as if new plucked.

Their squawks were as unnatural as the cries of the horses had
been and they circled overhead, plainly angry at being disturbed.
I did not like the sight of them. There was something foul about
their black bodies and those naked heads.

What had drawn them into the brush made itself plain within a
moment or two. For a noisome stench of something dead, and
dead for some time, arose strongly, as my horse half leaped, half
slid down to the water's edge.

He plunged his muzzle deep into the water, his companions
copying that action as speedily. I slid out of the saddle, made my
tether ropes fast to the nearest bush. Then, though I disliked the
business, I went to see what lay where the still-screaming birds
had been busy.

Bird beak and blazing sun had done nasty work, but there
remained enough to perceive that this had once been a near-
human form—though very small. A child—here? I tried not to
breathe as I made myself move closer. Whatever it had been
alive, it was no kin to Dalesmen. The body, where flesh still
remained, was furred with a bristly brown hair standing stiffly up
from the roots. The head and face were so destroyed I could not
trace any features, and for that I was glad. Both fingers and toes
ended in great hooked claws, in some of which clods of earth
still clung. The thing lay half in a scooped out pit as if it had
been digging frantically to escape whatever fate had struck it
down.

Using branches I broke from a bush, I rolled the thing farther
into the hole and tossed rocks and sand over it. I had no intention
of leaving it uncovered were I to camp here.

As I worked I kept glancing around. Whatever had killed this
creature might just still linger—though there was very little cover
about and I did not believe that the birds would have been
feeding, or my horses would have entered the oasis, had there
been danger.

I picketed my mounts as far from that rude grave as I could,
and I did not drink of the water myself, rather relied on what I

carried in my saddle bottle. The shape and size of the dead creature intrigued me.

There are many legends of things that have ventured or blundered out of the Waste in times past, of monsters and demons, which men, during the early days of our people in the Dales, had fought, killed, or been slain by. I had heard of great scaled reptiles with talons and beaks, of furred creatures near as tall as a keep tower, of smaller flyers with stinger tails carrying a fell poison. Then there were those in human form who could persuade a man they were kin, then ensorcel or kill him.

Riwal had been so enthralled by the Waste mysteries that he had kept records of such stories and had shared them with me. In his cottage he had bits and pieces of old images that he had found—some beautiful, some grotesque, some frightening. However, we could never be sure whether those had been made to resemble actual life forms or were the imaginings of artists who must have dreamed strange dreams. Nowhere could I remember having seen or heard of anything resembling the creature I had just buried.

Its wickedly sharp claws might have been employed for more than digging. With that thought in mind I drew my sword, set it point down in the earth close to hand as I opened my supply bag, found the tough trail rations, and chewed slowly, alert to any sound.

The birds continued to wheel overhead for a time, shrieking their anger. Finally they drew into a flock and, like a noisome black cloud, circled the oasis for a last time, then flew northward over the Waste.

The horses continued to graze, never raising their heads. As a rule their species could not be brought to approach dead things so easily, yet these three had not shied away when we entered the cut. I settled to my dry meal, reminding myself that I must never make the worst possible error—that of judging any life form I found here by the standards of the Dales. I had entered a new and different world.

After the flight of the birds it seemed very quiet—broken only by the sullen gurgle of the water, the sounds made as the horses cropped grass. There was no buzz of insect, no rustle of breeze through the twisted and curled leaves of the bushes. The heat of the westering sun seemed heavier. My mail burdened my shoulders, sweat trickled from beneath the rim of my helm.

Having finished eating, I explored this pocket further. What herbage grew made the most of the water's trickle. Along the banks grass was thick, bushes like solid balls, so intertwined with one another that I thought even a slashing sword could not have cleared a path.

The water issued from a rock-walled bank, the stone of which was smeared with a rusty-red stain reminding me unpleasantly of blood. Another warning against drinking here. That crevice was not natural, I decided, too well shaped—as if it had been set here to pipe in a flow of water for travelers. What kind of travelers?

Downstream I searched with care, but I could discover no signs that any had camped recently. The sand and gravel did preserve here and there formless prints suggesting that it was used by animals native to this harsh land.

What *was* the thing I had buried? I could not force myself to disinter it for another examination. Still, I was troubled by its presence. To establish a camp here, even for the sake of the horses, would be, I decided, too great a risk. This oasis must be a loadstone for any life nearby.

I did linger until the sun was nearly down before I let the horses drink a second time and then headed out into the open country, taking care to pick a way that led across the rockiest section I could find, so we would leave no trail.

Those heights, which I had marked as a goal, were now a black fringe across a rapidly darkening sky. I began to look for shelter, even if it were only an outcropping rock against which I could set my back in case of attack. I finally sighted a stand of stony spires set closely together, and toward that I turned the horses.

There was still light enough to perceive that this was the first indication something living here had needed a home or rough fort. What I had first thought to be spires of natural rock were a building. The structure had been so attuned to its surroundings that you could almost believe it was some freak of nature.

The tall rocks that formed its walls were rough, unworked, set vertically, but very closely, side to side, so that the cracks between were as narrow as their surfaces would allow. They were of the same yellowish-white as all the boulders I had seen hereabouts. What I did not expect was that the interior they guarded was filled by what looked, in this half-light, to be a vast, untidy nest.

Dried brush, clumps of coarse grass torn up by the roots, had been packed to such a depth that the top of the mass reached my waist when I dismounted. I prodded at it with swordpoint. Under the touch of metal the stuff broke apart, turned to powder, so dried and old it was.

Fastening the horses to one of the side pillars, I set about raking out that mess, using mainly my sword, as there was reluctance in me to touch any of the debris with my hands. At length I drew on my mail gauntlets before I dug into the lower layers.

Something hard rolled against my boot. I looked down into the empty eyeholes of a skull. Manifestly this was the remains of a human, or something near human. I put the thing aside and kept on with my task.

There were more bones, which I had no desire to examine, and a faintly evil smell that grew stronger as I delved deeper, throwing out the fetid, decayed material. I became aware of a persistent itching about my wrist as I tossed out the last I could grub free.

Washing my gauntleted hands with sand, I unfastened the wrist binding and turned back the supple linkage to bare what had become so much a part of me during the months since I had found it—that band of metal I had discovered by chance and which had saved me when Rogear had tried first to blind, and then to kill.

The band glowed; it was warm. The runes carved around it were bright sparks of fire. I stared down, near entranced, until on sudden impulse I thrust my arm into the space between the pillars. The marks flashed even brighter—yet I had had no warning of uneasiness.

Still, from the tall rocks, from which I had scraped the last of the nest, came an answering spark of light. I drew my small boot-top knife and picked out from a rock a scrap of the same blue metal as made up my wrist band, tucking it away in my pouch.

To keep my horses better tempered, tethered as they were away from grass and water, I crumpled journey cakes upon a rock. They nosed at them avidly, paying no attention as I made them secure for the night before I crawled into the space I had cleared.

There was only the one entrance, though overhead was no roof. The rocks tilted slightly inward so that the open space above was small. I pulled before the door itself my saddle and the bags of supplies, using them as a barricade. This night I wished that I had some comrade-at-arms to share watch and watch. Instead I must depend upon that faculty any soldier learns, the art of awaking into instant awareness at the least change in his surroundings. Once more I laid my sword, bare-bladed, at my side, while I sought sleep.

If any danger prowled the night it did not come near my refuge. However, I was awakened at dawn by that same shattering scream my mount had earlier given when he first sniffed the wind from the Waste. I crawled out to discover all three of the horses pulling furiously at their halters, rearing and pawing at the rocks.

Though I used all the art I knew to soothe them, I discovered, once I had loaded and saddled, there was little I could do with them. They were determined to head back to the oasis and perforce I had to allow that, since they needed grazing and water. They could have it as I broke my own fast.

Thus the sun was about an hour above the horizon when we set forth again toward the heights. Gradually the country changed. The desert stretch became a brown-gray soil that rooted clumps of grass, seared by the sun. As we passed, my led horses strove to snatch mouthfuls of the stuff, their elongated necks aiding them to so feed. Bushes were next, then trees, some of which my animals made wide detours to avoid.

I trusted to their instincts for they knew this land far better than I. Near midday I saw the first moving thing. The clumps of brush had become so thick that we must swing well to avoid them, and on such a side venture I caught a glimpse of more open land.

Crossing that was a rider. Though he was distant I could not mistake the glint of sun reflected from armor. His horse was unlike my three; there was no sign of the long neck.

He rode with the ease of a man who knew exactly where he was going. I did not think him a scavenger—though he could be

an outlaw. Or . . . this might be the very kind of contact I had
been sent to seek! I loosened my sword in its sheath and headed
out into the open willing to let myself be sighted, in spite of
possible risk.

Certainly his mount was of better stock than the desert-bred
nags I had selected, for, though he did not appear to be going at
more than a comfortable trot, he continued to draw ahead. Nor
did he seem aware that I followed.

Not too far before him stretched a spread of woodland. I
wanted to catch up before he vanished into its shade. If I were to
meet with trouble I desired such confrontation in the open. So I
urged my mount to a faster pace, though he snorted and jerked at
the reins angrily.

The stranger was almost under the shadow of the trees when
the ill-tempered beast I bestrode actively protested our chase.
Voicing one of those screams, he arose with his forefeet pawing
the air. The other two used their advantage at the same moment
to pull back on their lead cords. Perforce I was brought to a
speedy halt.

Viciously my mount continued to rear and kick, attempting to
attack his own companions. I had my hands very full striving to
control the three of them. What suddenly pierced the din they were
creating was a whistle, commanding, imperative.

My horses set all four feet to the ground again. Still their eyes
rolled to show the whites, ribbons of foam dripped to the earth
they had torn up with their hooves. However, now all three stood
as if as well rooted as the trees not too far away.

Taking as tight a grip on reins and lead ropes as I could, I
looked around.

The rider I had trailed had finally swung about and was
heading toward me, the gait of his mount a smooth flowing
gallop. Indeed that horse *was* different. As large as a lowland-
bred stallion, it possessed a strangely dappled hide such as I had
never seen before; shades of gray-brown merged into one another
so there was no clearly spotted pattern, only a suggestion of
such.

His horsecloth was not woven, but rather formed by the skin
of some beast—silver gray and also spotted. As he drew nearer I
recognized it for the tanned hide of a snow cat, one of the rarest

and yet most deadly and cunning beasts to roam the heights within the Dales.

He, himself, wore armor of the same silver-gray as the skin. The helm, which overshadowed his face until he seemed half masked, was surmounted by a beautifully carven crouching cat of that species. There were yellow jewels of eyes in the cat head, and, by some trick of the sun, they appeared to blink as if the thing were alive and merely resting on a perch, watching me curiously.

The stranger rode only a short distance toward me before he pulled up his shadow-patterned horse. My three beasts sweated, stared wild-eyed, gave the impression they were possessed by terror. Yet this other had, as far as I could see, made no gesture suggesting attack. His sword still rested in sheath, its heavy pommel forming the head of a cat, while the belt he wore was again of fur and its buckle a snarling feline head.

Though he had halted some distance away, I could see those cat heads clearly. They loomed as if they were the House sign of some clan.

We sat so for some moments of silence, eyeing each other across that gap he had chosen to keep between us. Now I was able to make out more plainly his features. He was young, I thought, perhaps near my own age. His face was smooth—but that was not strange, for many of the Dalesmen grew little or very scant beards until they were well past the middle span of life.

His skin was brown, and his eyes were slightly elongated, sloping up a little under straight brows. The more I studied him, the surer I became I had found one who called this Waste, or some place like it, his home. This was no strayed Dalesman. His accoutrements were too finely wrought, his mount a superb animal. Also, though he looked fully human, yet I did not need that light warmth at my wrist to tell me that this was one who possessed Power of one kind or another.

He regarded me with an equally intent study. I was certain he had not missed the sight of my hooves in the special stirrups I had devised. Did he know of any of my kind? *Were* there any of my kind or kin—or was I merely half-misshapen hybrid, and so, in the eyes of any true blood here, as much a mistake of birth as I was in the Dales?

I knew that without any warning it was useless for me to approach him closer. It was plain that my three animals held him in odd terror. They shivered, while foam still gathered at the corners of their mouths.

Since he had not drawn steel—did he think that I was so unworthy a foe, so helpless that he need not defend himself in that way—dare I accept him as neutral? There was no other choice. I would do what I had to.

Taking a chance, I dropped my reins and raised my hands palm out. The silk-fine mesh of my mail fell a little back from my wrist and the sunlight made a blue flame of that band.

Was it a passport, something that would gain me recognition in this place, at this time? I could only wait on the stranger's answer to me.

Joisan

As the light of day grew stronger my companions roused. The mist was gone and the protecting star about us faded. Jervon gave the animals each a small measure of grain, led them out to water at a hillside spring, while we opened supply bags for our own food.

With the mounts saddled, the packs on the pony, we headed away from the walls, following a hint of a trail, a shadow of a road, perhaps one so old that even the hills across which it cut had forgotten it.

Jervon led, heading westward across heights where there were no signs of any traveler before us, save twice a tumbledown hut such as were built by herders when they took the flocks out for summer forage. Those days of peaceful herding were past. We saw no one or any life, save for a blundering hill hen or two that ran squawking from under the very hooves of our horses, and once a glimpse of a snow cat staring arrogantly down from so high a ledge I wondered how even that venturous climber could have reached it.

We lit no fire that night since we camped in the open. It was plain that my companions moved with the wariness of scouts and took all precautions. As we sat closely together, more for the need for company than the warmth of our bodies, I asked whether they had ever been into the Waste.

"Only to the fringes," Jervon answered. "For a while we rode with scouts who were sent north to see if the invaders had headed down country. There was no sign of any Hound passing, though we combed the country as best we could. We saw the beginning of the Road of Exile."

The Road of Exile—Kerovan had mentioned that during those days when we had traveled to Norsdale, leading my poor people to safety. He had once traveled for a space along it, though he had not told me many details of that journey. Even that much of his past he had refused to share with me.

"Do any know where that leads?" I asked.

"Not that I have heard. We did not try to follow it. But neither have I heard of any other open road into that country."

During our day's journey I had had no chance to speak to Elys about my idea of early morning. Somehow I did not wish to mention my longing to master Power before Jervon. It was not because I feared he might object. Because of Elys he accepted much where any other Dalesman would have decried the very idea. It was rather that I was shy of making a plea for aid and did not know just how to phrase such.

During the next four days I had no better luck. The land was so deserted that, even though we traveled with all caution, we covered a goodly amount of distance in a short time. On the fifth evening Jervon pointed to the westward where there was a yellow glow across the clouds, differing from the clean sunsets I had always known.

"The Waste."

During our journey to the southwest we had searched diligently for any trace of a track such as the metal gatherers might have made, but had not sighted a single sign of such. Now, when we had unloaded the pack pony and Elys had collected certain dry branches, which she said would not yield much notice of a fire, Jervon did not unsaddle. Rather he proposed to ride out on a half circle, seeking again for trail marks.

As the yellow sky-glow faded, Elys and I spitted hill hens to roast, a more tasty meal than we had had for four days past. This was my chance and, as we worked, I made my desires known to her, hurrying lest Jervon return before I was done.

She listened, but when she spoke it was with a most serious note in her low voice.

"There is some logic in what you say. It could well be that this country has an influence over those born here—even if they have never had any reason to believe they had talents because fortune did not demand such efforts from them. As for learning the calling of Power—yes, I could teach you a little, if you showed aptitude, even as I was schooled in my girlhood and youth. But there is no time. This is not knowledge that one can pick from the air. It needs careful study. However, that does not mean that you cannot strive within yourself to awaken what may lie in you. Only you must be very patient."

After this warning she began there and then outlining to me some disciplines of mind I could practice, while I vowed that if I could win anything by following her teaching—that I would do. So from that hour forward I stretched my mind as a warrior stretches and exercises his body that battle skills may be known to every muscle over which he holds command.

We rode on in the morning, though Jervon had again found no guide, heading outward into a land that was grim and full of foreboding. I knew that the Waste must be a mixture of different kinds of land, but here it was all sand and gravel and bare rock upon which the sun beat with great waves of heat. We used the tricks of travelers in such desert land, seeking shelter during the worst hours, traveling in the early morning or in the evenings. We did not move at night, bright though the moon might hang over us.

Here there were too many oddly shaped shadows, strange sounds (though those were far away). It was better to camp, even though our traveling time was thus cut to a crawl, and be sure we were on guard.

By some favor of fortune we did chance upon meager grazing and water each day. Jervon remarked that, though there was no sign of any road, it might be that we had stumbled on some travelers' route—perhaps long forsaken.

I watched my gryphon anxiously, hoping it might in some way offer a clue as to whether we were headed in the right direction or not. I did not know what I expected, it was mainly hope that kept me at that quest. Only the globe remained ever the same.

Jervon wove a zigzag path ahead of us, still hunting a track, returning always to report he found none. Perforce, because we had to have some goal, we chose to head toward the line of heights in the west—those that loomed purple-black at night and brown by day. They were the only noticeable landmarks.

On the second day Jervon returned at a fast trot from one of his side expeditions. We had kept our horses to a walk for their own sakes and this burst of speed on his part suggested trouble.

"There is an oasis with water where there has been a camp," he reported, "and recently."

So slim a chance that that camp had been Kerovan's. Still I at once swung my mare in that direction, the others with me. The oasis lay in a narrow cleft, cutting below the surface of this sandy waste. It held greenery, dark and withered-looking. The water of the stream was not pleasant appearing either, rather dark and turgid as if it were a stagnant pool, though there was a slow, rolling current. However, our beasts drank greedily as Jervon pointed to where grass had been shortened by grazing and that not long ago.

"There is something else—" He beckoned us to follow him between two bushes.

I sniffed and wished I had not. There was the sweet corruption-smell of death here! The ground was disturbed, a pile of stones covering a narrow, filled-in depression.

"An animal would not be buried." Elys surveyed the stones. "But that space is too small to hold a man."

To my relief she was right, only a half-grown child could be in such a short grave. But a child—Kerovan could not have killed a child!

Elys's eyes were closed, she swayed, Jervon was at her side instantly, his hand out to steady her. She shuddered before she looked at us again.

"Not of our blood—it was not of our blood. Something strange—or perhaps *not* strange in this land. But whatever it was, it lived as a servant of the Dark."

I drew back involuntarily. The Dark—that signified the evil Powers and all who served them. Had Kerovan been attacked again by such force, which he spawned in the Waste?

"Leave be!" Jervon's order came harshly. "There is no need to fear the dead, do not mind search for it. We must not

meddle.'' It was the first time he had spoken so, with such a
show of authority.

She turned away. "You are right. And this is truly dead—for
many days I would say."

"Then Kerovan—" I stumbled over one of the rolling stones.
He must not have been responsible for that death, though he
could have buried the corpse. I held on to that belief as tightly as
I could. I hoped that he had not fronted again—and alone—a
dire danger of the Dark.

"I do not believe," Jervon continued, "that this is a place of
good omen."

The three of us withdrew from that grave place, as far down
the cut as we could, allowing our mounts, who showed no
distaste for their surroundings, to graze through the hottest part
of the day. When the sun was westering we started on.

It was when we topped the far bank of that sinister hollow that
what I had waited for so long happened. The gryphon flashed
with more than the sun's reflection. At my cry the others drew
rein, while I shifted in the saddle, this way and that, my attention close fixed upon the ball—until I thought I judged in what
direction it flashed the brightest.

My companions willingly granted me the lead and I pushed
Bural at a faster gait to where a circle of pointed rocks rose
abruptly from the sand-drifted ground. Lying to one side there
was a mass of dry stuff, which had plainly been dug from the
core of the rock huddle. Powdery, disintegrating wood mingled
with remains of long-withered vegetation. Perched on the highest
point of that moldering heap sat a grinning skull and I thought
that I sighted other bits of brittle bones in the decayed mass.

"Someone made camp here." Jervon slipped from the saddle,
went to peer within the circle of rocks. He stirred the dark heap a
little with the toe of his boot. "This may once have been a nest
lying within that."

"The nest of something large enough to hunt such prey?"
Elys gestured toward the skull.

Jervon stopped to view it the closer, though he did not touch
it.

"Very old, I think. Also what laired here once must have been
gone for a long time," came his verdict.

I cupped the crystal between my palms. Now heat flared

from it, startling me into a cry of pain. I let the globe fall, to swing at the end of its chain. Though I made no move of body it continued to move. In spite of my disgust and, yes, a growing fear, I, too, dismounted, advancing unwillingly toward the heap of debris, where that hollow-eyed skull rested—by chance or design.

Then . . .

There appeared in the dark eye hollows of the skull (I could not be so preyed upon by illusion even here) an answering fraction of light. My shaking hand was at my mouth, keeping back a cry of panic to which I refused voice.

The crystal now lifted from its place on my breast, pointing outward, pulling the chain that supported it into a taut line, as if it strained for freedom. I had said it would be a guide, now it drew me toward that ancient, time-worn thing of bone.

Unable to control the gryphon, I knelt, my hands going out, in spite of my efforts not to move. I was not going to touch that dry and years-leached bone—I was not!

The crystal became a ball of sparkling light, so bright I could no longer look directly at it. While to my ears, or perhaps within my head, came a very faint sound, like a far-off solemn chanting, such as might mark some ceremony. I wanted to put my hands over my ears and run as far as I could from that skull.

No skull—no! Air curdled about the yellowish bone, took on visible substance, building up a thin and unsubstantial vision of a face, a head. The eyes, the sharply jutting nose—so pointed that it might be likened to a bird's beak—overhanging a small chin, obliquely set eyes . . . No human face!

There was an urgency in the light-sparked eyes, a demand made upon me—but one I could not interpret. There had been something lost, which must be found. There was danger to be faced—there was—

The wisp of face vanished. While the bone it had built itself upon—I gasped! That, too, was crumbling into ashy powder. I cried out, "What is it that you would have me do? What do you want?"

The chant of that far-off ritual ceased, the terrible demand faded. Now the englobed gryphon lost its blaze of light, fell to rest again near my heart. Of the skull nothing remained.

"It wanted . . ." I stammered, turning to my companions, but I had no real explanation for them.

Jervon's face was impassive, Elys stared beyond me into that hollow among the rocks from which the skull and the rest had been cleared.

"There *was* something there!" I was obsessed with what I had seen. But had they also shared my vision?

"One who dies during some task laid upon him for good or ill," Elys said slowly, "clings to a shadow of life, unwilling to depart to new roads until that task is fulfilled. I think that such a shadow clung here. It is now gone—for good or ill."

"But it did not tell me what it wanted!" I found I could accept her words, accept them so completely that now I wished the skull back that I might again demand of whatever shadow was tied to it what I must do and where. For now I bore a burden also—though that might be an illusion only I could perceive.

"There will come a time when you shall know." Elys did not say that as one promises enlightenment to calm a bewildered child, rather as one who is sure of the truth.

I rose to my feet, my hand moved, as it so often did for reassurance, toward the gryphon. Then I jerked my fingers away before they could close about the globe. I wanted to rid myself of the thing! That is, one part of me did, while, deeper in me, arose an excitement that demanded that I yield to an unknown force, that I throw aside all those old fears and wariness of my people and go forth—to grasp . . . as yet I did not know what.

We did not linger long at that strange nesting place but went on, and soon there came a welcome change in the land. The arid desert gave way to growing things.

An arrow shot by Jervon brought down a creature not unlike the deer of the Dales. Thus we ate fresh meat and were able to drink the water we found in a much more wholesome oasis. Here were the signs of older camps and we believed we had chanced upon one of the regular rest sites of either scavengers or outlaws. Since the grazing was good we decided to remain there while Jervon once more went out scouting.

I was certain in my own mind that Kerovan had sheltered among the rocks, also that he had been in the narrow valley earlier. Inwardly I was discouraged. There was no trail to be followed through this wilderness and I could neither guess his destination nor direction. The gryphon—no, since its actions with the skull, even that I distrusted.

Though I tried talking with Elys, her answers were so random that I began to believe she either had thought better of her agreement to aid me, or that the episode of the skull had sent her into deep speculations of her own.

I sat back on my heels to look about me. This rough pasturelike land was normal to Dale eyes, at least more so than that portion of the Waste we had crossed. I remembered tales of the scavengers—that scattered across this country were cities or fortresses so blasted that all that remained were lumps of congealed metal, which they hacked free to sell. The metal itself was uncanny, for sometimes it exploded when touched with tools, killing those who would master it.

Who were the Old Ones? What kind of lives had they lived here? That skull, when it had taken on the semblance of life, had been more avian than human. The dead had not been in our form entirely—had it been more—or less—than us?

"Who were the Old Ones?" I had not realized that I asked that aloud until Elys, shaken out of her preoccupation by my voice, answered.

"I think there were many different kinds of them. She who taught me a Wisewoman's knowledge once said that they knew too much, tried too many uses of the Power. That they could change and did change into many forms. You have certainly heard legends . . ."

I nodded. Yes—the legends. Some were of monsters against whom our Dale forefathers had fought with fire and sword. Others—taking the seeming of fair women and comely men—enticed the venturesome away, some into permanent exile, others into visits from which they returned so bemused and bewildered that never again did they fit into human life, but went wandering, seeking that which remained ever hidden from them until their longing ate them into death.

"The use of Power," Elys continued, "can be the deadliest fate laid upon one. It is somehow bred into us, maybe doubly so into *them,* that the more we know, the more we must continue to seek. I think that those ancient ones learned, tampered, attempted too much. Their thirst for knowledge became the only mover in their lives. So it would follow that they might not be bound by any code of right or wrong—only by their own wills and desires . . .''

The truth of that I had already seen proven when Rogear had used the force of his will to bend me for a space into a tool—save that my dear lord had followed, to prove himself stronger. Yes, Rogear and my lord's own mother—others—had played with Power, drawing it greedily to them. However, in the end, it had turned upon them, eaten them up. Perhaps to bring upon them their endings.

"Can one use Power and still escape such consequences?" I made that a half-question, a new fear moving in me. Was I already, in my great need to gain my will with Kerovan, tainted with this hunger for the unknown? What had seemed to be a straightforward plan of action when I had ridden out of Norsdale was now confused. I was nibbled upon by doubt, which grew stronger. Was Kerovan—*could* he be right? Was it knowledge derived of the Dark and not the Light that would grow between us if we kept a bond and built upon it? Must I resist what lay in me clamoring for fulfillment?

No! That belief I refused to accept. I remembered again that strange man who had appeared out of nowhere when my lord had been so beaten down by the Dark, all those months ago. Neevor—he had said that I had the key, that we were fated to use it together. And for good—surely for good. I must allow no such doubts to creep into my mind.

Jervon returned just before sundown, excited and eager. He reported having found tracks of three mounts, one he thought ridden, the other two led. "There was a fourth also," he added.

"Three of the horses are still there grazing free. There are packs also—but no one camps. I believe that someone met with the traveler—their trails lay close together."

I was on my feet at once, heading for Bural. "Kerovan—he may have been taken captive!" In my mind churned the many dangers that could have befallen him.

"I do not think so. There is no sign of any attack. The horses are of the desert breed the scavengers usually use and they are peaceful. It is a good situation for a camp." Now he looked to Elys. "Also there have been safeguards placed."

She raised her eyebrows. "Of what nature?" she demanded sharply.

"None of a kind I have seen before. There are four peeled wands, each set upright in the earth at the outer limits of a well-seized grazing field. One, to the north, has fastened to it a tuft of horse hair. That to the south bears a patch of snowcat fur. To the east is one with an eagle feather, to the west one bearing boar bristles. I did not touch any. However, they manifestly have a purpose and the horses do not stray past them."

I glanced at Elys for an explanation. She looked as baffled as I felt.

"Where did he go? The man of that camp—it is Kerovan!" I did not know why I was so sure, perhaps mainly because I wanted to be.

"There are hoofprints—leading on westward into a wood. I would have followed but Agran here"—he drew his hand down the neck of the horse he bestrode—"would not approach it. He was as wild with fear as if a red bear reared in the way reaching for him. It is plain that was forbidden territory and Agran recognized it."

"But if the horses will not follow—then we can go afoot," I persisted.

Jervon regarded me gravely. "Lady, I would not try to enter that place whether astride or on my own two feet. It warns one off, I believe that some power rules there. We can but camp and wait at that place—to dare more is to achieve nothing."

I refused to believe him—then. We did ride on to that strangely marked camp and saw the horses as placidly grazing as if they were in a fenced field, never venturing beyond those wands. I paid only passing attention to those; instead I set Bural on the way to the wood.

She shied violently, near tossing me from the saddle. Twice we fought a battle of wills until I was forced to admit that I could not make the mare venture near the shadows of the trees.

My companions had gone their own way, establishing camp in the same hollow where the vanished traveler had left piled saddle and gear. Jervon tried the experiment of turning our own beasts into the square with the three desert horses and they appeared also to respect the wand barrier so that they need not be put on grazing ropes.

Only I was far too impatient to remain in camp awaiting a return that might or might not come. Having proven I could not

ride into the wood, I was determined to attempt it on foot, with
the turf torn by hoof marks for my guide.

My start was brisk enough, and neither Elys nor Jervon attempted to argue me out of it. It was not until I was some
distance along my chosen path (so was I strengthened in stubborn determination) that I realized I could not move fast, nor
could I touch any of those hoofprints with my boots. Rather,
without any volition, I was zigzaging back and forth just to avoid
that.

An uneasiness was growing in me for which I could not
account. I persevered but against a growing sense of danger, of
opposition, so that my pace grew slower and slower, in spite of
my will to push on.

It was not that I was fronted by any visible wall forbidding
entrance to the wood. No, rather my energy was steadily sapped,
my will itself weakened with every step I fought to gain. I
decided that I was not repelled by fear itself, rather a growing
awareness that I was intruding rashly, rudely, on private ground,
that I ventured where I had no right to go without invitation.

Even though I had come near under the outstretched branches of
one of the tall trees, I realized that my hope of traveling farther
was done. This *was* forbidden ground. Reluctantly I turned back,
faced toward camp. Then it was as if a strong force swept me
up, a storm of wind (though not a leaf rustled, none of the tall
grass rippled) pushed me away, heavy at my back. I had dared to
approach a guarded refuge—the wood was a sanctuary—but not
one for those of my kind.

Kerovan

As I sat with what I hoped was an appearance of ease, the sun shining on that band of metal, I was certain the stranger's oddly set eyes widened. For a moment, perhaps two breaths, his gaze held on that. Then he dropped his reins in turn, the shadow steed standing quiet, all four feet planted rock fast, as its rider's hands arose in an answering gesture of peace. At least in this much he followed Dale custom.

Cautiously, half fearing that my horses might come to life and bolt, I slipped from the saddle. None of the three moved as I watched them warily before advancing through the tall grass toward the cat-crowned man.

He waited until I was a sword's length away before he spoke—soft slurred words with a lilting cadence. He might have been reciting some formula. I shook my head, then replied in Dale speech:

"Greeting to a sharer of the road; may the—" I hesitated now. I could not wish him Flame Blessing—such words might be an insult to one who worshiped other powers. Nor could I, in all honestly, call upon the Flame myself, since I was marked as one with no right to the belief of true men.

He frowned. For the fist time there was a shadow of expression on his impassive face. Had a faint tinge of surprise also

57

crossed it for an instant? When he spoke again he used Dale speech, accented, but clear.

"Where ride you, man?" He made the word "man" sound like a title of disrepute.

"In search of—" I hesitated again. To inform the first comer of my reason for riding the Waste was folly.

"In search of—" he prompted. Now it was true he wore an expression and it was grim. "Old treasure, of scrap heaps to burrow in, scavenger?"

His hands dropped, not to seize sword as I had first thought, rather to gather up reins. I knew he was preparing to ride on where my mounts would not follow. At that moment I knew fear. For I had a strong feeling if he went I would not again see him or discover more of his kind, while it could well be he represented just those I had been sent to find.

"I am not a hunter of old metal—a scavenger." I hastened to say. "I ride with a message."

"What message and to be given to whom?" He was plainly impatient.

"The message I do know—but to whom it is to be delivered— of that I am not sure."

"Riddles!" he snapped scornfully.

"Not riddle but ignorance. I am out of the Dales where there has been war for two years and more . . ."

He had been on the point of turning his horse, now he stayed that movement.

"War." Again there was scorn in his tone. "One petty lord man against his fellow, quarreling over half a hillside of near-barren land."

His contempt for the Dalesmen was open. I half agreed inwardly that he was right. That was all that war had been for years—hot family feuds in which men died, to be sure, but there was no wide ravening of the countryside.

"This is true war," I made haste to explain. "Invaders from overseas such as we have not seen before, using new and terrible weapons." There was no need, I decided, for me to explain that most of those weapons had been by now rendered impotent through some lack we did not understand. "All the coast they hold and now they sweep farther inland. Always they bring reinforcements. We die and there are few to fill our empty saddles, or even horses to wear those saddles."

He leaned a little forward, his eyes narrowed. By some trick of the light they yet showed, within their depths, tiny glints of flame such as I had seen earlier in the cat eyes of his helm crest.

"So—why do you then come to the Waste—you in warrior mail? Do you run?"

Temper unleashed or leashed I had long ago learned to use as a weapon. I did not need to show any inner fire in answer to his taunt upon this occasion.

"I bring a message, as I have said." I decided there was only one way I might achieve my purpose after all—and that was with the truth. "We have taken prisoners and they have talked. Their story is that what they seek is a source of power, and it lies to the west. We think that they believe this. Therefore, it is not our Dales that is their final goal but perhaps—this—" I made a gesture to include the meadow in which we stood. Once more the wristlet blazed. "Your land—and perhaps those you name kin."

He made a sound deep in his throat, a snarl such as a cat might voice. Now he pointed to my wristlet.

"Where got you that?" he demanded.

"By chance—I found it in a stream in the Dales."

He smiled, the lift of his lip resembling a cat baring fangs—though the teeth he displayed were no different than my own.

"And where got you those?" This time he pointed to my hooves.

I answered steadily enough.

"My birthright—or birth curse. I have heard it said both ways in my time."

Again those narrowed eyes studied me closely. When he spoke some of the hardness was gone from his voice.

"I think you may have found those who will listen to your message—or may find them after I take council. Your animals" —he glanced disdainfully at the fear-struck desert horses—"cannot follow our trails. Their breed would die of terror were one of my people to approach them closely. I go now to my pack lord. If he wishes to see you I shall return—Man of the Dales."

He pointed now to the north.

"There is water there and good forage. If you wish—camp

and wait." He had turned his mount, now he looked back over his shoulder.

"I am Herrel."

I was startled. It is one of the strong beliefs of my people, who know the Power only slightly, that to give one's name to a stranger is a dangerous thing—since a man's name is an important part of himself and he can be influenced through it. Still this stranger had just, by that standard, shown great trust in me. I answered as quickly.

"I am Kerovan." To that I added no title or lordship, for such were mine no longer.

He sketched a salute with his free hand, then rode without looking back again, while I followed his advice in leading my now-more-biddable mounts on toward that campsite he had indicated.

I did not have to wait long. Herrel returned and with him another like him, save that his helm crest was an eagle with half unfurled wings, his saddle cloth a netting into which feathers had been woven. He sat his horse a little aloof while Herrel told me that I was bidden to speak with their lord. The second rider busied himself by driving four wands well into the ground, each being topped with a tuft of fur or feathers. Herrel, indicating them, told me that they would keep my mounts within bounds as well as any fence, but that I must go afoot.

So it came that I paced as might a captive between the two of them into the dusk of that dark wood. I did not allow my hand to brush near my sheathed sword. From now on I must be doubly wary, though I did not sense from these two, as I always had in Imgry's camp, the waves of hatred that my appearance fired in the Dalesmen.

Once within the first screen of trees, the way was not hard going. In fact there was a path or narrow road, wide enough for only one horseman, so deep-trodden one might believe it was a highway used through many years. To my advantage, my hooves were no longer constricted by the boots I had worn so many years in concealment. In fact I was glad to stretch my legs by this tramp. The many scents of the forest were heady. I drew deep breaths, and I discovered that I was growing lighter of heart and less wearied than I had been since I entered the Waste.

What did begin to impress me was that I saw no other life save the three of us who moved silently, for the hooves of the horses awakened only the slightest of sounds. No bird hopped on any branch, nor did I spy, along the outer edges of the trail, any beast's prints. The greenery was very dark nor had I elsewhere seen such trees of so huge circumference of bole. Their bark was black and deeply ridged.

The path we followed wove a meandering way, turning often to avoid such an obstruction as one of those trunks.

How long we traveled I had no way of knowing. My two escorts held their curiously dappled steeds to a walk, while around us the silence grew, the light became more and more dusky. Twice we passed stones, set upright, no normal outcroppings, for they had been wrought upon by man.

The tops of each of them had been carved with diabolical skill—I say diabolical for the creatures sculpture had evoked out of the rock were grim. One was a head, or perhaps better a skull, with a huge beak looming out to threaten any passerby. That bill was also a fraction agape as if about to seize on the unwary. There was something of a bird about it, also a bit of a long-snouted reptile. The holes, which had been left to represent eyes, had insets, so deep within I could not see whether they were gems or not (though how, in the absence of sunlight, any gleam could have been awakened from such was a mystery). I only know that red pits of utter savagery regarded me.

Neither of my companions so much as turned an eye in the direction of that looming guardian. Nor did they, either, regard the second such we passed. Where the first had been beaked or snouted, this was a life-size death's head possessing close kinship to a skull of my own race. The thing had been more graphically and disgustingly carved as if far gone in decay, stretches of rotting skin portrayed across cheekbones and chin, a nose half sloughed away. Once more there were eyes to watch, these yellow.

I made no comment as we passed these posts. For I was determined not to allow my companions to believe I found anything strange in this wood. To my own pride I owed that much, so I clung to an outward show of self-possession as I would to a battle shield.

We had left the skull post at least five turns of the path behind when Herrel leaned forward to sweep out an arm. As if he had so loosed the latch of a door a mass of branches lifted, swung to one side, to allow us out into the full light of day once again.

The wood still stretched like encircling arms on either side, and, by a distant mark across the horizon, formed another barrier there. However, directly ahead lay a section of land as wide as any Dale holding I had seen. Planted fields were guarded by low stone walls from pastures in which horses, such as Herrel and his fellow rode, grazed. There was the blue sheen of a pond or small lake farther west. Near that stood the first building that was not a long-abandoned ruin that I had ever seen in the Waste.

Stone formed the walls of the first story, but, rising above that, logs were set in tight company. The strangest thing was that these logs were apparently not dead and seasoned wood. Rather branches jutted here and there and those bore living leaves. The branches were thickest near the top of the walls, and spread wide as if they so formed the roof.

From the point where we had issued out of the wood, running directly toward the building, was a continuation of the forest path. Here in the open, however, the way was much wider. Perhaps four horsemen could have ridden it abreast.

He who had followed me on the trail did not urge his mount forward and we proceeded by the same line of march as we had kept under the trees, save that Herrel slowed a fraction to allow me to pace beside him. For the fisrt time since we left my camp he spoke:

"The lodge." He gestured to the building.

Any Dale keep whose lord abode within its wall would have flown his banner from the highest point. None such flapped here. Rather in a line flanking the front of that half-alive structure, there was planted in the earth a series of poles, all perhaps twice my height. From the top of each fluttered a narrow ribbon of color. The closer we drew the better able I was to recognize the devices these bore. Whereas the lords of High Hallack used for their heraldic crests either some fanciful monster, or an object suggesting a deed of valor performed by some ancestor, these carried very detailed pictures of well-known animals or birds.

A boar, a rearing stallion, an eagle, a mountain cat, a snouted and armored lurker of the river—there were a full twenty banners and not two alike. Save for my escort, however, there were no signs of life except four men, stripped to breeches and boots, at labor in the fields. Not one of them raised his eyes from his task to mark our passing.

Herrel swung out of his saddle and dropped the reins of his horse. The animal stood as if tethered.

"Wait!" He flung that single word in my direction, then passed beneath the outgrowing, bushy leaves of the building to push in a massive door. He who had been my other guide or guard, swung his own mount around and rode off. Nor did he look back.

I studied the strangeness of the keep for want of any better occupation. There were windows set on either side of the door on the lower floor. Each was covered by a fine latticework of branches perhaps as thick as my thumb. However, they were of worked wood, showing no leaves or twiglets.

My attention was drawn to a stirring among the leaves above, certainly not induced by any wind's rustle, for not the slightest breeze blew. I caught sight here and there of a small head—then two or three more—that could be viewed only for a moment, disappearing again before I had real sight of them. I thought though they were not of any species of animal or reptile I knew—and they were not birds.

They left an impression of a long, sharply pointed snout, ringed by fangs, exposed as if the creature possessed no concealing lips. Above that were the eyes, bright, inquisitive, knowing . . . Yes, *knowing*.

Almost the whole of the brush wall facing me was a-shake now. Numbers of the creatures, small as they were, must be gathering, right above the door. I had a sudden hint of what might happen should an intruder attempt entrance there against the will or orders given to such sentinels, guards, or whatever they might be.

As abruptly as he had disappeared, Herrel returned, the door left open behind him. He gestured for me to come. Nor did he glance above to where boughs creaked under unseen weight. The watchers remained at their posts, as, trying not to show any interest in them, I passed under that overhang and came into the hall of these Waste riders.

I had expected to walk into gloom, for those tightly latticed windows suggested that they admitted very little light. Instead I discovered a green glow, while at intervals along the stone walls there were baskets of metal—not the torch rings of the Daleland. In each of these rested a clutch of balls about the size of an egg, all of which glowed to give fair lighting.

The hall itself was enough like that of a keep to make me feel that these horsemen lived a life not too different from what I had always known.

Directly facing me stood the high table. However, this did not have just three or four chairs of honor. Instead there were twenty, each with a high-carved back, none set above its fellows. There was no second table for servants of the household, only that one board.

A wide hearth took up nearly a third of the far wall, cavernous enough to hold logs that must be nearly the size of those forest giants we had passed among. Along the other wall, which was broken by the door, were bunks on which were piled cloaks and coverings made of the cured skins of animals. A chest stood beneath each sleeping place.

There were no wall tapestries, no carved panels or screens. However, on the expanse of stone against which the high table was situated, a star was outlined in red-brown, the color reminding one unpleasantly of dried blood. The center of that was a mass of runes and symbols for which I hurriedly averted my gaze. For it seemed to me, that, when one viewed it directly, they came to life, wriggled, coiled, moved as might headless serpents in their death throes. I glanced to the band on my wrist. Its blue sheen neither waxed nor waned. Perhaps that meant that for me (at least now) there was no danger, no Power of the Dark here.

I was given little time to look about, for a man, seated in the chair directly before the center of that wall star, moved. He had sat so utterly motionless that now he startled me as he leaned forward. Both elbows were planted on the table, his forearms outstretched along the surface of the board. He presented the appearance of one who had no reason to try to impress a visitor, he being who and what he was.

He did not wear mail, or even a jerkin, his chest and shoulders being as bare as those of the field laborers. Though he was seated he gave the feeling of height and strength—the wiry strength of a good swordsman. A sword did lie there, lengthwise on the table, both of his hands resting upon its scabbard.

The scabbard was leather, horsehide, while the pommel of the weapon was in the form of a rearing stallion, such as I had seen depicted on one of the banners without. To his right a helm also rested, its crest the same design, save larger and in more detail.

He was dark-haired, and there was a likeness between him and Herrel, which revealed, I decided, some kinship—if not of close blood, then of race. It was difficult to judge his age, though I believed him older than my guide. There was about him such an air of inborn command and practiced Power as would reduce Imgry's bearing to that of a fumbling recruit new come to camp. Whatever this warrior might be otherwise, he was a long-time leader and user of Power.

I do not know whether he was used to staring others out of countenance at first meeting, but the look he turned on me was a heady mixture of contempt, a very faint curiosity, and much personal assurance.

Little by little I was learning how to deal with the unknown. Now I left it to him to break the silence. This might just be a duel of wills set to test me, he who spoke first forfeiting an undefined advantage. How long we faced each other so I do not know. Then to my surprise (which I fought not to show), he flung back his head and gave a laugh carrying a hint of a horse's neigh.

"So there is sturdy metal in you, hill-hugger, after all."

I shook my head. "Lord"—I granted him the courtesy title, though I did not know his rank—"I speak for certain of the Dalesmen, yes, but if you look you shall perceive I am not wholly hill-hugger." I advanced one of my hooves a fraction. If my half-blood should prove a barrier here as it was in the Dales, that must be my first discovery.

He had very level black brows, straight and fine of hair. They now drew together in a frown. When he spoke it was as if a faint, far-off ring of a stallion's battle scream hung behind his words.

"None of us may be what we seem." There was bitterness in that.

Then it happened. The air thickened, wrapping him in mist. When that cleared, it was pulled away by force, as if blown by the great arched nostrils of a horse. For there was no longer any man in the chair. Rather a war stallion, such as any fighting man may see but once in a lifetime, planted forehooves on the board, still nudging the sword. Its head, crowned by a wild mane, was lowered until it near overreached the far edge of the table in my direction. White teeth showed as it voiced the scream of a fighter.

I gave no ground; afterwards that memory sustained me. The thing was no hallucination, of that I was sure. Also the red fury in its eyes might signal a death warning. In that moment, in spite of my daze, I understood. I fronted a shapechanger—one who could at will, or in the heat of some emotion, assume animal form. Not that of any ordinary beast, no, this was a manifestation of the Were—one of the most dreaded of our ancient legends.

There was a deadly snarl to my right. I dared to turn my head a fraction. Where Herrel had stood a moment earlier, there crouched a huge snow cat—tail lashing, fangs displayed, burning eyes on me as its muzzle wrinkled farther and farther back.

Then—

A man again sat at the table fondling the sword. I did not need another glance to assure myself that the cat had also disappeared.

"I am Hyron," the man announced in a flat voice as if he had played a game that no longer amused him. There was a weariness in his tone also. He might have been very tired at the rise of each sun, the coming of every night. "We are the Wereriders. And you—what are you? Who are you? What do the hill-huggers want of us that they dare send a messenger?"

"I am Kerovan." Once more I made no claim of lordship or rank. "I was sent because I am what I am—a half-blood. Therefore, there were those who believed that you might give me better attention."

"A half-blood—one they hold in low esteem. And so they must hold us also—thus why would they wish a pact with us?"

"Lord Imgry has a saying to fit the need," I returned steadily. This horseman's taunts would awake no visible anger in me. "He has said that a common enemy makes allies."

"A common enemy, eh?" Lord Hyron's right hand had closed about the hilt of his sword. He played with the blade, drawing it forth from its sheath a fraction, snapping it back again sharply. "We have seen no such enemy."

"You may, my lord. And, if things continue to go so ill in the

Dales, sooner than you think.'' With as few words as possible and as simply as I could I told him of what we suspected to be the eventual purpose of the invaders.

"A treasure—a Power . . .'' He tossed his head with an equine gesture. "Poor fools and dolts. If these invaders found any such they would rue it bitterly in the end. Whoever dispatched them on such an errand is well disordered in what wits they possess. The Waste itself would fight with us.''

I felt Herrel stir rather than saw him move. His lord's gaze shifted to him. The cat-helmed warrior said nothing. All I perceived was that he and his leader locked gazes, though I gained the impression that between them communication passed.

There was a need, I sensed, not to speculate too far concerning the talents of the Weres. They were not of the kind to take kindly to any who pried into their ways. But that this period of silence was important I was sure.

Nor was I too surprised when there appeared from behind us several other men, drawing near to Herrel and me as if they had obeyed some unheard summons to council.

A loud click ended that period of silence, as emphatic a sound as if the fist of a man had come smashing down. Hyron had given a final slam to the sword, smashing it back into the scabbard with full force.

He arose, not as a threatening stallion, but in man guise. Yet still he leaned across the board even as the stallion had done.

"There is much to be thought on,'' he said. His frown had returned full force. Also there was a quirk to his lips as if he tasted something sour, perhaps his own words. "There is nothing in the Dales for which *we* choose to fight. On the other hand''—he hesitated as if turning some thought over several times to examine it the better—"there was once a geas laid—and perhaps that has brought us to this meeting. If we consult and discover that we indeed have a common enemy—that your purpose can answer ours—'' He broke off with a shrug. What he said had no real commitment, but I guessed I would get no better answer. Then he asked a question.

"Whom did you really seek when you came so boldly into the Waste, Kinsman-by-half?''

"Whoever there might be who would listen, Lord.''

Now he raised a forefinger to scratch along the line of his beardless jaw.

"You are forthright enough," he commented. From his tone I could not judge whether he thought me a fool for using the truth. "That being so—there are others here who might be interested in your warning." He smiled and I heard muffled sounds from those about me as if they shared his amusement. Did he want me to beg him for directions to those "others"? Somehow I believed that if I did that I would lose any advantage I had held in this interview.

"This you may tell your Lord—or he whose scheme brought you to us—" He folded his arms across his chest, once more tossed his head so that the crest of his hair fell in a lock over his forehead. "We shall certainly consider all he has said. If we make a decision in his favor, he shall hear so from us. There will be a price for our services, of course. We must have time to think of that. Years ago we once sold our swords and sold them well. Those who bought had no reason to claim they did not receive full measure. If we choose to bargain again, your Dalesmen may find us worth any price we ask."

"That price being?" I mistrusted this horse lord—not because I thought him a follower of the Dark, for I knew he was not. Still, legends say that there were those among the Old Ones who were neither good nor evil, but whose standards of right and wrong are not our measures.

"In due time and to your lord's own face shall we state that," he countered. "Also, if you wish to gather an army you need other allies." He suddenly pointed to my hooves.

"Why not," he asked, "seek those with whom you can claim kin?"

I knew that I dare not show ignorance now, that to do so would lessen me in their sight. My mother's clan came from the northernmost Dales—there must lie the mixture that had made me what I was. So if I did have kin there I would find such.

I managed a shrug. "We have no maps of the Waste, Lord. I took the westward hills for my guide—that brought me here. Now I shall ride north."

"North." Lord Hyron repeated. Then it was his turn to shrug. "The choice is yours. This is not an easy land, none does ride or walk here without due caution."

"So I have already discovered, Lord Hyron. My first meeting with a Waste dweller was his body—"

"That being?" He asked it idly, as if it did not matter.

Just because he would so dismiss my gruesome find, I described the mauled thing I had buried and was only halfway through my story when I felt the whole atmosphere about me change. It was as if I had brought portentous tidings without being aware of it.

"Thas!" It was a name, a word I did not know, and it exploded with force from Herrel. The indifference of Lord Hyron had vanished in the same instant.

Joisan

ELYS STOOD ON A SMALL RISE FACING THE FOREST LAND. SHE WAS frowning and the hands that hung by her sides twitched slightly. I thought that she was disturbed, that she felt some need for action, yet she was not sure what. Jervon had brought the packs and our saddles close to the mark of a recent fire and was again off collecting wood. A small pile of branches lay at Elys's feet also but she made no move to pick them up again. I paused beside her, turned also to face that line of trees that was so well protected against any invasion. Now that I regarded them more intently I could see that the leaves were darker green than those I had known in the Dales and they grew very thickly together.

"There are no birds." Elys said abruptly.

For a moment I was at a loss. Then, thinking back, I could not remember having sighted, since we left the Dales, any wing-borne life. The Waste was indeed a barren land. Still—why Elys should now be seeking sight of birds puzzled me.

"In such a wood—yes, there should be birds," she repeated; her frown grew heavier.

"But—I do not remember seeing any since we came out of the Dales."

She gave an impatient shake of the head. "Perhaps over the desert—no—there would be few to wing there. But this is a wood, a place to harbor them well. There *should* be birds!'' She spoke emphatically, her attitude one of foreboding. Then she glanced at me.

"You did not enter there after all."

"Jervon was right—there was a barrier. As if a keep door was closed and no visitors welcomed."

Her frown lightened a fraction. My answer might have supplied a part answer to her puzzle.

"There is a keep of sorts, I believe, in that wood. If that be so—then the land *is* closed, save when those who hold it wish otherwise. It will open to their desire only."

I did not like the idea her words conjured in my mind. "But"—I spoke my thought aloud, trying to reassure myself, perhaps have Elys agree with some hope or comfort—"I cannot be sure that it was Kerovan who camped here, who was enticed within there . . ." Even as I spoke that denial I knew that any hope of it being so was folly.

"Enticed . . ." Elys repeated thoughtfully. "No. If he entered there he did so willingly. These are not of the ones who entice, they have no need to do so. They are—strong—"

"What do you know or guess?" I demanded eagerly. "Have you then found some trace—some clue . . ."

"I only feel," she replied. "There is Power there, but I cannot say with any truth what it is. There is no sense of ill, but neither is there any of a force that is friendly, or beneficial. It is just—Power." She made a small gesture of bafflement with one of her hands. "But I wish that there were birds."

"Why?" I still could not understand her preoccupation with them. Nor why the presence—or absence—of birds might be so important.

"Because"—again she sketched that gesture of helplessness—"they would be here if all was well, judged by our own world. Without them that wood must be very silent, a secret place—too secret . . ."

Jervon called and we turned toward the camp. But she had wrought upon my imagination. As I went I found myself straining to hear a bird call—one of those things I had taken so for granted in the world I had always known that I had not been aware of such until it was missing.

Back in the campsite I looked longingly at those other saddle bags, which had been left behind by the missing traveler. If I could only rummage through them, perhaps so discover for certain that they were Kerovan's. Yet I could not bring myself to do that. I was sure, far too sure, that this was his camp—but a small hint of hope did remain battling within me and I feared to quench it and allow the dark suspicions that prowled among my thoughts entirely free.

As I sat beside the fire Jervon had kindled I still strained to listen, hoping for the comfort of the usual noises of the world. Even those made by the grazing horses, the thud of their hooves as they moved about was a reassurance. There was also the crackling of the fire . . .

Elys had been far too right. That wood was ominously silent. Not a leaf stirred, no branch swayed. The growth was rooted like a dark green trap, set to swallow up a reckless venturer at its own time and in its own way. Behind it, now cutting off the setting sun, bulked that dark line of heights. Perhaps they stood guard on the very end of the world. One could believe any weird fancy here.

I was too restless to sit still for long. Twice I sought the small rise where I had found Elys, ever watching the wood. Only the horses moved within the oddly marked square of pasture. When I looked back over my shoulder I saw that Jervon had taken out a whetstone, was using it on his sword balde, though he continually glanced up and around with a keen measuring look such as a scout would use in unknown and perhaps dangerous territory.

Elys remained by the fire. Her back was straight, her head up, but I could see even from my perch that her eyes were closed, and still she had the attitude of one listening intensely. It was said that the Wisewomen at times were able to detach a part of their inner sense, send it questing in search of what could not be seen, felt, or heard—by the body.

Where was Kerovan? Who had he gone to deal with inside that silent wood? Why had he been welcomed within and I refused entrance? Had he arranged a meeting with one who did sentry duty there?

I was so impatient for some news of him that I could have raged in my frustration. The sun was gone, the sky was beginning to dim—though bright colors still spanned the sky with broad bands of brilliant hue.

Twilight always came to the Waste as a time of brooding evil, or so I had found it in the past. The shadows of these trees lengthened across the open meadow, crept and crawled toward us. Even as there had been in that thick mist that enclosed the ruin where I had met with my present companions, so here now grew the feeling that something—or things—used those shadows for sinister purposes, and that a threat of peril hung here.

Yet the last thing I could have done—a thing I could not force myself to think of doing—was to get to horse and ride away. Slowly, with heavy feet and a feeling of growing chill within me, I left the rise to return to the fireside. As I went I shook my head against those irrational fears—but I was not able to so rid my mind's sensing of that brooding, watching something . . .

Jervon had put aside his stone, sheathed his sword. The world was all the more quiet when the scraping of his whetstone ceased. He came to Elys, dropped on his knees behind her. His hands went out to rest, one on each of her shoulders.

I saw her quiver at his touch, as if he had drawn her back out of some trance. Her eyes opened, yet she did not turn her head toward him.

"There is trouble?" he asked softly. I was on my feet again, looking at once to the wood.

Her eyes, though they now opened, remained blank. She did not focus on anything before her. At last one of her hands arose to close about his where it lay on her right shoulder. Again she shivered.

"If I only knew more." Her cry held passion, even a note of despair. "Yes, there is something—something wrong—wrong—or else so different from us that there is no understanding it!"

Startled, I wheeled to look at that wood, for I thought only of it. Was Kerovan returning, perhaps accompanied by whoever dwelt here? But surely Kerovan, for all that strangeness in him since he had summoned Power (in spite of himself when he fronted Rogear and the rest), was not so unhuman as to be what Elys apparently now sensed.

"Who comes from the wood?" I demanded of her, all my fears aroused.

"Not the wood." There was still enough of the lingering after-sunset light to see clearly what she did. She pulled out of Jervon's hold, set both hands palm down on the earth where

there was a patch bare of grass, leaving only the naked soil.
There she leaned forward, her weight upon her arms and hands,
while there was very strong about her that air of listening, of a
need for concentration.

So tense she was that I found myself also kneeling, watching
her hands against the earth as if one could expect a sudden
upheaval of the soil there.

"Under"—she spoke so softly that I barely caught her whisper—
"under . . ." I was sure I saw her hands whiten across the
knuckles as if she exerted her full strength to hold down a force
under the ground that was struggling with a matching effort to
win free.

Then she threw herself backward and away, scrambled to her
knees, seizing upon Jervon's arm to drag him with her.

"Up—and back!" That was no half-whisper, rather close to a
shout of warning.

I also scrambled backwards, at the same time heard a mad-
dened squealing from the horses. They were racing, their eyes
wild, kicking out at each other, milling around within that square
marked by the wands.

While the ground—! The ground itself was trembling, shaking
and rolling under my feet, the earth shifting as if it were as light
and fluid as water, Jervon had drawn steel, so had Elys. Swords
ready, the two crowded back from the spot where they had been
a moment earlier.

The flames of the fire flared as wildly as the horses moved,
spitting sparks into the air while the brands upon which they fed
shifted this way and that.

I saw the earth rise like a wave, hurtling outward, striving, it
would seem, to sweep us from our feet. Jervon and Elys were on
one side of that surge, I on the other. I could not keep my
balance as the wave sent me wavering from side to side. Now
there was a second peril. Between me and my companions the
soil spun around and around like batter stirred by a giant spoon.
As it so spun the circle of that whirlpool reached farther and
farther out gulping down first the fire, then the unknown's
saddlebags, then one of the poles—that with the tuft of grey-
white fur—breaking so the unseen barrier that had confined the
horses.

It was then I turned and ran, but not quick or far enough. One of the horses had found the opening and raced straight at me. I threw myself to one side, toppled and fell. The earth curled about me in an instant, trapping my legs, flowing waist high, engulfing my flailing arms. I sank as into quicksand, soil filling the mouth I opened to scream, forcing itself into eyes I tried to blink shut. I had but a single half-conscious moment to draw a deep breath and try to hold it, as the ground took me down into darkness.

Choking, I fought again for air. I could not move and my fear was such that I cannot now remember much of what followed, mercifully perhaps. Then—I could once more breathe freely! My smarting eyes teared, striving to clear themselves of the earth clotted on my lashes. I could see nothing but deep dark—and a sharp fear lashed at me—was I blind!

No—it was not completely dark. There was a glow—very faint—against my breast. I tried to raise my arms to brush away the burden holding me flat on my back and discovered that, twist and struggle though I might, my wrists and ankles were secured in some fashion.

However, those welling tears had cleared my eyes enough so that, with the aid of the faint glow, I discovered I was no longer encased in the earth. Rather I lay in an open space—though plainly I was still a prisoner.

The glow—with a great effort I raised my head and saw that it spread from the globe of the gryphon, which nursed a small core of faded radiance.

"Elys! Jervon!" I spat out earth and called. My only answer was a dull echo. Once more I fought against whatever held me, and, by twisting my hands as hard as I could, I became aware that each wrist was ringed by bonds to keep me firmly captive.

Captive. Then that action of the earth, which had been in force to engulf our camp, was a trap! And any trap in the Waste meant—

I fought the fear that followed like a sword thrust of ice cold. The Waste harbored life we could not even begin to imagine— what had taken me?

For some moments I lost control, flopping about as best I might, striving in sheer terror to tear apart what held me. My wrists burned from the chafing of the loops about them, earth cascaded from me in powdery puffs, until I began to cough and strangle, and so was forced to lie quiet.

Then I became aware of a noisome odor. Such was not natural to any earth I knew. It was the stench of some beast's unclean den, of old decay and death. I gagged and fought sickness rising sourly in my throat.

Beast . . . den . . . More fear awoke from such scattered thoughts to nip at me. But beasts do not bind their captives. This was the Waste—said that other, the fear itself—anything may happen here.

Gaining such control as I could summon, I once more called aloud the names of my companions. This time, through the echo, came another sound—something brushed against the side of a narrow way—a scraping. I gulped, and in spite of my efforts to master my growing terror (for in my mind formed the picture of a giant scaled thing crawling through the dark), I closed my eyes. But I could not close my ears—or my nose.

There was other life here now—rustling. The odor was such to make me gasp and choke as I had when the soil had closed on me. I felt a tugging at my wrists, my ankles. There were hands (or were they paws?) fumbling about my body. I was firmly grasped by a number of such—what, I dared not open my eyes and try to see.

They raised me. Then I was being carried through a passage so narrow that at times my body brushed walls on both sides, continually bringing a rain of dust and clods down upon me. While that terrible foul odor never ceased to assault my nose.

I think that at least once I lost consciousness entirely and perhaps that may have lasted for some time. Then I was dropped with force enough to awaken pain from many bruises—and left to myself. I became dully aware that now there were no longer bonds to hold me.

Slowly I opened my eyes. The foul smell was still strong. Only the rustling had ceased, nor did I sense any of my captors close by.

It was still dark, a thick dark, broken only by the gleam of the gryphon. I had lost my helm, my hair had fallen about my shoulders and was matted with earth, sour smelling and sticky. I moved my hands cautiously, half expecting to be rushed by those whose prisoner I was. My sword was also gone, as was my belt knife and dart gun. Apparently my captors recognized the threat those weapons offered and had good reasons to be wary. I still wore my mail and the rest of my clothing was intact.

Wincing at the pain of my many bruises, I levered myself up, moving with great wariness since I could not tell how large was the place in which I lay. I half feared I might strike my uncovered head against a roof.

As I sat so, my hands out on either side to support me, turning my head very slowly to peer fruitlessly into the dark, I gained the impression that, far from now being in a tunnel such as the one I had earlier been dragged through, I was in a hollow of some size, perhaps a cavern.

I continued to listen and so became aware of a sound, which my still-dulled senses finally identified as the drip of water. The moment I thought of water my dust-filled throat became a torment. I did not attempt to get farther up than on my hands and knees. In fact even that much effort made my head whirl like the churning earth that had brought me here. So I crawled a little at a time, seeking the source of the sound.

It was mainly by a stroke of fortune that I found it, since the glow of the gryphon was so faint and I could not even be sure I was heading in the right direction. One hand, edging forward for the next advance to my painful journey, plunged down in liquid so cold it brought a sharp gasp from me.

The gryphon, dangling forward, showed the dim outlines of a small basin or hollow, perhaps worn so by ages of such dripping. The drops themselves fell from somewhere overhead to splash into a catch pool, which I could have covered with my lost cloak.

I drank, splashed water on my dust-covered face, drank again, a cupped palmful at a time. The water was as cold as if drained from some unreasonable block of ice. But, as it flowed down my parched throat, it brought with it a return of my courage.

When I had drunk my fill, I felt strong enough to stand, balancing myself with feet slightly apart and hands outspread at my sides. Once on my feet, I stood listening with all my might, for I could not rid myself of the idea that whoever had dragged me here might well still have me under observation and any move on my part would provoke an attack.

There was nothing to be heard but the constant drip of the

water. At last I took the globe in one hand and tried to use it as a
torch. But the dim light showed me nothing. I felt wary of
advancing blindly into the unknown. Yet to remain where I was
solved nothing.

It was plain I needed some way to locate the spring again after
I was through exploring. Now I considered my clothing as an
answer to that. Beneath my mail shirt was a quilted leather
jerkin, under that a linen chemise, all the protection I had against
the rub of the link-mail. I fumbled with the lashing of my
protective shirt, stopping every second or so to listen. Then I
dropped the quilted jerkin on top of my body armor, skinning
off, last of all, the linen.

Once more I donned leather and mail, then considered the
linen. It was stout stuff, well and tightly woven, made to resist
hard wear.

Had I been left my knife I might have had an easier piece of
work, but I had to use the edge of my belt buckle, even tug at
the fabric with my teeth, before I could start a tear. Then there
was a battle to make a second slit, a third. Working at this so
determinedly was settling for my nerves. At least I was doing
something that was for my own help. Finally I had a ragged coil
of frayed cloth, tied into a line.

One end of this I made fast with the tightest knot I could
fashion to a sharp stone that helped to form part of the basin
wall. The anchorage being in place, I walked forward, step,
pause, step, until the cord pulled taut warningly. There was still
nothing ahead of me, even though I took off my belt and swung
it forward as a lash, hoping so to encounter a wall. Defeated in
that direction I edged to the right, determined to make a complete circle about my anchor.

I had gone perhaps a quarter of that distance when a barrier
did loom out of the dark, barely visible in the globe light. A
wall—so close I could touch it with my hand. Running my
fingers along its surface I moved on several steps. The cord grew
so tight I was afraid of pulling it loose. I stooped to near floor
level where my boots had kicked some small rocks. There I
found one to which I made fast the other end of the line. Heaping
several more of the rocks on top of that one I left it so, intending
from here to keep to the wall as a guide.

The wall was all rock, not packed earth, rough enough to be

the natural wall of a cavern. Yet it ran on and on without end, save that once it curved to form a side chamber.

At last I did come to a second section of wall that met the first at a right angle. This I also used as a guide. I had, however, taken only a few tentative steps along beside it when I halted. The rustling sound, the noisome smell—both were back! I was no longer alone.

Hastily I wrapped one end of my belt about my fist, leaving the buckle end dangling. This was the only weapon I could improvise, but I could flail out with it through the dark and defend myself so. I set my shoulders against the wall and stood waiting, hoping my ears could give me warning of an attack.

There came a grunting, which rose and fell—it might even have been speech of a kind. Only I could not center it at any one place in the dark. Suddenly I thought of the gryphon globe—the light from that could betray me. However, I had no time left now if my ears did not play me false.

I heard their rush, the pad of feet racing toward me. Tense, I let the globe swing free. Poor as its illumination was, it might serve if the creatures came close enough. Also, I had the belt whip.

I was hardly sure whether I could detect movements or not, but I swung the belt and felt it strike home. There was a satisfactory squeal—perhaps I had done more damage than I might have hoped for.

Skidding across the floor, to come to a stop just beyond the toes of my boots, was a dark hunch of a body. I swung the globed gryphon, needing to see the nature of my enemy. The thing gave a cry and flopped hastily away. I gained only a quick impression of something much smaller than myself, covered by thick hair or fur, not clothing, though it had four limbs, a body, and a blob of a head not too far from human kind.

The stench that arose from it was nauseating. I swung the belt once more, hard, hoping to catch it again before it could dodge. My blow failed, I only heard the buckle clang against rock.

There followed a determined attack and I lashed out again and again. Whether the things were used to being met by resistance I could not tell, but their grunting rose to a screeching as they dodged and flopped, so near the limit of my vision I was mostly only aware by touch when I caught any of them with my lash.

I had no idea how many of them there were, while I had ever the thought that if enough of them made a concentrated rush at me I could hope for no escape.

For some reason I could not understand they did not try that, making only scattered, darting attacks as if they were being held at bay by more than just my clumsy belt. Then an idea began to grow in my mind that it was the gryphon that must bother them. I could now try a great gamble, which might lose me what little advantage I had, or I could keep on beating the air about me until my arm was tired past raising (it was already beginning to ache and it took more of an effort to forestall those rushes).

If I only knew more about the nature of the Power the globe employed! I had seen it in action, yes, but both times it had been animated by one who had some knowledge of such energy— which I did not. Neevor's promise—that to me it was a key— flitted through my mind. But it was not a key I needed now—rather a weapon.

With the belt hanging ready in one hand, I ducked my head to free the chain of the globe so I could swing it, though at a much more restricted length, like my improvised whip.

I whirled it up and around my head. To my vast astonishment, the result was the same as that of whirling a flaming torch to increase its fire. There followed a burst of light—the gryphon was lost to sight in the brilliant flare—the beams of which shot far farther than I would ever have dared hope.

For the first time I saw the enemy clearly. They stood hardly higher than my shoulder as they shuffled backward in haste. However, they retreated still facing me, hands or paws out-stretched and sweeping through the air in my direction, as if their desire to cut me down was so great they must continue to wave those handlike extremities from which sprouted huge, sickle-shaped claws. Their bodies were completely covered by a bristly growth, which looked coarser than any fur or hair, more like fine roots, while there were pits in their rounded skulls though they did not appear to hold any eyes. Their faces became muzzles not unlike that of a foreshortened hound's, showing great fangs of teeth—hinting ominously at what their diets might be.

In the light of the globe they squirmed, cowered, raised their clawed paws to cover their eye pits, while they shrieked and cried out as if I had handed them over to dire torment.

Then, cutting through all that clamor, there sounded a single long, high-pitched whistle. The noise hurt my ears—as sharp as a knife thrust into my head.

The things' heads swung about on their bowed shoulders, turning almost as one in the direction from which the whistle had come. Then they moved, scuttling away at a speed that took them out of the range of light into their normal dark. I could hear the thud of their feet as they ran until there was nothing but silence once again.

So I had withstood one attack. Only I gained no sense of triumph from that, being sure that it *was* only a first one and that those under-earth dwellers would return. Which meant that I must find some way out before they mustered up will or desire to try me again.

I held the globe closer to the wall straining to see any opening, knowing better than to forsake it and head out into the open blackness of this place.

That whistle—and the things had answered it as hounds do their master's call. It might well be that these creatures, who had tried to pull me down, had brought me here, were tools or servants of someone else, undoubtedly infinitely more dangerous. Why they had been called off when they need only have tired me out . . . Unless . . . I weighed the gryphon in my hand. If I only *knew!*

I leaned one shoulder against the wall, the globe cupped against me. My encounter by battle, brief as it had been, had left me with an aching arm and a body, I was surprised to find now, shaking as if I had lately crawled out of my bed after a long illness. I realized it had been a long time, or so a gnawing within me testified, since I had eaten. Water I had found—but food to strengthen me . . .? Where in this dark hole could I hope to discover that?

The wall seemed endless as I shuffled on, my pace very slow, for I also stopped every few steps to listen, always fearing that the dark-loving creatures might not come so boldly next time, rather would creep upon me stealthily. The globe gave off a warmth that battled the chill beginning to eat into me. I kept glancing down to reassure myself of the light—which had now faded to its first dim glow. The gryphon was once more visible, its sparks of eyes seemingly raised to meet mine. Suddenly I realized that I was whispering to it.

First just Kerovan's name—which I said over and over in a sing-song as if it were a spell that could lift me through all care and danger. I tried to raise in my mind a picture of him as I had last seen him.

What followed was—no, I cannot ever find the words to describe what happened. It was as if some energy had hurled me back against the wall with a bruising force. I had—somehow I had—linked thought for an instant with my lord!

Frantically I stared down at the gryphon, fighting to hold onto that instant of communication—to know—to feel . . . I had not been alone. He . . . it had been as if he stood beside me. If I only could once more . . .!

"If I knew—if I only knew!" I cried desperately to the gryphon. The globe was a link, but chance only had made it, and now it was gone. That it was my own ignorance that stood in the way made my heart pound, brought tears of rage to my eyes.

Rage would not help. I did not need Elys to warn me against unshielded emotion. One commanded oneself before one learned to command Power. That was part of the long training she had spoken of—years spent in learning mastery, of how to nourish talent.

Will might control talent, but one had to center will, shut away all else, put all one's energy into forming of one's will a weapon as strong as steel. What could I do with my will? This was the hour in which I could bring it and me to a testing—a testing that could mean life or death.

Kerovan

As I STOOD THERE IN THE HALL OF THE WERERIDERS I COULD INDEED
feel the touch of danger—yet this was not a threat aimed at me.
No, it was something inherent in that single word Herrel of the
cat-shape had uttered, the word that had burst from him when I
had described the mutilated body I had discovered in a dismal
oasis of the Waste.

"Thas." It was Lord Hyron who repeated that word now,
and his voice was low, hardly above a whisper. I watched, for
the second time, air begin to curdle about him. Whether he
willed it or not this time, his shapechange had begun. Then,
perhaps because he was able to control a near-compelling emotion, he was man again.

"Watch the ground," he said to me with the force of one
delivering a necessary warning. "For the earth itself is Thas
land, and they have the rule of the under surface of it. They are
no friend to any who can wear *that* without harm!" He pointed a
long forefinger at the band about my wrist. "That they are now
found near here—that means matters are on the move—matters
that have long been dormant."

He shook his head until his mane of hair near blinded him
with its fringe across bright eyes.

"You are neither one thing nor the other, you who call yourself

83

Kerovan. Learn what you are, and that speedily, or you shall be
reduced to nothing at all—not even bones left to dry in desert
air.''

Such was the farewell the lord of the Wereriders took of me,
for I was not invited to be a guest under that bush roof. I had
been offered no greeting cup when I came, no stirrup cup when I
left. It was as if here I was less considered than even the most
humble of landsmen. I did not allow my temper to take edge
from that, for I was not wishful to remain longer in a place
where I could never be sure which shape those about me wore
was theirs in truth.

The sun was well west when I came forth into the clearing in
which that half-living keep stood. None of the Wereriders had
gathered to see me off. Only he who called himself Herrel
followed me out, to mount again, and stood waiting to escort me
from their holding. Perhaps in some way they were as suspicious
of me as I was of them. My last sight of the keep showed me
that the branches that clothed its upper stories were waving as
energetically as if storm-tossed, while from them numerous small
shapes sprang outward, heading in great racing leaps for the
wood. Did they go to hunt by night, I wondered, as I trudged
beside Herrel's shadow-dappled mount? Or were they to form
another part of my escort? I sensed in them a source of peril I did
not understand, but thought it prudent that I be wary of them.

Once more we threaded that path through the wood. This time
the gloom had deepened until now and then I stumbled, half-
blinded by the dusk, though neither Herrel nor his mount had
any difficulty in keeping the trail. It crossed my mind that those
of the feline breed had excellent night sight, so that this man
who could will to be a furred, fanged hunter on four paws might
well share that sense.

I speculated, as we went in silence, as to how it might feel to
be a shapechanger, to taste at desire another kind of life far
divorced from that I myself awoke to each morning. Did the
instincts and thoughts of a man remain alive in the mind of the
beast, or were such dulled and forgotten after one endured the
change? Was there in truth a real alteration of body, or was that
only a forceful hallucination which the Weres were able to
impress upon others? Had I indeed seen Hyron as an actual
stallion ready to savage me, or just what I was meant to see?

So musing, I tried to recall such legends of the Weres as the Dalesmen knew. But all our stories were so old, so overlaid with the horror of people who had faced such a mixture of nature, that I really knew very little. I would have liked to have questioned Herrel—asked him what it meant to be two different natures fused into one. In my own way was I not this also? Did *he* ever consider himself so apart from normal mankind as to be cursed, walled off from any small pleasure of life? No—that burden would not touch one who walked among his own kin, who had the comradeship of those who shared his own talent, if one could call it that. Also I knew better than to ask such questions of a stranger.

Our winding path so disguised the length of the journey that I was not sure how close we were to the outermost part of the tree wall when there came a thin, high chittering from the left. It was the first sound other than the faint thud of hooves and the scarcely heard pad of my own feet to break the silence.

"Wait!" Herrel reined up.

I, who was behind him on the narrow path, obeyed his order. He leaned forward, his head turned a little toward the nearest of the tree branches.

Again, imperative, came that sound. I heard Herrel whistle— not that command note that he had used to stay the panic of my horses, but rather as if he summoned.

From the branch toward which he had been looking sprang a small creature, certainly of the same species as those abiding in the roof of the Were keep. It balanced on the Were's shoulder and gave a series of sharp squeaks, as if it spoke to him in its own tongue.

At last he held out his arm and the creature ran along it with the sureness it might have used on a stout branch, leaped out, vanishing in the walling mass of green. Herrel looked to me.

"Thas," he said tersely.

"Here?" Though I still did not know the nature of that enemy, the reaction of the Weres earlier had made very plain this was a threat even they respected, not to be taken lightly.

"At your camp." He prodded his mount from a walk to a trot, so that I must run to keep up. However, it was only a very short time before we burst free into the open land. There was more light here—much more, for the western sky was striped with color. Only, what I looked upon was such an area of disaster as made me think for a moment that I *was* the victim of hallucination.

The ground where I had made my camp was now a raw mass of new cut ruts and hollows, of great circular scars, laying bare piles of soil. Where my horses had grazed there were no animals, while from the broken ground there arose a stench of foul decay strong enough to make me gag.

Down on his knees in the midst of that churned and torn sod was a man in Dalesman's armor hacking at the earth with heavy jabs of his sword, sending broken clods flying in all directions. At his side a woman, also wearing mail but without any helm on her dark head, used the edge of a small arm shield to aid in the frantic digging.

As we broke from the wood, and I ran toward that mass, she glanced up—then reached to catch the arm of the sword user. The man turned his head to note us, but he did not pause in his digging. It might have been that any halt in his labor could be, for some reason, fatal.

The woman arose to her feet, shaking free a scoopful of earth she held in the shield. There was light enough to see her face clearly, and I was startled, for there was that in it I recognized—though I could not have set name to her. I felt, as I had not ever before in my life, that her kind was kin—to me who had no kin. Was she another inhabitant of the Waste, but closer to man in heritage than Herrel and his kind?

She spoke as I came up to her, not to me, rather to the man still digging.

"There is no longer any use, Jervon. She is lost to us."

She then turned to eye Herrel and to him also she spoke, sharply, as one who had the right to demand answers.

"Warrior, what manner of peril is it that can turn solid earth into a whirlpool and engulf a traveler so? Who casts such a Power spell and for what purpose?"

He continued to sit his mount, though he met her gaze squarely, a faint frown on his face.

"Thas," he replied.

"And what are Thas—or could it be who?" she persisted, with the same tone of command.

"Deep earth dwellers. The inner parts of the ground are theirs. It is their given talent to command it to their desires when they

wish. As to why they set such a trap here—'' He shrugged.
''The Waste holds divers species, we go our own ways, following the demands of our natures. Though this is the truth: it has
not been known for many seasons that the Thas venture outward
from the mountains where lie their chosen burrows. Though they
may well have delved so without our knowing of it, they run
their ways very deep. Also, we of the Waste meddle not among
ourselves.'' His answer was chill, as if he meant it as a reproof
for her persistence, her open questioning of a matter he plainly
thought was none of her concern.

She stepped across a deep rut, advanced closer to him. Her
companion had arisen, his soil-encrusted sword still in hand. I
had seen his like in the Dales, for he was plainly a man of that
pure blood. Though he wore a helm, it carried no House badge.
Still there was nothing about him that proclaimed ''outlaw.''

''These burrows, which the Thas run for their purposes,'' the
woman continued, ''how deeply may such lie and where?''

Herrel shrugged again. ''Who knows? Or cares. We have
never had any traffic with the earth-dwellers—their ways are not
ours.''

''Nor do you want to meet them, I presume.'' There was a
note of challenge in that. She was using a tone sharp enough to
bring blood to the cheeks of any fighting man. Certainly she
stood in no awe of Herrel. If she knew what he was . . . I had a
strong suspicion that she did. Perhaps she had had dealings with
his kind before and knew best how to gain answers. ''Why do
they seek to entrap those who offer them no harm?''

''We do not know. Thas are Thas. But such as this''—he
glanced down at the churned earth, what had been a camp and
was now only a morass of disturbed soil—''I have not seen
before. There is—'' His frown grew deeper.

''Perhaps you wish to say that there is something new—
an awakening somewhere in this land,'' she answered him.
''Shapechanger, have you been so long safe in the refuge of your
kind that you do not sense a stir—or know that there is a new
element ready to invade the Waste? Old things can be stirred into
life by those having the proper key—and the power to turn such.
If this is done wrongly, then all, no matter who or how they seek
to stand aloof, can be drawn in—into a battle where forces,
blindly awakened, cannot be easily controlled—or laid—again!''

Herrel had been studying her face. His mount moved restlessly, sidled away from her. I did not believe the Wererider had any fear of the woman, rather he was moved by an instinctive wariness, which was a part of his heritage.

"You have Power," he observed. "Ask any questions of those or that which you can summon. We have no dealing with the Thas, nor"—now he looked from her directly at me—"do we want any with those who can awaken aught here. Carry no assurances of any aid now to your lord, Dalesman-by-half. If the Waste stirs we shall have other affairs to deal with."

With no more words and no backward look, he sent his mount trotting for the wood, the horse's hooves throwing up clods of the loose earth as he went.

It was my turn for questions. Who were these two, and what did they mean about another who had been trapped in the earth? Again it was the woman who spoke.

"You are Kerovan." She did not ask, she named me as one she had known well.

Her familiar use of my name was disturbing. Had she and this fighting man been sent after me by Imgry (who was the type, I was sure, to always strive to make certain any plan by a double protection)? He could very well have caught within his search net this woman (I was sure she possessed the talents Herrel had recognized by instinct) and dispatched her also, with the same orders he had given me.

"I am Kerovan," I admitted, "and you?"

I waited for her to tell me of Imgry, but all she answered was, "I am Elys, and this is Jervon."

The Dalesman only nodded. He stopped to catch up a tuft of grass and began wiping the soil from his blade.

"We came," the woman continued deliberately, "with my Lady Joisan."

I froze. Of all the explanations I had been prepared to hear that one was the most impossible. For a long breath I could not believe I had heard her aright. Joisan here? But—where—and why?

As I looked around wildly, Elys then added, "She was engulfed—in that . . ." To my growing horror she pointed to the hole where Jervon had been digging.

"You—you lie!" I was caught now in such bewilderment I

could only deny and deny that such an impossibility could be so. This was trickery, the kind of trickery those of the Waste might use to entrap one. "Joisan is in Norsdale. I set her free—she is safe—she is . . ."

That which welled in me now was an anger deeper, a fear greater, than I thought any one could hold. Now I knew—fleetingly—why I had felt so cold. *This* was the fire that had been in me, that I had willed so fiercely into an inner prison.

Jervon strode toward me, his sword point rising, aimed at the small hollow left bare between my chin and my mail.

"My lady does not lie," he said with dangerous softness. "The Lady Joisan was here and the whirlpool of the earth swallowed her down. She came out of her concern for one Kerovan, who, it would seem, lacks any concern for her."

Madness . . . either they were—or I was—mad! Hallucination—could this be some spell born perhaps from that meeting in the Wereriders' Hall? To have any dealings with those who possessed Power was always dangerous and tricky. This could be some subtle attempt to try and influence me by awaking emotions I dared not allow to trouble my mind—or my heart.

Save that now Elys told me in detail of how the two of them had met with Joisan in the Dales, and of her great desire to find me, of how they decided I might have gone into the Waste because of a scrying in which Joisan took part, of how they had come here to what they believed was my camp—and then of the attack . . .

This was all true! I could not deny it any longer, and at that moment I could have thrown back my head and howled like any winter-haunted wolf. That Joisan had followed me! She had no part in my life—just as I had no right in hers. I was bound to a dark past, perhaps a worse future. She must be free of me.

That *she* had been taken, buried, caught in an evil web of the Dark spawn because of her mistaken value of me—that I could not bear. Only I must—I had to accept the truth, hard as it was.

I crossed the ruts to the hole where Jervon had dug so fruitlessly and then I looked up from that shallow pit to ask just one question. Though I already knew what the answer must be and how I would stand condemned by it, in my own eyes, as long as I lived. "How long?"

Elys had followed me. Now her fingers just touched my arm. I did not deserve any sympathy, but I was still too frozen without, too a-fire within, to reject her out of hand.

"I do not believe she is truly buried."

I glanced at her, turned my eyes once more to the earth. There was no use in her trying to reassure me thus. Joisan was gone into the Dark. I was just beginning to realize what a loss was mine. I had believed when I rode out of Norsdale that I had armored myself, that I accepted in full the bitterness of what my life would be from that day forward. Now I knew that I had not sensed even a hundredth part of what fate had brought to burden me as long as I walked the earth that had taken her.

Now Elys's fingers tightened their grip. She gave a tug, which brought me to look at her again.

"She is not dead." Her words were quiet but delivered with conviction, a conviction I could not accept, caught as I was in my inner hell.

"Lady"—I spoke in the same quiet tone also, with a remnant of the old great hall courtesy—"you well know there is no way she could be buried so and still live."

"We shall see—and I promise you this shall be true seeing."

She made a summoning gesture with her other hand. Jervon had already gone to where a saddlebag lay half-hidden in up-thrown soil. From that he brought her a wrapped bundle.

Twilight was now upon us, but when Elys let fall the wrapping there appeared a concentration of what light was left, centering on the thing she uncovered, a silver cup that shone with a moon's full light, as if the moon's beams themselves had been forged into it.

I watched, dull-eyed, as she mixed pinches of dried herbs, which she took from small bags carried in her belt pouch, shifting them into a very small measure of water Jervon poured from a saddle bottle. I saw her lips move soundlessly as she twirled the cup. Then she held it out to me.

Against my will I accepted it. Not that I denied she could use some talent to so summon sight of Joisan, but because I was so sure of, and so feared, what I might see. On my wrist blazed the band, rising to a glow that matched that of the cup—no warning there—could it be a promise? I would not allow myself to believe that.

Holding the moon between my hands I looked down—into its hollow bowl.

As I had expected—darkness. No! The liquid within had taken on life of its own, swirled, though I held the cup steady. Now it climbed the wall of the hollow, filling it to the brim. Still I stared at a surface that remained dark. Then . . .

A glow—so faint—still it held steady there. Perhaps the urgency of my fear and desire gave power to my sight at that moment when I longed so, needed this so much. There—there was the gryphon! The small beast was alive with light, and behind it—I fought against the dark, I tried to compel greater sight with my will. I *must* see! Slowly, very slowly, I did. There was only a shadow of a face, but the eyes were open, it was the face of the living—Joisan!

Hallucination, meant to deceive?

No! Somehow I was certain that the gryphon, that my wrist band, would not allow a false vision. I saw Joisan alive. She was not dead, crushed in the earth. But where was she—and how might I find her?

The liquid began to subside, fall back in the hollow. I cried out, "No! I must see—learn where she is."

Too late, as one part of my mind was forced to accept. Now there was only a small portion at the very bottom of the cup. The vision was lost.

Elys took the cup out of my now shaking hands. I looked to her as I had not done for a long time to anyone—with pleading—for she was my only link with Joisan.

"Where? And how may I come to her?" My tongue seemed thick, swollen, so I could hardly mouth those questions.

With the tutored prudence of a Wisewoman, she went from me to pour away the liquid—not upon the churned soil, but beyond, where the ground was still undisturbed, gesturing with her other hand. Only when she had done with such ritual did she again face me.

"One is only shown what the Power can produce at that moment. And," she looked about her somberly, "we have used the talent in a place that has been disturbed by that which is certainly not friendly to us, which may not be of the Light at all. It is best now for us to push on—away from all influences that may arise here."

"But where is Joisan?" I did not move from where I stood in the deep ruts of the freshly turned ground.

Jervon was at work, pulling some pack bags out of the dirt. Those I had brought had completely disappeared, but apparently others, carried by their party, had been so near the edge of the disturbance as to escape burial. There was no sign of the horses.

I crossed the disturbed ground directly to Elys, determined to have from her any hint that would aid me to find my lady.

She did not look up, rather busied herself with the rewrapping of the cup. I could already guess her answer. There are limits to all talents. Perhaps hers had been reached when she had shown me that Joisan had survived. In what direction Joisan had vanished, except down, or what further peril threatened her—those one could only imagine. I strove, with all the force of will I could summon, to keep certain dire mind-pictures out of my thoughts.

Jervon had piled up what he had salvaged. Now, facing east, he put two fingers to his lips and whistled. The sound carried as clearly as had those notes Herrel had used to quiet my horses. Elys, the wrapped cup cradled against her in one arm, now raised her right hand in a summoning gesture.

I turned to look in that direction. Twilight was fast upon us now and I saw nothing. Then, pushing through a rim of brush, a horse trotted, to stop short, snort, and plant its hooves hard in the ground, expressing plainly a refusal to advance any nearer that evil-smelling spread of torn earth.

Jervon, voicing those sounds an expert horseman uses to soothe an excited and frightened beast, advanced slowly toward the animal. Twice it snorted, the whites of its eyes showing, once half wheeling as if to make off again. However, some strong tie between rider and mount held fast, so that the Dalesman was able to lay hand flat against the sweating neck. The horse, after one more toss of head, nosed against the man's shoulder, allowing him to comb its mane with his fingers.

Elys followed him, still making beckoning gestures. Before she reached her companion, a second horse appeared at a slow and reluctant pace. Thus they summoned to them two that were excellent mounts of the type used and cherished by the fighters of the Dales. After them trailed another, a smaller mare of mountain breed, and lastly a pack pony. Of my own desert mounts there was no trace. Probably suited to this land, they had joyfully taken their freedom once they had fled. I divined that, by long association, these two who had companioned Joisan in her search had established close communication with their own horses—and perhaps those in turn had influenced the mare Joisan had ridden. For I recognized it to be one of the sort commonly seen in Norsdale. I had no hope that my own would ever appear.

Because at the moment I did not know what lay before me now, I went to where Jervon and Elys were stroking the sweating, still-frightened horses, using soft words of reassurance. The man glanced at me.

"Elys is right—we had best move on. Even these know better than to stay where the Dark has been at work."

We brought saddles and packs and made ready, though the dark was gathering fast. Then, on Joisan's mare, I swung out across the open land, away from the forest of the Weres, the place where Joisan had last been. I did not want to leave, but neither could I linger on there. If I only had some clue. . . . My hands tightened on the reins and my wrist band seemed to flare with a last flicker of light.

Though the dusk became thicker, Jervon, who had drawn up beside me, leading the pack horse, did not pause. Then Elys came even with him, so we three rode abreast into the night.

Both their mounts suddenly whinnied and broke into a trot, my mare following. It was so we reached a waterway, cut deeply into the surface of the plain. The water which had worn that gully was now but a small stream running through a narrow middle channel. However, the banks, down which our horses half slid when we allowed them their heads, gave one a sense of protection. We made camp there as the full dark closed in. For want of any better hope I had come this far—what I would do next I had no idea.

There crossed my mind what I had said to Hyron, that I would ride north and west in quest of my own kind (if any such existed). That declaration had small meaning now. Once before I had sought Joisan across this same imperiled country—when she had been taken by my enemies. I knew without any question that now I must seek her a second time—save that I had no trail to follow.

If you traced the tangle of our lives back to its beginning, where did the interlocking of our fates begin—that interlocking which had now endangered her twice over? Was it because she had been axe-wedded to me in both our childhoods—or because I had given her the gryphon and so made her of importance to Rogear? Had my life not touched hers with these dangers she would have never fallen to this last peril.

If she had not believed that she had a duty to me, because she was my lady (even though I had fully released her from her vows), she would never have followed me into this new danger. Therefore mine was the fault, and if she could be saved, I must do it. At the moment I know that this stood above any task Imgry had set on me. What did I care for the Dales, even in their death throes, when Joisan was lost in some web of the Dark?

Joisan

IN SPITE OF MY TIRED BODY, OF MY HUNGER, OF THE NAGGING FEAR
that I was trapped forever here—so that the very dark itself
pressed against me with a force I could almost feel, I forgot for a
space all this—for I was possessed by this idea of the use of will.
So slender and frail a thing as thought alone—might this indeed
be for me more of a key than . . .

A key! It was as if I came fully alive, waking out of a
nightmare-laden sleep. Neevor had said it—and I had marshalled
only human thoughts of locks and doors—not of this! If I were
right. . . !

Once more I set my shoulders against the support of the wall,
ready to do battle in another way—with a part of myself. I
cradled the globe, high against my breast, dared to take the
chance of closing out my senses for a space, all that lay about
me, centering my attention only on the gryphon—on its red eyes.

Now I did not fight to reach Kerovan—no. This was of even
greater importance in the here and now—my own escape. If
will—my untrained will—held any force, all of it must be fo-
cused on my key!

"Out!" I do not know whether I whispered, cried, shouted
that aloud, or if it rang only through my mind, answered by the
strain I laid upon myself. "Out!"

Slowly, with such an effort as even an hour before I had not believed lay within me, I envisioned a wall such as that against which I now leaned—save with one difference. In it was an opening—a door . . . out!

The globe blazed with heat, it burned. Still I held and willed that heat away from me. I had no body, no pain, I had only a will—a will demanding obedience.

Out!

Once more the globe burst bright with fire, dazzling me by shooting forth white rays. Those shifted, though I did not change the position of my hand or what it held. The rays joined into one, became an oddly thick rod of pearl color—as if the light had taken on tangible substance.

I turned in the direction it now pointed, began to walk, keeping—with every fraction of energy locked on it—the picture in my mind of what I sought, of what I must find. At that moment nothing in the world must be allowed to exist save that ray of light. I would have been easy prey for the creatures of the dark—had they chosen to move in upon me then.

The ray crooked, turned, struck, as a spear is sent flying at a target—not the wall but a crevice, a long, vertical crack. Into that spun my radiant spear and I followed. The way was rough and I stumbled over loose rocks and slippery gravel.

Just as my arm had tired when I had used the belt lash over and over, so now my will was beginning to falter. The ray rippled, no longer so solid. This narrow crevice sloped sharply upward and I climbed; each time my footing shifted the light dimmed a fraction as the focus of my thought was disturbed.

It began to seem that I had been trapped forever in an evil dream, condemned to ever climb over a constantly shifting footing where I fought for balance. The fingers of my left hand were raw-tipped from scrambling for holds on the wall, while my other wrist was stiff and numb as I held the globe out before me. The illumination from it grew fainter; I was nearing the limit of the compulsion I could put upon my will.

Now the gleam was hardly brighter than it had been back in the cavern. I was forced, in spite of myself, to climb and climb without knowing what a misstep might bring. Finally the impression came dimly, through my exhaustion, that my path was leveling out once again. Also, the stench that had polluted the lower region was gone. I lifted my chin a fraction, drew a deep, sobbing breath. Surely what had touched against my cheeks just then had been a thin current—of fresh air!

Hope gave me a last spurt of energy. I pushed forward to half fall out of the crevice into a very different place, where I stood amazed, staring about, first in bewilderment and then in growing wonder.

This still lay underground, though far above was a circular opening to the sky. For I was sure the dark expanse I sighted, with those points of light, could be no other than night sky and distant stars. However the cavern was filled with a pale illumination that did not come from any torch, lamp, or fire. Instead the walls themselves gave off a diffused glow, pale and wan, but enough for me to see.

The chamber, cave, or whatever it might be, was a hemisphere with a level flooring. Round walls curved up on all sides. Such perfect symmetry could not be of nature's devising.

The floor was divided by a large number of low partitions, which followed no logical pattern, cutting across or joining each other to form a crazy maze of sharp-angled spaces. There was no design nor could I imagine any purpose for such a meticulous network of squares, triangles, and other odd forms. Some looked far too small even to set foot into, others were wide enough to provide short paths, which led nowhere.

I decided to edge along the outer walls and thus seek any exit. For to reach that roof opening was far beyond my ability. But there did exist an unwalled space between the first of the maze walls and the circumference of the cavern.

It was not until I squeezed into that space and set out that my hand (which I still slipped along the curve to steady me, for to my rising concern I was growing more and more unsteady on my feet) discovered this wall was not as smooth as it looked. Instead it bore a regular series of indentations. Peering more closely at them, I decided they were runes, though in what forgotten language they had been wrought must remain a mystery.

When, as a child, I had visited Norsdale Abbey with my aunt and had there been allowed to delve into the archives, I had seen manuscripts that reproduced fragments of inscriptions from the places of the Old Ones. Though for my own people these remained a tongue locked against their knowing, these discover-

ies had been preserved because they marked this or that place
that had had some influence upon the Dalesman.

How fiercely I longed to be able to read what was inscribed
here. Perhaps the very information I needed—how to get out—
lay in those lines under my fingers. However, even though I
could not master their secret, I continued to slip my hand along
over those lost messages as I went.

I had won a good third of the way around that curved rise, and
as far as I could see ahead, there was no break in the wall,
nothing to let me out into the world, the sky of which hung so
tantalizingly overhead. I was tired.

At last, my legs shaking under me, I perched on one of the
maze walls and let my hands fall to my knees. I was thirsty and
my thoughts kept running back to that pool I had found in the
dark, the icy sweetness of the water there. This place was utterly
sterile and dead. No water—no food—I had come to the end of
my escape way to discover but another trap.

Nor did I believe that I could summon up once again that
strength of concentration to bring the globe alive. Even as I
rested there my energy seeped away as though I were deep
wounded, losing heart's blood. My confidence drained in the
same way, I huddled where I was, apathetic, in a state of
uncaring.

I could not have slept, but I must have fallen into a half-
dreamlike state, for I did not blink and look about me again until
I realized that the gray light of the chamber was changing.
Glancing up I could no longer see those pinpoints of stars.
Rather, there came a paling of the sky. In that outer world I
could not reach, a new day must be at dawn.

The sight of that portion of sky now was a dull torment to me.
I might as well wish for wings, such as the gryphon sported, to
raise me out of here; there was no other escape. However, the
sight of day broke through the state of uncaring that had held
me. Somehow I wavered to my feet, stood swaying. My mouth
was dry—my whole throat parched and raw. Almost I could turn
again to the dark way that had brought me here, return to seek
the basin into which that blessed water dripped in constant flow.

The rest of the curved wall was still to be explored, to no
purpose. I turned unsteadily and viewed it all—no break save
that ragged seam through which I had first come. To go stum-

bling in and out of that crazy mixtures of spaces on the floor was utter folly.

Drawing on a very small store of strength, I began again to move, without any real hope, only because I could not simply sit and wait for death to enfold me. The light above grew ever stronger. Day did not pierce to the walls of the chamber, there the gray still held. Then a sudden sharp flash to my right brought my head around.

Daylight had awakened a glittering response from edges of those low dividing walls that were immediately under the dome opening. The response was one of rich color.

I stood in wonder to gaze at gem-bright sparks of red, of gold, of brilliant green, of purple, amber, blue—winging from stone that only moments before had been lifelessly dull. It looked as if a casket had been opened above, loosing in careless profusion such jewels as even the wealthiest of the Dalelords had never hoped to possess.

There was—I began now to perceive it—some arrangement, some pattern about those sparks. They lay thick in some places, thin in others, not at all in a few sections. A design perhaps, but one (the idea awoke sluggishly in a mind that had been overtired by my earlier efforts) that could only be properly viewed and understood if one could see it from above.

Could a person standing on one of the low walls see it? I leaned back against the curved wall, an uncomfortable position, to consider that. What good could it possibly do for me to make such an effort? This was only another unsolvable mystery and nothing to give me any aid.

The glitter grew steadily stronger. I could almost imagine that I saw mists of color flaring upward even as flames arise from wood being consumed. There was certainly something of import out there, tenuous, but perhaps having more substance than light alone.

In spite of my telling myself that this was a useless puzzle beyond my solving, I began to make my way, creeping from one of the enclosures into the next, toward that spread of radiance. While I was still some distance from it, I scrambled up on top of one of the dividing walls, teetered there, hands thrown out to balance me.

At first I thought that if there was any design I could not reach

a height high enough to discern its outlines. However, the longer
I traced one color to the next, or the joining of the glistening
walls that. formed the base, the more I began to perceive that
what I looked at was in reality the representation of a symbol I
had seen before—carefully lined upon a sheet of very old parchment in the Abbey library.

The general outline was that of a winged creature, but not a
bird or any of the fanciful, monstrous beasts Dalesmen were
pleased to use to identify their House clans. The outspread
wings, the point of one of which stretched quite close to the wall
on which I now perched, were blue. Seeing that color gave me a
little heart. It was well known that those places of the Old Ones
that held Power that was safe, or at least unharmful, to my race
were always touched with that color.

A round globe rested between the wings, the expanse marked
by a circular center for the maze. This glowed amber-gold.
While to the fore and back of that were other colors in bright
gem shades, as if the thing wore a double crown, one at either
side of what might represent either a bodiless head or a headless
body.

The longer I stared at that pattern the clearer it became, while
the colors were now bright enough to dazzle my eyes. I wavered
back and forth on my perch, my weariness fighting against my
will. Only I was as one entangled in a strong spell, for I could
not turn my back and move away.

My hands closed about the gryphon globe, half expecting that
to be afire, gathering force from what I looked upon. Perhaps I
was too exhausted, had drawn too much upon its energy in the
cavern, for it did not awaken.

If I were enspelled, that bondage held, not only held, but drew
me. Still I did not walk straight toward the center; rather it was
as if there was another in command of my movements. For some
reason, I did not find this either strange or frightening.

My path from one space to the next was odd, sometimes I
circled, sometimes I retreated a step, a whole square, a curve,
then went forward at a different angle. I think I laughed
lightheadedly when it struck me that I might seem, to any
onlooker, to be engaged in the movements of some formal
dance, such as we foot in the Dale keeps at mid-year when the
kin gather for feasting.

Back, forward, sidewise, straight, my feet moved, sometimes having to squeeze into a space where my battered boots scraped both sides of the dividers. Still, to all things there comes an end, and at last I stepped across the final one of the low walls to stand in that golden center, not knowing why it was important that I be here, only that it was.

The light thickened as it streamed upward, walling me in with a veil I could no longer see through. It made a curtain, but I did not stir to sweep it aside; I had reached the place I was meant to be, from here there was no going on.

Now all my great weariness of body and mind settled in full force upon me, actually bearing me to the pavement, so that I wilted as if my knees were now as soft as the bruised flesh that encased them. I was thirsty, I was hungry, I was afraid. I would end here—there was no longer hope of reaching the world I had known.

I curled about in that gold-walled circle as might a child who has wept herself near to sleep. There was a dulling of thought and that pushed away the fear, banished the remaining scraps of wonder—then even memory. I watched drowsily, without marveling any more, the golden light grow thicker and thicker.

Now I could no longer see even the low wall from which it rose. The light billowed, began to spin, first slowly and then faster and faster. Because it made me dizzy to watch, I closed my eyes to shut out that whirl.

There followed a moment of cold, utter cold, sharp enough to bring a cry of pain from me. Then a feeling of deep horror that I was—elsewhere—in a place where no one of my kind should ever venture. Through this nowhere I was swept, or pulled, or pushed. I felt all three such urgings. The terror of the nowhere seeped into my head, drove out the part that was truly me. My inner self, so threatened, fled thankfully into deep darkness and I knew nothing at all.

I opened my eyes. There was no curtain of golden light enclosing me. Instead sunlight wrapped me round, so warmly that my mail shirt was an overheated burden, and my skin stung from a beginning burn. I sat up.

This was not the full light of day, through some opening overhead, that bathed me in heat. I did not still lie in the round of the circular chamber—I was in the open again!

Did I dream? I pinched my own flesh sharply between thumb
and forefinger to test that—achieving so pain but no change in
what I saw. No rock walls here, rather tufts of coarse-bladed
grass and bushes. Not too far away a flock of birds weighed
branches—as they pecked eagerly at a bountiful harvest of scar-
let berries—so the whole growth, down to its roots, trembled and
swung under their assault.

Very slowly, still afraid that I might break this spell—which
was certainly good instead of ill—I turned my head. No, this
was not deserted country. There *were* walls, or the remains of
such. They stood at a little distance and it was plain they had
been tumbled by time, their stone much overgrown with moss.
One squat tower was actually topped by a small tree, which had
rooted itself there to take the place of a keep lord's banner.

How had I come here?

Just at that moment I did not care. What drew me was the
harvest of berries. I knew their like. Had I not gathered such
many times over—the excess being reduced to a thick jam for
winter use? They had never looked so plump, so abundant in the
Dales though. Now their sweet, yet slightly tart taste promised
delight to my hot, dry mouth. I started for the bushes on my
hands and knees, not sure I had strength enough to get to my
feet.

The birds wheeled up and away, scolding angrily, as I began
to raid their feeding place. I culled handfuls from the branches,
crammed them into my mouth, their juice relieving my thirst,
their substance my hunger. I ate without thought for anything
else, without prudence. If this *were* a dream after all, it was the
first one in which I had ever feasted with such satisfaction and
delight.

After the first edge was off my thirst and hunger, I allowed
myself time to survey my surroundings more closely. The bushes
I attacked (I was raking berries from the third bush by this time)
had been planted in order, in spite of their now sprawling
growth, at what had once been equal distance from one another—a
fact still visible.

Beyond stood several similar rows of trees. The closer I knew
also as a fruit bearer, though what it now bore was just beginning to grow pink. This was another native of the Dales, which
any keep-dweller, finding on his land, guarded and cherished.

So I was in what had manifestly once been a garden. Now I looked to the walls, the three-crowned tower—all were certainly part of a keep. Wonderingly (having eaten what was, for that moment, my fill), I pulled myself up, still caught by the puzzle of how I had come here.

When I had opened my eyes, I had been lying—right there!

There was a slab of stone much moss-grown. As I made my way back to it I saw that some of the green cover had been scraped away, was now in ragged tatters. It looked as if, when I had landed—or somehow arrived there—I had done so with violence. Now I knelt and tore loose more of the moss. Deep-carved right under where my head had rested was the symbol of the ball with the outstretched wings.

Sitting back on my heels, I tried to think logically. I had fallen asleep, or been rendered unconscious, in the deep earth chamber, curled in the midst of a three dimensional representation of what was carved here. Later . . . how much later?

I looked up at the sky. By the sun's westering position, the time must not be too far from late afternoon. Of the same day? Another? Or a still longer period? There was no way of my knowing.

The fact remained that some agency had transferred me from the cavern into the open, saving my life in the process. I could not be sure whether that act had been deliberate on the part of an unknown intelligence, greater and more far-seeing than my own, or whether I had merely stumbled on a process that would have worked for anyone fortunate enough to follow the conditions set by an ancient spell.

I was inclined toward the latter theory, perhaps because that was the more comforting. To believe that I was under observation, being moved at the will of some Old One, was enough to raise my neck hair and bring shivers in spite of the drowsy heat.

Very well—and for now it did not matter how—I was out of the cave chamber. Only where might I be in relation to the place that had turned into an earth whirlpool? How far was I from my late companions? I was certain I had not been somehow wafted out of the Waste itself, and I was weaponless, alone, with no horse or provisions, in country I did not know, without a guide. A series of facts that were enough to make anyone quail. I had only my own wits to depend upon. Night was on its inevitable

way and I had no wish to be caught in the open by any such
things as might run these ridges or crawl across the land.

The answer to a quest for shelter was, of course, the ruins.
Perhaps beyond those broken walls I could find a hiding hole, a
shelter until morning.

The wall nearest me had fallen in convenient gaps so I did not
have to seek any gateway. Through one of the gaps I entered into
a paved courtyard. Empty window spaces and three doorways
(one fringed by the rotting remains of a wooden door) broke the
inner walls. Darkish holes those were, from which I could be
spied upon, though unable myself to sight any lurker. The place
was alive with birds, and I remembered Elys's dissatisfaction
with the wood because it had appeared to harbor no winged
inhabitants.

Perhaps the berry feast enticed them. Still, where the ivy grew
on the wall of what might have once been the great hall of
whatever lord ruled there, there was a constant fluttering among
its vines, which suggested nests concealed there in goodly numbers.

I did not hear any pad of foot, any rustle of the drifts of last
season's leaves that lay across the pavement, but, as I turned
slowly, inspecting all I could see of the ruins, I found myself
indeed under observation.

By the rotted door sat a cat—not such an animal as was
esteemed in the Dales because of the slaughter it caused among
rats and mice that feasted on stored grain. No, this was half
again as large as one of those sleek-sided, striped tabbies. Also
its fur was uniformly a yellow-brown and, between its eyes,
boldly marked by a much darker growth of fur, was a V.
Another such brand grew on the upper part of its lighter breast
fur.

About an arm's distance from the first was a second of the
same breed, slightly smaller, a little more lithe of body, but
of the like uniform color of coat and markings. The birds appeared to pay no attention to these who might well be termed
natural enemies, rather wheeled back and forth overhead, intent
upon their own comings and goings.

The cats were not alone. Before a second door squatted a
small bear, sitting up upon its haunches and rocking a little to
and fro. Catching sight of that red brown form I stiffened. My
hand reached by instinct for a weapon I no longer carried.

This was a very small specimen of bear, to be sure. But if it were a cub and its mother was nearby—then I could have walked into a trap even more cruel than the earth one I had managed to escape. I knew only too well hunters' tales. Among the worst menaces to be found in the Dales were female bears who thought, or suspected, that their offspring might be endangered.

While both the cats surveyed me with that unwinking stare that their whole species turns upon my kind upon occasion— emphasizing the gulf between us (one I have always been certain they believe was set for *their* purposes)—the bear paid me only fleeting attention. It snapped at a fly, then set to scratching vigorously with one long clawed paw at its own rounded paunch. I found that somewhat disarming and dared to expel the breath I had been holding, without knowing it, ever since I had caught sight of the creature.

I had been far too cautious to try to move—now I dared edge backward toward the gap that had given me entry into this too-well-occupied courtyard. Clearly, as an intruder, I was better away. And I hoped with all my heart that I would be allowed my retreat.

"A female—very young—and very stupid . . ."

I stopped short to stare. No one had *said* that! Only the cries and twitterings of the birds could be heard. No one had *spoken*. Then—how had I heard, and who had dismissed me so summarily? For I was certain that those words had concerned me. I fumbled with the buckle of my belt, ready once again to use it weaponwise as I had against the creatures in the dark. Only— who was the enemy here?

"To be young is a state through which all pass. And this one is not truly stupid—I think—only untaught. Which is another matter altogether."

I turned a gasp into a gulp. My hair had worked loose of its braiding since I no longer had a helm to hold it in place. I reached up with my left hand to brush away a straying lock that I might keep close attention upon those three—two cats, large, a bear, undersized. There was, I would take heart oath on that, no other life here—save the birds. And those I discounted at once.

The smaller of the cats arose leisurely and approached me. I stood my ground, even dropping my hand from the belt buckle. It advanced until it was just beyond reaching distance from me, settled again into the same dignified stance as its companion held, tail tip curled decorously over the front paws. Those unblinking yellow eyes were lifted to mine, caught—and held—my gaze. Now I knew!

"Who—what are you?" I had to moisten my lips with my tongue and use effort to ask that question. My voice echoed back from the open eyes of the windows and sounded far too small and tremulous in my own ears.

There was no answer. Still I was sure I had not been mistaken. The speaker had been this animal—or the larger one behind it. One had commented disparagingly upon me, the other had replied with more tolerance. And I had caught that speech in—my mind!

Kerovan

I WAS BUSIED WITH MY THOUGHTS, MAKING MY DECISION AS JERVON and I worked together without words, hobbling the horses after they drank, leaving them to graze through the night. When the moon arose I stood watching it, remembering the silver of the cup—a cup that could have been carved from that pure disk. Tonight the stars also seemed unusually bright, gems flashing in the cloudless sky.

Beyond the valley of the stream the land lay open, save for dark clumps of trees or brush here and there. I was used to the Dales with their protecting ridges. Now, having on impulse climbed to the edge of the river cut, I stood watching shadows grow darker until each and every one of those growths appeared lapped in a pool of dark. The sky was alight, fresh and open— but this land was secret, it held no easy road for such as us.

A rising night wind blew against me. I had taken off my helm so that the wind tugged at my hair, dried the sweat that had gathered under the band of my headgear, cooled me—perhaps too much. Silver and black was all this land—silver above, black below. It was that darker part that held us.

Inside me something awoke, stirred as if from a long sleep, then was gone before I could seize upon it. Memory? No. I had ranged the Waste twice before, yes. But never in this direction.

It was not possible for me to recognize the land before me. Yet . . .

I shook my head firmly against such fancies. What I needed was clear-cut purpose, a centering in on what was the most important thing in the world—to find Joisan. Though how . . . Reluctantly I returned to our fireless camp where the others had settled. I came to stand before the two of them.

"She must be found," I said bleakly. "Since my own horses are gone, I shall of a necessity take hers."

"We ride with the morning," Jervon answered me as one who stated the obvious.

"Go with safety. Bear with you my heart thanks that you have served my lady."

"You do not understand." Elys's voice came through the night that veiled her face. "We ride *with* you."

For a moment I tensed, so filled was I with the guilt I had drawn about me like a cloak. Since it was because of me Joisan had come here at her great peril, what part of any rescue venture belonged to these two? I was willing only to welcome anger— and to turn it against others since I burned with it myself.

Then the Wisewoman added: "Her way was our way—of free choice. We are not about to turn from it, now that it has brought this upon her. If you choose not to ride in our company, that is for you to decide. Still we shall go."

How had Joisan so tied these two to her? Or—suspicion crawled where anger had opened a way—were they indeed Imgry's eyes ready to turn me from my road when they had the chance? Well enough. I could watch and wait, be all fair words and thanks, and still keep my own path. Unless . . .

This Elys had the Power, and through that might be a way to my lady. I could not disdain any chance, however small, of a guide.

"You speak," I said, "as if you have a road in mind. But how can that be?" Something of eagerness broke the right cover I tried to force on my feelings. Had I been jealous in part because these two had been my lady's friends when I had left her without any outward show of feeling? I clenched my hands at my sides until my nails cut into the softer flesh of my palms.

"I know nothing of Thas—save they are of the earth. But . . ."

I remembered! By the Warmth of the Flame and the Flash of Gonder's Spell Sword, in that moment I remembered!

"The mountains! The Werelord said their dens were known to be among the mountains!" I swung about, but even the brightness of the moon could not show me now these distant ridges against the far sky.

"The mountains it is then," Jervon said, much as one speaks of riding to a market to price wool, though I was sure he was not as pragmatic as he sounded.

This was a time when I could not, for Joisan's sake, push aside any suggestion of aid. I must accept what was offered and be grateful—honestly grateful—that it was given.

I had thought that I could not sleep, that I must lie and remember too much—and fear far more. However, sometimes the body defeats the mind and brings it under domination. I found that my eyelids grew heavy and . . .

No—I did not dream. Or if I did . . . But I did not! It was no dream—nor was it any sorcery summoned up by Elys in some mistaken hope perhaps of lightening my inner burden. I was sitting up, my hands half raised to my head. There was the moon and the stars, and around me the dark. I could hear the rasping sound made by a grazing horse not too far away.

"Joisan!" I scrambled up, blundered forward a step or two— my hands outstretched to grasp something—someone—who was not there. "Joisan . . . ."

She had been there, or here—or . . .

I rubbed my forehead dazedly. Out of the dark I heard movement, whirled about. "Joisan!"

"No."

A single word of denial. One that I was hot to dispute.

"I—I saw her." I stammered. "She was here, I tell you!"

"He is ensorcelled?" It was Jervon's deep voice in the night. Then came an answer from the Wisewoman.

"He could not be—not with such a safeguard as he wears."

There was a glitter of ice blue, the band on my wrist. Of course it had not been sorcery! I had seen Joisan—she had stood with bared head, her hair clotted with earth, smears of it across her face. There had been wonder in her eyes and between us—the gryphon! I had seen her.

I must have repeated that, for Elys replied to words I did not remember uttering.

"A true sending. It was surely a true sending."

A sending! I shook my head, tried to believe that my sight of her had been more than a willed vision. But once more logic awakened in me. I dropped down on the ground, clasped my head between my hands—then changed and held the wrist with its band flat against my forehead. I closed my eyes and tried with all the force I could summon, all the will I knew, to reach out—to touch—to see . . . Only there was no answer—nothing but the moon above and the black land below.

A hand rested on my shoulder. I strove to shake it off but the clasp clung.

"Let be!" Elys spoke with authority. "This is no land in which to open any gates. Let be—I do not think you are an utter fool!"

Did I indeed feel in that moment, even as she spoke, that something—a faint trace—a sensation that my frantic searching had touched what should not be disturbed except by fools? I could not tell—though I shivered as I might have had a breath of winter wind swept across the gully and wrapped itself about my shoulders in a lash-cut. I dropped my hand, stared hard-eyed into the dark, knowing that my chance was gone and I would have no value to Joisan should I now—as Elys had pointed out—play the fool.

Perhaps I had never before been driven so . . . unless it was when I had trailed Rogear into the Waste. The ferment within me urged me on and on during the next two days. Had I traveled alone I might neither have eaten nor slept—until I fell from the saddle of a horse ridden near to death. Still it seemed that the heights toward which we headed never drew any closer. My worst fear rode with me, that suspicion that perhaps we had chosen wrongly, that we were not heading toward my lady, but away.

Was it that constant nag of fear that brought back the dreams? I never returned in sleep to that place where the gryphon-man lay. Mostly I was in the company of those whose faces I could not clearly see, whose murmuring voices I did not understand, yet in me strained the need to both see and hear. From such dreams I awoke as weak in body as if I had run for a day, sweat heavy and sticky on my body.

I did not tell my companions of these dreams. In fact I spoke very little. Still striving to free my mind from a prison of dark thoughts, I made myself watch both of them. I asked no questions concerning their past, though such questions began to crowd my mind.

Elys was a Wisewoman, more than that—for she wore the mail of a warrior with practiced ease and I saw that a sword was as familiar to her as it was to anyone who was trained in such usage for many years. Thus she was a strange puzzle—for Wisewomen and weapons have never consorted together from all I had ever heard.

By her appearance she was not of Dalesblood; perhaps her talent therefore was the stronger. Yet her tie with Jervon was very close and easy, acceptable to both. Jervon, though he was plainly of keep-kin, had no visible taint of the Old Ones—and I did not believe he was one who bore my own curse. Together they traveled without many words between them, but I was more and more aware that theirs was so strong a bond that at times it seemed as if one could read the mind of the other.

It was Jervon who interested me the most. All Dalespeople accepted Wisewomen—after a fashion. Those are born of our own blood with a talent they enlarge by learning. A girl with such a gift apprenticed herself early to one well practiced in herb lore, in minor Power control. She was thus set apart from childhood, knowing thereafter no kin-tie, even among those of her birth family, making no marriage, rearing no child, unless she in turn took an apprentice. Her knowledge was her whole life.

A Wisewoman's arts are of healing and peace. None goes armed, none speaks of battle as Elys had made mention of skirmishes and alerts, inquiring of me how went Imgry's training of the new forces. She was two things—each opposed to the other. How could this be?

Also, how could Jervon, who lacked any pretense of talent, accept her so wholly, feeling none of the aversion that was bred into all Dalesmen—that wariness, the latent fear of the unknown raised by the constant awareness that we dwelt in a land which was not truly our own?

This alliance of theirs—my thoughts returned ever to the strangeness of it—was by Dale standards unexplainable. Jervon was neither servant nor guard, that I had learned early during this endless ride west. They were equals in spite of their differences. Could one take two such opposing people—as one would take two different metals—and forge from their uniting a third stronger, more powerful than either alone?

Jervon accepted Elys for what she was. Could anyone so accept—me, in the same fashion?

They both spoke of Joisan, not as if they wished to add to my burden, but naturally, as if she had been brought into that shared companionship of theirs. There came a time (did my face so reveal my inner struggles) that Elys broke the silence in which I rode with an abrupt comment.

"She wished for more."

Anger touched me, and then bewilderment. More of what? Lands? Heritage? For both of us those had been swept away by the fortunes of the war. I had given her her full freedom—I held her by no promise. What then was "more"?

If this clear-eyed warrior woman could indeed reach into the turmoil of my thoughts, did she not realize that I knew Joisan was something apart, precious—something I could not bind to me. Being what I was I would ask nothing. Not all were as accepting as she—as Jervon . . .

"Men fear that which has no substance, better they should look with clear eyes, open minds," Elys continued. "Joisan told me of your heritage, that you deemed it a dire thing you cannot escape. But have you not already faced it in part—faced and defeated it?"

"I did not defeat it, Lady," I flared up in answer. "What I wrought was against enemies—enemies who had taken my lady to bend to their will. Nor did I alone do that thing. There was another Power that took a hand—which used me as one uses a sword. Am I then to be commended? Because I am what I am, I was only a doorway . . ."

Memory moved. Who—what—had I been at that moment when a Power that certainly I had not summoned had turned against Rogear and my mother? I had not been Kerovan then, but another—another who was greater, stronger, whole in spirit—

everything I was not, as I knew when he had withdrawn, and had never been nor could hope to be.

"Be not so swift to deny," she countered. "There are often skills that lie sleeping within one until destiny—and need—awakens and draws them forth. You think meanly of yourself and"—there was a note in her tone that brought a flush to my cheek, a hot retort to my lips though I did not so interrupt her—"perhaps you find that to so think is a protection, a ward against doing what you were born to do. One cannot stand in the end against one's fate."

To that I made no answer seeing that if I spoke now what I deemed to be the truth she might only say again that I hid behind an excuse, as she had just accused me of doing. Nor did I find that I liked either of these two the more (for I brooded upon my conviction that they found in me perhaps not the monster the Dales would name me, but someone so poor-spirited that I was not of the breed to have honestly earned Joisan's regard). Perhaps I should have been glad of that verdict, seeing that it would afford me an added excuse to hold aloof—when and if my lady was safely found. Only, contrarily, its affect upon me now was to arouse a determination to prove that I was not less than Jervon in my ability to accept. Though the acceptance would never be mine—it was Joisan's.

On the second day the country began to change—even as desert had given way earlier to grassland—though the hills still seemed farther away. While we did not see again any such silent and thick wood as the Wereriders' sanctuary, there were more trees. Also, we forded one good-sized river, making our way across on the remains of a stone bridge, enough of which still stood above water to give us dry footing.

Hereabouts were signs that this land had once been under cultivation, perhaps very fertile. There were fallow fields walled with stones set skillfully in place, and twice we sighted towers standing as watch points. We made no attempt to explore these, for their surroundings suggested that they had been long abandoned, and there was a fever burning, in me at least, to keep pushing on.

In midafternoon of the second day we came near a third such tower, only this was surrounded by a clump of dark trees (most of which were unseasonably bare of leaf, but with branches so

matted and entwined as to form another kind of defense). The
band on my wrist warmed. I pulled back my mail sleeve to see it
emitting blue sparks, visible even in the sunlight. Elys reined up,
watched that tower as one looked upon a defended enemy position. She had caught her lower lip between her teeth and a frown
of concentration drew her brows closer together.

"Swing out!" she ordered, emphasizing that with a gesture to
her left. "Can you not also feel it?"

Perhaps because I had been for so many hours wrapped in my
own thoughts, I had not been too much aware of what was round
about. Now her command startled me into attention. I hunched
my shoulders, tightened grip on the reins so that the mare sidled
under me. It was as if an unexpected blow had struck out of the
very air—one I had no means of countering.

The only words I can find to describe what chanced are that in
that moment I had been attacked by a wave of pure evil. Evil is
the only name for the foulness of it. Cold it was, wholly inimical
to my kind of life, or at least to that part of me that could claim
kinship with humanity. I sensed a subtle movement in my mind,
a feeble assault, as if what had launched that blow (perhaps
intending invasion) had been drained through centuries until its
force was only a faint shadow of what it had once been. Something coiled out there behind the dark of the trees, the tumble of
stone, something full of poison against the soul, as an adder is
full of poison to discharge against living flesh.

We rode on, making a wide circle around that ill-inhabited
place. However, we had not gone far (though the pressure I had
felt had faded entirely away) when there came the sound of wild
screeching. Coiling up from the tower, in the form of a giant
serpent rearing to strike, came a spiral of birds.

Once aloft they wheeled, to fly directly at us. I saw, as they
drew near, that they were of the same breed as those foul
scavengers I had found at the desert oasis. Their raw red heads,
armed with those murderous curved beaks, were stretched forward like spears, aimed at us.

Arriving just above us, they circled, continuing to screech, a
clamor loud enough to hurt the ears. From the flock some darted
down, two and three at a time, skimming just above our heads. I
had flung up my arm in an intuitive gesture of protection and the
band on my wrist blazed like leaping flames. Our horses went

wild, screaming in pure fear, tossing their heads frantically, as if they expected that their eyes were about to be plucked out of their skulls. There was no trying to hold them. Instead we gave them their heads and they ran, directly west, until we came to cover under a stand of trees. The birds followed, settling on branches above, still shrieking what may have been dire threats in their own tongue.

However, the branches prevented them from attacking us, and they raised stronger cries of rage and frustration. We discovered, as we threaded a way among the trees, that those winged demons did not seem disposed to follow beyond the very edge of the wood.

It was our hope, though there was no path, that we were not wandering in circles as we ducked down in our saddles to avoid being brushed out of them by low-hanging branches. Such ferocity in an attack made by winged things was new to me, and I marveled that they had not scored us with beak and talon. They might well have been trained, as were falcons of the Dales schooled, to hunt on command—or else they themselves possessed both a malicious form of intelligence and a purpose in harrying us.

"I trust," Jervon commented, throwing out an arm to ward off a branch, "that they will not be awaiting us when we reach the other side of this cover. Never had I thought birds were creatures to fear. But those—they could and would tear a man's face from his skull—given the chance."

"Your ward is strong," Elys spoke to me, and nodded to the wrist band. It still shone, but the fire that had awakened to life there as we had approached that tower was less brilliant. "However, what lay there was not only birds . . ." She turned her head a little to one side as if she were listening.

All I could hear were the cries of feathered attackers growing steadily fainter as we drew away. I regarded the band of the Old One's metal with the same thankfulness a warrior, pushed to a last stand, looks upon his sword. I had been very well served since chance had brought it to me.

"No," Elys continued. "Something more than birds laired in that place. Though whether it is strong enough to leave its den and come into the open by daylight . . . Most things of the Dark use the night for their cover—unless they are masters of evil arts.

That . . . force is no longer strong as it once was. But I think
that we had better set as much distance between us and its
lurking place as we can before we camp.''

We made a slow passage but we did win at least to the other
side of the covering wood. No birds had flown above to lie in
wait as we had half feared. What we discovered was something
far different—a broad road, better laid than any of those in the
Dales, showing only small signs of erosion at the extreme edges
of the smooth surface.

The highway came up from the south, but at the very point
where we emerged from among the trees, it took a sharp,
curving turn to the west. On either side it had been cleared of tall
growth, so that anything or anyone traveling there would proceed
in clear sight—an idea I did not find very much to my present
taste.

I had seen a similar highway once before. The Road of Exile,
which led into the Waste not far from Ulmsdale, resembled this.
It had served those Old Ones who had passed from the Dales
into a place and future we knew nothing of. Never would I forget
how Riwal and I had sheltered from a sudden storm in a ruin
standing beside that road and the vision that had come to me that
night—the march of the Old Ones, only half seen—but felt,
yes—felt! That heavy sorrow, which had sent them roving, arose
from their ghostly passing to touch me and turn the whole world
into a place of loss and heartbreak.

Here, however, lay a brightness, which that other road had
lacked. Age had lain heavy on the path of the Exiles; here abode
a feeling that this highway might still be in use, that at any
moment a party of warriors, a train of merchants's ponies, might
come trotting into view.

Elys slipped from her saddle and Jervon gathered up the reins
she released. She walked forward until the very toes of her boots
touched the slight crumbling of the surface edge. There she stood
for a very long moment, neither looking up nor down the way,
but rather with her head bent, studying the surface itself with
care, as if she sought some lost object that might lie there.

Out of curiosity I followed her, my mare treading behind me
as I hauled on the reins. A moment later I, too, sighted what had
caught and so held her attention.

The actual surface of the road was unbroken and smooth.

However, inlaid in it were many symbols, arranged so that any who walked or rode upon it must, of necessity, tread on them in passing.

Some were undoubtedly runes, unreadable, as far as I knew, to any now living. Once more I was reminded forceably of Riwal, of how he had spent most of his life in eager search for a clue that would unlock for him the knowledge scattered in the Waste.

Among the markings of the runes were also designs that had no resemblance to writing. I saw stars of Power, their five points always filled with symbols. There were also silver outlines of footprints, not only of men (or some race nearly human) but also of beasts—hoofprints, the pad marks of what must have been outsized cats, the pointed toes of birds.

These last, judging by their length, must also have been giants of their species. The prints and the star points both glistened under the sun rays as if they were inset with some burnished metal, or even with tiny gems, though there was no color other than the silver of the Moon's mirror about them.

Elys knelt, holding her hand out, palm down, over the point of one of the stars that was not too far from the edge of the pavement. She did not touch the surface of the road, merely moved her hand slowly back and forth. For some reason I could not understand, I was drawn to kneel and copy her gesture. In turn I put out my right hand.

My wrist band warmed gently, though it did not continue to blaze into fire as it had when we neared the tower of the birds. And—there came a calming, an easement of my mind and spirit. No one did actually stand now behind me with a comrade's hand laid on my shoulder. Still it seemed to me that I had this comfort, that what we had found here, sorcery as it surely was, held no terror or possible harm—might in fact work for our future good. I said as much.

Elys got lightly to her feet.

"This is indeed our way," she said soberly. If she had felt the same touch of comfort as had come to me she did not show it in either face or voice, for she spoke as one who faces a task or a test. "This holds a power meant to protect those who travel. We have perhaps been led here without our realizing it. The Old Ones have many mysteries and secrets—it could be that we have, in some manner, been selected to be hands and feet for them—for the doing of a task. If this is the way of it then the road is their reassurance—safety for us.''

I wanted instantly to protest that I was no one's servant—either that of a Power or a lord. Though I had come at Imgry's bidding, it had been of my own choice. The belief that I might be now used by another was one I resented hotly.

Joisan was my only concern. I was back at the side of my mare, ready to mount and ride—not *to*, but *away* from this road to which we had been led—if Elys guessed rightly. Only—where would I ride? And—Joisan . . .

Elys looked over her shoulder, directly into my eyes.

''You fight, thus wasting your strength; accept and hoard that. Do not believe that I also do not know what it is to be a stranger among all who are kin to one another. Once I had a father, a brother—neither could nor would accept me for what I am. I learned that through hardship and heart sorrow. You must also find your road and then hold to it. There are no easy paths for such as us.''

Perhaps something in my expression silenced her. She still gazed at me and then turned away, and I did not look after her or speak. This was my own battle that I must face.

In the Dales I knew that I was distrusted—hated—for what I was. I had managed to set that behind me for a space, just as I had left Imgry and his camp. At that moment I still longed—in a part of me—to ride away, turn my back on the road and all that it stood for, even on these two who had learned a secret for living cruelly denied to me, a secret I was perhaps not even wishful to learn. That was the human part of me. What if I forgot the Kerovan who was? What would be my way now? Would it lie as straight as the road heading toward those distant heights—taking me out of the past?

And Joisan—but, no, Joisan was not to be left in the past, she was not to be forgotten. She was—I must admit it to myself now if I never did to any other—she was all that was real now in my world.

Joisan

I STOOD ON STONE AND IT WAS SOLID UNDER ME. I FELT THE COOL OF the breeze that tugged at the ragged, earth-smeared loops of my hair where the braids had come apart, I heard the nervous twittering and calls of the birds. All this I could believe in. But the rest—could one walk half in, half out of some spell? There had been enough behind me in the past hours that could lead me to believe that I might indeed no longer be able to think straight and clearly.

"Untaught—and no longer a cub. There is nothing but folly in such a one." A new voice in my head, a contemptuous voice. "It was not so in the other days."

Slowly I went to my knees that my eyes might be on a closer line with the bland gaze meeting mine. Beyond the cat, the bear yawned, its small eyes ignoring me. Surely—surely it had been the bear that thought-spoke that time!

These—these animals—I had no other way to name those who transferred speech directly into my mind—how . . . I fought down my fear. This was the Waste, I must always remember that and be warned. In a place where remnants of Power had been loosed for more generations than my people had built and lived in the Dales, how could I—dare I—marvel at anything that I might encounter here? Cats—a bear—who thought-spoke—these

119

were no more extraordinary than the means by which I had been lifted out of an earth-walled prison into this outer world again.

"I—can—not speak—as—you—do . . ." I returned haltingly.

Now the smaller cat yawned with the same boredom the bear had shown. "Why state that which is so plainly true?"

That *had* come in direct answer to my speech! I had not fallen easy prey to hallucination, unless it was so strong a one, or a spell, that it carried this semblance of reason.

"Allow me time." I did not wonder at my pleading with the cat; at that moment it seemed very natural. At least there was my old liking for its kind to make this easier. I still distrusted the bear. "I thought I knew a little of your people—but this—"

"Our people?" There was disdain in that. "You have never met with our people, witling." The yellow eyes narrowed a little. "Our like does not live with yours—or has not for more years than it has taken these walls to loose their stones."

I searched for an apology. It was plain that if this cat knew of those who roamed Dale keeps, it considered itself of a different breed altogether.

"Your pardon," I said hurriedly. "I have seen some like unto you. They are of the Dales. But I do not know you, and if I have offended, then please understand it is done in ignorance."

"Ignorance? If you are ignorant why then do you wear the key? That opens doors without, minds within." Now the voice was impatient as well as condescending. My furred questioner plainly found me one she considered of inferior intelligence—I deduced that this was the female of the pair.

The gryphon! A key—Neevor had said so. My hand closed about the globe. It would seem that even these chance-met animals knew more than I about what I carried. I wondered if they could tell me, but, before I could search for the proper words, that other voice growled into my mind.

"It is time for eating, not talking. This one has no Power, is indeed a witling. Let it go away and stop troubling us. What it does with itself is no concern of ours."

The bear had gotten up onto four feet, was swinging around toward the same wall gap through which I had earlier come. Now it lumbered toward it, never looking back, plainly divorcing itself from me and my concerns. Still neither of the cats seemed inclined to follow it.

I had found the words for my explanation, very glad that that
red-brown body had disappeared. It was far easier for me to feel
more comfortable—or as much at ease as my situation would
allow—with the cats alone.

"I do not know the Powers of the Old Ones—perhaps the ones
who once lived here . . ." I gestured about the courtyard.
"This"—I held the globe out a fraction so that the sun shown
full on the gryphon within—"was a gift from my lord. It has
powers, that is true, but I am not one trained to use them. I do
not even know what they may be. Please—can you tell me where
is this place—and why—or how . . ." I floundered.

One part of me stood aside in pure wonder at what I did, that I
sat on my heels and strove to talk to a cat. The rest of me urged
that this was the only way for me to learn what might be of great
importance to me—that I could no longer live by Dale ways or
judge by Dale standards, but must accept all that came, no
matter how impossible some of it might seem.

More than cats—yes. And I—was I less than any like me they
might have once known? I suspected as much.

The smaller of the two—the female—still watched me with
that unwinking stare. She weighed me by some standards of her
own and I suspected that I was so discovered to be sadly
wanting.

"You say you do not know how to use the Key, yet you came
here by the ——" The concept, which followed words I did
understand, was one to now leave me completely baffled. I had a
faint impression of what might be wings beating the air, but that
passed through my mind so swiftly I could not be sure I was
correct.

"I was trapped underground," I explained, as I would to
another person had I been welcomed into the ruins by one of my
own kind. So I told my story—of the whirlpool in the earth, of
the place of dark, of how I had beaten off the creatures and then
found my escape by way of the gryphon, which, as I talked, I
held cupped in my hand. To touch it so gave me strength, a
feeling of reality, a link with the world I had always known.

I described the chamber of the low walls, and of how I had
lain down in the middle of it, only to find myself transported
here. While I talked the two cats watched me, nor did either of
them use mind speech to comment upon, or to interrupt my tale.

"So I found myself out there." I pointed to the gap through which the bear had gone—to that overgrown garden where I had discovered food and drink.

"It is true—you are as blind as a newborn kitten." The female again. "You play with things beyond your knowing. All you *do* know is that you are hungry and that you want to find your way out—that you—"

"Kittens learn." A milder mind-voice cut through this petulant recital of my lacks. "She will learn. Remember, it takes her kind much longer to grow from kitten to hunter—"

"Meanwhile she meddles foolishly with that which could bring notice—trouble for not only her, but for others. It has been very long since any one used the——" (again those words which had no meaning for me). "How can we be sure that the alarm of that has not belled, to awaken much it is better not to have any dealings with? Let her go and take her Key. *That* in itself is bait enough for many a Dark One. Such need only sense its presence with a least hint—and then—!"

The cat before me raised a paw, pads spread a little so that the claws (which were formidable looking even in this smaller animal) hooked out into the open. A threat—I thought—or at least a firm warning.

Her mate arose and stretched forefeet well before him after the manner of his kind.

"So the Thas are setting traps." His comment meant nothing to me. The female looked around at him, her eyes became slits, her lips wrinkled back to display fangs as sharp as her claws.

"Earth-worms!" Now she spat. "Since when do such crawlers dare face the light?"

"Since when have they stirred at all—this side of the Barrier—after the Spell of the Hour was set? Their earth-moving has not spread hither for a long time. Nor have they dared leave the Range of Shifting Shadows. This one certainly did not draw them; they were already burrowing where they had no right to be. Who knows what they plan in their murky, earth-slimed minds? Or who gives them orders? For they dare not the Light unless there is some strong will urging them on."

His range of questions apparently struck his mate as having importance—though they meant very little to me. She set her paw back on the ground and her attention shifted from me to him. I tried hard to sort out from the information I had so gained what I could.

Thas—that name I impressed in my mind. It must be that of the creatures I had battled in the dark. They had been formidable surely and I could still bring to mind the memory of their claws reaching for me. Yet—now I was a little startled at the realization— they had not pulled me down as easily as they were armed to do. I did not believe that it was my flapping efforts with that belt that had held them at bay.

"The gryphon." I was thinking aloud rather than addressing myself to the cats. "They were afraid of the gryphon's light. Then they were whistled away—"

"That is so. And who whistled? It was the Key that defeated their first purpose—perhaps was a bane also to that which loosed them at you," the male cat assented. "Do not forget the Key. Whether you dealt with it out of knowledge or out of fear and need, you have used it—and it brought you here." He looked to his mate, and I believed they were exchanging some confidence that was close to me.

The female growled deep in her throat. I thought that that warning or protest was not aimed at me. Now she drew back to the doorway beside her mate, settling herself as if she were withdrawing from proceedings that were not to her liking. The male spoke to me again.

"You are not of the old blood, nor are you one of those who come seeking what they call 'treasure'—bits and pieces of things— some of which are better forgotten. Them we have seen—and small value do they get for all their grubbing. The real things of Power are near all safe-hidden. Why then have you come into this land, bringing that with you which can arouse both Light and Dark?"

"I seek my lord." So I told them the other portion of my story as I might, and had in part, to Elys and Jervon. Elys—Jervon— my mind turned to them. Had they also been caught in the snare of the Thas? I had not found them in that place of utter dark— but that did not mean they had gone free. For their sakes I hoped that I had been the only one so completely entrapped.

Thus I spoke of Kerovan, and when I mentioned that he shared heritage with the Old Ones, the male cat drew a step or two closer, as if this was of importance and he must hear every word. I talked of Neevor—and *that* name wrought a change in both animals. Once more they looked one to the other in silent communication.

Now the female mind-spoke.

"Trouble—trouble indeed. Old truces broken if *that* One has interested himself in this. An ill day for all of us if the sleeping wake—there will be more than Thas overrunning, or underrunning this land."

"Neevor cannot be of the Dark Ones!" I challenged her for the first time. I was sure of what I said.

"That is very true. Only we have had peaceful years in which Dark and Light did not strive against one another, drawing even the least of us into their battles. Each, long ago, withdrew to their chosen strongholds and did not trouble with us, who bear no allegiance to either, as long as we did not intrude upon them. Now the Thas move, they lay traps. Those worms of the deep earth obey orders—whose orders? You speak of one who calls himself Neevor—upon occasion—telling us that he wanders abroad and takes action. This lord of yours—what is *he?*"

Her eyes once more narrowed to slits and her ears had flattened slightly against her skull, but she did not snarl. Instead she voiced an order, sharply, as one who is well used to being obeyed.

"Show me the Key, show it to me closely!"

Before I thought, so imperative was her demand, I slipped the chain over my head and held out my hand, the globe resting in the hollow of my palm. Within that crystal, not clouded now with any radiance, the gryphon was plain to be seen. I had a strange fancy, lasting for a breath or two, that the small image held a form of life, that it made contact with the two cats who paced forward and stood with their noses close to the ball.

"Sooooo." That was like a hiss in my brain. "He is *that* one!"

The male spoke first. The head of the female was still outstretched, her attitude one of sniffing, as if the ball gave forth an odor, which it was imperative that she detect.

"It cannot be!" She jerked back her head. "The time for that is long past—the very way forgotten. Not even Neevor can walk into that hall and greet him who sleeps there. Sleeps? Surely not—too many seasons have come and gone—the life force must have departed out of him long since!''

"It is true"—the male paid no attention to his mate's comment, rather mind-spoke me—"that you do not know what you hold. There is more to the Key than any one of us can sense—it is a very special Key. No wonder the——" (again those words I knew not) "brought you here! If that Power awakes again, indeed the hills shall dance, the rivers turn in their beds, and the very land will be rewoven.''

"Take it from her!" demanded the female. "Take it and cast it into some pit—or better still—set it under a stone. Turn her out . . . Such a thing is not for this witling to play with, or for anyone to hold!" Now she did openly snarl and her paw arose with lightning speed to hook what I held out from my fingers. I jerked the globe back against my breast just in time.

"We cannot take away what has been given." But there was a growl sounding from the male's throat even as his thought-words reached me. "GIVEN—remember?''

"She can loose—she can use—" Now the female's thought-speech ended. Instead the squawl of a cat about to launch itself into a fight arose.

The male shouldered between us, even as his mate crouched to spring. I had hurriedly once more dropped the chain over my head.

"If you tell me what you know of this—of how I may use it safely," I began, eyeing the female warily. She was no snow cat to be sure, a huntress large enough to bring down a horse, kill an unwary human. Still, her mounting fury, linked with those claws and fangs, could cause grievous hurts if she indeed sprang for me.

"No!" The male made answer. "There are many Powers, one does not play with any. Perhaps it was meant that what you hold should be returned to this land in the guardianship of one who is ignorant. On your head will the consequences be, only if it is loosed. This much we must grant you as long as you wear that—you may shelter here.''

"In safety?" I looked with meaning from him to the furious female.

He moved a fraction forward, urging her also with his shoulder. "From us you need fear nothing. We do not strive to meddle.''

The female growled, but her anger was plainly fading. She sent no other thought to me. Her mate added, "This place is safe—for now—if we give consent. Rest—and wait. There must be some plan in which you are to play a part—or Neevor would not have moved. No, chance does not send the Thas into making traps—bring him who is your lord hither—give you the right to wear and use—that."

Now the female did speak.

"We have no part in such plans, we want none!"

"We may believe now we have no part," he corrected her. "We are not movers and shakers, doers and undoers—but many times such, even as we, are entangled in the nets of Great Ones. Let be! In truth, by the old promise and the covent, having come hither by the———" (those words once more), "you have a right to claim refuge. You have followed a road long unused but none the less important. Yes"—now his eyes slitted in turn—"we are not kin, nor comrade ones to your kind, nor have we, in many years, sworn aid to anyone. But because you have come to us by certain ways we are bound to shelter you. You are free to stay, or go, whichever you wish."

Abruptly then he vanished in a long, graceful bound, the female swift behind him, leaving me alone in the ruined courtyard as the sun sank behind the heights, its light lost in the shadow of what had once been a watch tower.

Wait—he had said wait. For what—or whom? I did not altogether like the sound of that. Had it been really a command? He had also said that I could go at my desire, though I was not about to strike out across this countryside among growing shadows and the coming dark of night.

There was no evil here and it was shelter of a sort. I cupped the globe tightly between my hands. What I had heard was tantalizing, but that I could get any more information out of the cats was doubtful. Oddly enough, now that they were gone, a loneliness touched me. There was no fear—just that emptiness.

I looked at the gaping doors. No, I had no mind to enter into that place. I would spend this night right here in the courtyard under the open sky.

So I harvested armloads of grass, pulled from the thick growth in what had been the garden. This I made into a nestlike bed. Once more I ate berries, found a small stream of water and drank my fill, washed my hands and face, combed all I could of the soil from my hair, and made up my mind to try to wash it clean with the coming of the morning.

I would have liked to have set a fire—I had a spark-striker in my belt pouch—but I sought no wood for one. It seemed more prudent to me that the dark of the courtyard remain. I wanted no advertisement of my presence. The cats had said this was a safe refuge but I did not want to test the truth of that. What they might deem enemies and what I could fear might be two different things altogether.

As I stretched out on my bed, my arms beneath my head, looking up into the darkening sky, I sought to plan what I must do when morning came. The cat's word—that I was to wait—I did not care for that . . . unless I had some idea of what I waited for. On the other hand, without any guide, supplies, horses—what was I to do? To go wandering off, without any aim, across a land that was far more hostile than it looked—that indeed would be rank folly.

It seemed to me, now that I had a period in which to think through events since I had left Norsdale, that so far I had been singularly favored by fortune. The meeting with Elys and Jervon— had that really happened by chance alone? Or had I, by my choice in Norsdale, my determination to cling to Kerovan, set in motion a series of events that linked, one with the other, to foster some action determined by a will beyond my reckoning?

It is never pleasant to believe that one is moved here or there by that which one does not understand. As a child I had come and gone at the bidding of my uncle or Dame Math. Then later I had been the one to give orders, to decide the fates of more than myself when I led the survivors of Ithdale into the wilderness. I had many times been uncertain of my own judgment. Still I had had to make decisions and sometimes quickly, so that I grew more confident and sure of myself.

My lord had never said do this, do that. Though according to Dales law I was as much his servant as the youngest serving wench in his hall. He had stood beside me, been like my right hand or my left when there was need, but never intruded his own orders unless such was for our good, and then in such a way that his suggestion came not as a direct command, but rather as if I, too, must see the logic of it even as he did.

Was it the Waste and its ghostly shadows that now made me doubt my independence—think that perhaps after all I had made no real choice that was of my own wishing? How far back did such an influence then exist?

Had it come about long years ago when my uncle chose my lord—when I, a child of eight, was axe-wedded to a boy I had never seen? Or did the entanglement, which I now feared existed, start when my unknown husband had sent me the gryphon? Or did it follow after the invaders' attack upon Ithdale? Or—had our fates been decided even in the hour of our births?

Did any living thing have complete freedom of choice in this eerie country—or was what I had said to Elys the truth, that we who were born here had other heritage than human, were bound to Powers whether we knew it or not?

I knew that there was only one major truth in my life, and that was that Kerovan and I were meant to be one in the same manner as Elys and Jervon—each bringing to that unity different gifts and talents—so that the whole was greater. That Kerovan would not, or could not, admit this, did not release me, nor would it ever. No words of his, no action he might take, could make me other than I was.

Shutting my eyes upon the sky, I drew into my mind the memory of his face. The vision had not faded any during the many days we had been apart. I saw him as clearly now as I had on that morning in Norsdale, when he had put aside all I offered to ride away, as clearly as I had when trapped in the cave I had sought and had seen him. Now I strained to bring about once more *that*, only it did not come, no matter how much I willed it.

With Kerovan thus with me in memory, the only way I could hold him now, I drifted into sleep, holding fiercely to this small piece of comfort—the single one I knew.

I was warm—I must have slept too near the fire. Trying to edge away from the heat, I opened my eyes upon a dazzle of sunlight, which struck full upon me, turning my mail into a highly uncomfortable covering. As I sat up, my hair caught and tangled with the withered grasses on which I had slept, and I tried to shake that mass free as I looked, heavy-eyed, about me.

From the high position of the sun I must have slept clear through the night and well into the next morning. The birds still flew in and out of the vines, making a rising din with their chirpings and song. Otherwise the courtyard was deserted. There was no sign of either cats or bear.

My body ached. Though there was the padded jerkin between my body and the mail, still I missed the under-shirt I had torn in the cavern. I itched and felt as unkempt and dirty as any vagabond. I longed for cleanliness of skin, for fresh clothing. If I only had the saddlebags I had left in the camp the Thas had engulfed!

I arose slowly, stretching, wanting to feel more alert and lithe of limb. Once on my feet, I stood with my hands on my hips looking about.

This ruin must have long been just that—an abiding place for only birds and animals. Today, in the warmth of the sun, I no longer sensed that feeling of intrusion that had come upon me when I first entered the courtyard. This was only a shell from which life had long departed.

"Halloooo?" I did not know just why I tried that call. My voice was not loud, but it echoed emptily in a way that kept me from trying a second call. The cats—almost I could believe that I had dreamed them—still I knew that I had not.

Before I went to seek food and water I determined to know more of this place and I eyed the nearer tower speculatively. If the flooring within it remained intact I should be able to climb to a point high enough to see more of the country. That survey was imperative before I made even the shortest of plans ahead.

Thus I stepped through the door, which had the hanging fragments of a one-time barrier. Within, the sunlight was abruptly cut to dusk. The windows, even though no shutters remained, no parchment covered their openness, still admitted very little light, while the walls between the windows (which were wide on the courtyard side and narrowed to slits on the other) were bare stone. There were no remains of any furnishings save a couple of long benches—each fashioned to resemble an elongated cat—the head upstanding at one end, the tail erect at the other, the four supporting feet ending in clawed paws.

One of these was set against the far wall and I mounted on it to peer out of the narrow window. The same vines that overhung the courtyard also grew here in profusion and I could see very little through the veil they formed.

The floor of this large chamber was covered by paw marks in

the dust—those of the cats, and some that could belong only to the bear, while there was also a strong animal smell in the room, though it had not been used as a general lair, for there were no beds of drifted leaves, no signs of the inedible parts of prey.

I passed under the archway, which gave into the lowest floor of the tower, and found what I had hoped, a stairway leading up, one side against the wall. The other, which lacked any guard rail, was open, while the steps were unusually narrow, hardly wide enough to take the length of my boots, and the rises were not as high as one would expect. However, the stones were sturdily set, though I tested each before I placed my full weight upon it.

So I climbed, emerging into another chamber as bare as the one below. Then, finally, into a third above that. Here were more window slits, and I made my way toward the closest through even deeper gloom, for the vines were thick curtains I had to push, break, and tear in order to force an opening through which I might view what lay beyond.

It would seem that this hall had been built with one side just above the edge of a sharp, down-dropping slope. There were trees rooted precariously on it, as well as a lot of brush, but where it reached the level at last, the land was wide open.

Across that, as straight as if someone had used a sword blade to cut a path—the tip of which touched heights to the west—was what could only be a road. Only this was such a road as I had never seen in the Dales, where tracks, of necessity, were narrow because of the many ridges.

Not only was it dazzling white under the sun, but broad and very smooth, though there were glints of glitter on its surface, flashing now and then. The highway lacked any travelers as far as I could see. It was just there—startling on that dull plain. There were wide stretches of open ground on each side as if all cover had been deliberately pruned away. To discourage ambush? But who had come this way in such fear—and against what or whom had those wayfarers needed to so protect themselves?

Kerovan

THIS ROAD, WHICH I KNEW AS WELL AS ELYS DID, WAS NO TRACK such as ran through the Dales. It carried the mark of sorcery even more than that which the Exiles had used, and it ran toward the heights. Though I had determined to ride west, now I was reluctant to set out upon such a way, easy as it was to travel. Not so my companions, for remounted, Elys swung out upon the pavement, nor did Jervon linger, but was at her side, the pack pony on a lead, already past me.

I mounted the mare, fighting inner turmoil. To take such a path was to expose myself to—to what? Was I such a one now as started at shadows, drew steel at the sloughing of a wind through tree branches? This shaming fact I could not yield to. I sent the mare on, where the click of her shoes on the stone of the way sounded overloud.

Whoever had laid out the way that highway traveled had paid no attention to the contour of the land, had allowed no fact of nature to dispute where it would run. Hillocks had been cut through, leveled back to allow passage, surfaces smoothed. Its making was a feat of labor that I do not think the Dales, even if all their manpower was summoned to the task, could ever have equaled.

As the pavement provided the easiest of footing, we made far

better time than we had riding cross-country. Nor did we see any
signs of life, except a bird or two—not flying in that threatening
coil of the evil flock but high and alone. The country apparently
was very bare hearabouts, or else all that lived near kept their
distance from the road itself.

A little before sunset we came upon a place where the pavement curved out at one side, forming an oval section that was
still attached to the highway, as a piece of fruit might lie next to
a bough. Elys turned her mount in that direction and for the first
time in some hours spoke, raising her voice to reach me where I
still trailed a little behind.

"This will afford a safe campsite."

Most of the surface of that oval was covered by one of the five
pointed stars, so that the space might lie under some protection,
a kind we should welcome, I guessed. There might not be any
inns or other shelters along the highways, but those who had
built it had arranged such places as this for the safe rest of the
travelers.

Here the surrounding land was wide open, covered mainly
with a tall-growing grass. We put our horses on picket ropes,
allowing them to graze to their content. There was also (within a
stride or two of the road) a basin in which water bubbled up from
underground. The water was not only very clear and very cold,
but it possessed a flavor all its own and . . . Can water be
perfumed? I had never heard of such, yet when I rinsed my
hands and then cupped them to make a drinking cup, I was sure
that I caught a faint scent—like unto that of a garden of fresh
herbs lying under the full-drawing rays of the sun.

Nor did we have to light a fire to brave the draw-in of the
dark. For with the coming of night that star in which our camp
was set began to glow faintly. There was a warmth in the air.
Whoever had fashioned this wonder we would never know, but
to me it was a fitting answer to all those who claim that only evil
comes from the use of that which belongs to the Old Ones.

Elys sat crosslegged in the very heart of the star after we had
eaten from our trail supplies. Her eyes were fixed on the road.
At first I believed that, in truth, her sight was turned inward, and
that she was near in a state of trance, which made me uneasy.
With the coming of the dark a feeling of Power, which I had not
sensed as we rode under the sun, gathered to hedge us in. One's

skin prickled with uneasiness, one's hair seemed to stir with a force of deeply pent energy.

I looked from Elys's closed face to the road. In me something came alert, waited—Would this highway also prove to be "haunted"? Would we see and hear tonight the passing of some who had long gone before? There came another thought into my mind. Power such as I now felt could certainly be drawn upon. Suppose we tried again to scry—might not the result be that I could see Joisan, learn enough to be guided directly to her?

"The cup . . ." I began, though I knew that breaking through her present deep absorption might alienate rather than lead Elys to agree to my plea.

She did not turn her head, she did not even break her forward stare by so much as a blink. But her answer came readily enough.

"Not here. I have not the strength to hold what might answer. I am not so learned . . ." In her voice there was an unhappy, longing note. "No. I could not control the forces that await here. They have not been tapped for long and long—that does not mean they have grown the less, rather they have built in strength."

My disappointment was tinged with a fraction of anger. Still I knew that she was right. One should not meddle to raise any Power that one did not know one had the ability to control. It was very certain that our present surroundings, benevolent as they seemed, might hold a violent response to any witchery, no matter how mild or well intended.

So I sat in silence, nor did I stare as she did down that road, which promised so much and yet which we dared not trust. I did not care what ghosts might walk here. They were no kin of mine—that I chose to be so. I was myself—alone—as in reality I had always been. Yet, sometimes with Joisan . . .

To think of her brought pain that was not of the body, rather an inward ache, as if I had hungered all my life and now understood that I must continue to hunger until I died. There was Joisan . . .

I no longer saw that band of metal on my wrist, on which I had idly centered my gaze. Rather, there arose before my eyes a girl's face, the skin sun-browned, thin . . . Perhaps no man who did not look the second time would call her beautiful. No man—but I was not a true man, and, to me, she was as radiant

as the fabled, much-courted daughters of keeps such as the
songsmiths sing of—those before whom men paraded in their
pride, fought monsters, and courted death-danger that they might
be noticed and admired.

She had such courage, that brown girl, so wide and deep a
heart, that even an outcast who was also a "monster" had been
invited into the warm core of it. I need only have said the right
words and she would have come to me willingly. But I did not
want willingness out of duty—I wanted . . .

I wanted something else, not pity, not duty, not that she came
to me because we had faced evil together and come unharmed
out of that battle that we had fought. I did not know just what I
wanted—save it was something I had not found, nor really could
put name to.

Then I heard, even through my cloud of self-pity, a soft sound
from Elys, a deeper gasp that could only have come from
Jervon. Startled I raised my head. The road lay radiant in the
night. Each and every mark along it was alive with silver fire,
even though the moon was not yet high.

Also—perhaps the cause was induced by some trick of that
light, but it seemed to me that part of the patterns moved. There
was a glow that came and went along the patches that resembled
the footprints of man, beast, and bird, almost as if things now
trod upon them, clouding them for a second here and there as an
invisible foot pressed, was again lifted, while those symbols in
the corners of the stars glowed stronger, a light haze arising from
them as if candles had been set ablaze.

I put out my hand, without being conscious that I did, until
Elys's fingers clasped mine. Also, I knew without looking, she
must be linked with Jervon in the same manner. We were *not*
alone! There were travelers on the road though we might not see
them, even as those other ghosts had passed into exile long ago.
They did not approach us. Perhaps they journeyed, not in another dimension of space, but in time itself. Great concerns we
could not comprehend drew them on. We dimly felt their concern—
or at least I did.

Twice I stirred as a touch reached me. Slight as it was, that
contact held the sharp impact of a blow. For that single instant I
had been on the brink of knowledge and understanding. Yes, I
almost knew—then the meaning was lost and I was left as empty

as when I had put Joisan from me to ride alone out of Norsdale. Only this had nothing to do with Joisan, rather it came to me as a greeting, a meeting with those I understood, who knew and welcomed me—but to whose attention I could not hold because I was only a part of what they were in full.

I do not know how long we sat there so hand-linked, watching what no human eyes could ever catch in full. There came at last a time when the prints no longer glowed, dimmed, glowed again, when our sensing of those hastening travelers faded. Elys's fingers slid out from mine. My hand fell limply, to lie on the stone.

We did not speak to each other—had we even seen or felt the same things? I never knew. Rather we separated in silence, all at once full spent, worn from the watching, wrapped ourselves in our cloaks to sleep. Nor did I dream that night.

However, I awoke later in the morning than my companions. Jervon had already brought up the horses and had them saddled, the packs ready. Elys knelt, was busy dividing supplies into two pouches. As I sat up, she gestured to a portion of journey cake set aside, giving the packet that held the remainder to Jervon.

He stayed where he was but Elys arose, to stand before me as I sat chewing the dry cake, wishing that for once I had a bowl of porridge hot from the pot, such as I had seldom tasted since I rode from Ulmsdale years ago.

"Kerovan," she said abruptly. "Here we must part company."

At first I did not even understand her. When I did, I stared at her open-mouthed. There were dark bruises left by exhaustion under her eyes, and her face seemed gaunt, as if she were fresh out of some battle. Her hand went out in a small gesture—not to summon power, rather one that expressed helplessness.

"We—we have been forbidden . . ."

I was on my feet, my food forgotten. What had happened as I slept away the rising of the sun? Who had forbidden?

She no longer looked at me but to the road, white and straight under the sun. I saw a longing, as deep as the heart-wrenching sorrow that I carried (perhaps with such ill grace) in her face. She might be regarding all the wonders the world can offer, piled in a heap before her, and yet know that she could touch them not.

"This way is not for us . . . not yet—not yet . . ."

The sadness in her eyes was near a sob in her voice.

"But you—you said . . ." I found myself floundering for
words as might a child trying to learn from an elder the why of
an inexplicable change in plan.

"When I told you that we would ride together—then I believed I spoke the truth. Perhaps—perhaps we, Jervon—I—have
been weighed and found wanting." Her disappointment was
hurtful for any one to see. "Believe me, it is not for us to go on.
This is your road only, Kerovan. Perhaps we played our part
merely in companying you to this place, even as we earlier
companied your lady. There must be some reason behind the
pattern of our meeting with you both. Whatever that was, it is
now fulfilled. But if we have in any way served—then remember
us, Kerovan, in those days when you come into your heritage. It
may be that we shall . . . No, you ride alone, for that is where
you go—to accept your own fate, whether you believe it or not.

"If there comes a time later"—her expression did not change,
still I read a thread of hope in her voice—"when we shall be
made free of this way, and none shall say us no—then, when
that time comes, look for us, Kerovan, be sure we come with
glad hearts. What we shall do from this day forward is wait—
and struggle and learn—until the road lies open."

I clasped her hand and her flesh was chill. She said no more
but mounted. Then I clasped hands with Jervon also. He had eyes
mainly for Elys, as if whatever burden she bore, he would seize
upon as his own if he could. I was left with no words at all as I
stood and watched them go leaving Joisan's mare and the pack
pony, on which they had loaded the bulk of their own supplies, a
last gesture of good will for me.

Back down the road they went, leaving in me a vast loneliness, a sharply growing need. Still, such had been the force of
Elys's words and manner I could not have found any argument to
stop them.

I did not at once start in the other direction along that road,
which Elys had said was to be mine alone. Rather I settled on
my heels after I had seen them out of sight, they never turning
once to lift hand to me again. Not until now had I been aware
how much their company had meant during these past few days.
I had ridden into this Waste telling myself that I was my own
man (though I chose to go on Imgry's errand), that in all High

Hallack now there was not one I wished to comrade with, or who cared if I might come to trouble. Save only my lady—and her I had thought safe as anyone might be in this grim and war-torn land.

There was nothing, I had thought, which I any longer desired to have, to hold, to know. As if he who had been Kerovan of Ulmsdale was dead—only a husk of him walked, rode, spoke.

I had always known I was different. They had told me early that my mother could not bear to look upon me and thus I had been sent to the very edge of my father's holdings to be fostered. There I had had but two friends—Riwal, for whom the Waste and its secrets were a lodestone, the attraction of which he never tried to deny, and Jago, a crippled man-at-arms who had taught me the ways of war—and later died treacherously at the hands of his enemies who were also mine, those enemies I faced in time and fought.

No! Even at that battle with the Dark I had not been Kerovan of Ulmsdale; instead I had been filled by another personality, one who was out of another place (or else another time), filled with great force, one who used me as I myself would draw a sword. Save, when that presence withdrew, its will accomplished, it took with it that part of Kerovan that had warmth, a love of life, a belief in himself. Now I was empty, and only with the going of Elys and Jervon (having witnessed the strong bond between them) did I realize how empty.

My fingers sought the wrist band of the Old Ones, as one of the Dames of Norsdale might tell her prayer hoops. Only I repeated no prayers, for though as any rational person I acknowledged there were Powers beyond the comprehension of my kind, still I called upon none such. The truth was I knew not which to call. Or whether any such would still concern themselves with a husk of a man who was lost inside his empty self as much as he would be lost in the world which was theirs.

To linger on here was no answer. Nor did I altogether believe Elys's assurance that this was the road I must take to some unknown confrontation with the future. However, it had its safeguards, and was a means to reach the heights. I mounted the mare that had been Joisan's, fastened the lead rope of the pack pony to my saddle horn, and at last rode on.

The sun awoke silvery glints from the patterns laid in the

stone. Those varied ever (though there were always the many
foot, paw, and hoof tracks cutting sometimes even across symbols). I noted that all those prints pointed in the same direction—
forward, none returned—as if all traffic here lay in one direction
only—toward the mountains. Just one more mystery to add to all
the others.

I kept the mare to a walk. For about me, as I rode, there clung
the feeling that I was not alone (perhaps that had been allayed
yesterday when I did have human comrades), and neither did I
believe that I passed unobserved. So I found myself watching the
prints far more than the way before me. In the sunlight they did
not change as they had in the night, when it appeared that
invisible feet fitted and left their outlines.

This close watch on the pavement caused a feeling of de-
tachment in my mind, induced a dreamy acceptance of all lying
about me. When I suddenly realized that, I knew a pinch of fear.
Was I being so ensorcelled by some long-laid spell?

Deliberately I turned the mare to the edge of the road, urged
her to step off onto the turf. Unexpectedly she tossed her head,
fought me, mouthing the bit angrily, planting her hooves and
refusing to go. Was it the firmer footing of the pavement she
wanted? Or was she under the guidance of another, even though
I held her reins? Perhaps the sorcery I suspected already had her
enthralled.

Even for me it no longer seemed strange that I should close
my eyes for an instant now and then, and feel (when I was not
looking on the emptiness around me) that I was riding in company, though none of those I sensed appeared aware of me in turn.
Or, if they were, my presence meant nothing to them as they had
urgent and pressing affairs elsewhere.

That feeling of urgency came to possess me also. The first
slow pace I had set the mare became a trot without my conscious
urging. She held her head high, her tail switched from side to
side, as if she were a parade mount, proud among her kind. The
pack pony crowded up on my left until he paced abreast of us.

Though we certainly traveled more swiftly than before we had
taken the road, those dark heights to the west were very slow in
drawing closer. It was as if they in turn retreated before our
advance.

Nor did I sight any more ruins such as the towers. This part of the Waste might have always been forsaken wilderness had not the road traversed it. At intervals there were those ovals such as we had used for a campsite. Each had its basin of water, a good stand of grass inviting a traveler to rest. I drew into one at nooning, allowed the mare and the pony to graze, ate my journey cake washed down with water. Then I simply sat, no longer thinking, just accepting that this is what must be.

Lord Imgry, the Dales, the Wereriders, even Elys and Jervon, faded and diminished in my memory. I spun the band about my wrist. Holding that, I summoned up (first with an effort, and then with a fast burst of clear inner sight) my vision of Joisan. So vivid was that, I felt she actually stood somewhere ahead, waiting for me, a serious, questioning look on her face—the same expression I had seen there so many times during our last days together in Norsdale.

"Joisan! Joisan!" I awoke to the fact that I was calling her name over and over as my fingers slipped around that band.

Within me . . . No! I was not just a husk of a man after all! The dream that had held me most of the morning shattered at that new force astir within. I saw again the churned earth and Jervon digging in it; I watched a cup fill itself to the brim and my lady's face show mistily, surrounded by the heavy dark but still with the blazing gryphon in her hand. Hurriedly now I reclaimed the mare and the pony, swung into the saddle. There was a purpose in all this, as Elys had suspected. I might see only the beginning of it at the moment, but there would be more later and . . .

What more that might be, or how I was so important a part of it, I did not yet understand. Yet the urgency now fastened full upon me and my thoughts no longer drifted. Rather did I make a speedy return to what once I had been—a scout of the Dales' force, marking not patterns upon the road, rather the country through which it ran. For the first time I saw that indeed my morning's ride had brought me well ahead. There lay foothills not too far beyond—forming the fringes of the heights.

On those hills were odd outcroppings, which did not look to be natural in such places. I had thought this part of the land held no ruins, but I saw them now—and so many that I might be approaching the remains of a town as large as one of our own port cities.

The sun, however, was well westward, when I came close

enough to see those tumbled walls clearly. Above them, on a tongue of higher ground licking to the east, stood towers, more walls—plainly a keep. It was of course a site such as any builder would choose for a place of defense. So perhaps there had been those also among the Old Ones who had not found life so safe that they could neglect such positions of prudent safety.

As I drew rein to gaze upward, make sure that the keep was indeed a ruin (and not perhaps one hiding such a peril as that tower around whose territory we had so carefully ridden), I caught a brilliant flash from the top of a broken wall a little below the tower itself. I raised my hand as a shade for my eyes and felt growing warmth about my wrist.

The band burned. For a moment or two I thought I had actually seen a small tongue of flame leap from its surface.

Now I dropped hand to sword hilt, even though I well knew that whatever might lie in wait there might be impervious to any steel, even that forged from Waste metal itself.

At that moment there sounded an ear-punishing squall. Out of the brush that rimmed the flat land between the road and the rise on which stood the keep, a tawny, brown-yellow body flashed in great ground-covering bounds, heading for me. Behind it came a second.

Very faint and far away, nearly drowned by the animals' challenge, I thought I also heard a shout. My sword was out. The creatures coming for me moved fast—like arrows of gold shooting through the tall grass. My pack pony snorted and jerked back on the lead rope. However, the mare showed no fear, though she sidled around to face head-on those who came.

Both halted short at the very edge of the highway, panting from the effort that had brought them at such speed. I half expected now that one, or both, would launch into the air in a characteristic leap at prey. For I could now see they were feline, not as large as the cunning and formidable snow cats to be sure, but still big enough to cause some trouble if they did attack.

I studied them as they made no further move, to my astonishment. These might be kin-cousin to those cats living in the Dale keeps save they were much larger and of a uniform yellow-brown I had not seen before. Both of their heads, between the large eyes and on the upper breasts, showed distinct V marks.

Since they had stopped and now were settling in a seated

position, I felt slightly foolish to be holding bared steel and thrust
my sword back into its sheath. Their behavior was certainly not
that of ordinary animals. I reminded myself once again to expect
anything in the Waste. Also they were certainly *not* as formidable as—

"Do not be too sure of that!"

The cats had not made a sound since their initial squalls. Nor
were those words *sounds*. They had formed in my head, and
came as a clear answer to a thought *I* had held! In spite of my
belief that the Waste could hold any surprise, I found it startling
now to have my mind invaded by a coherent message—and it
must have originated from one of the animals, now regarding me
round-eyed.

"What do you want of me?" I strove to form that as a
mind-question and then discovered it was far easier to ask it
aloud.

"Nothing." The reply was both clear and curt.

"Nothing? But you cried—you came . . ."

The smaller of the cats, a female, turned her head a fraction to
look back over her shoulder at the slope down which she and her
mate had just descended.

"*We* want nothing. Wait—you shall learn who does."

Wait? For whom? That the cats might be allied with some
other Waste dweller was not out of reason. I glanced at my wrist
band. The metal was still warm; however, the flame I thought I
had seen in play was no longer there. I was sure that I had not
received a warning of evil to come, rather it had been another
message—perhaps a recognition of another Power.

I slipped from the saddle and stretched. That saddle was not
an easy perch for my heavier body. Both the mare and the pony
watched the cats, but I detected no sign of fear such as my desert
mounts had displayed at the coming of the Wererider.

"How long must I wait?" I asked after a moment.

Now the other cat also turned his head to look up-slope. I saw
there a wavering of brush, as if someone, or something, was
fighting a path through tough growth. A figure burst into the
open, running and dodging among piles of stone that marked old
ruins. From this distance it appeared human enough. Though that
also could mean nothing. It was well known that many of the
Old Ones were human in appearance, enough so that they could

couple successfully with Dale folk and produce offspring such
as myself. Was it not true that my mother's clan had been
rumored to have had such ancestry, and it was not only her
sorcery that had warped my body, but also her blood?

The runner sped from the last fringe of taller growth and
sprinted now through the grass that grew tall enough to brush
those flashing legs knee high. Sun glinted on mail. But above
that—a tangle of long hair was bunched into ragged braids
flopping across slender shoulders. A woman!

Elys? But how . . . ? That first explanation went in a flash.
This hair was not the black strands of the wise warrior-woman. It
held the deep red-brown of autumn leaves in the high country.
Only one had such hair—only—

I was running too, not aware of it until my boot snagged on a
grass-hidden root and I nearly sprawled full-length upon the
ground. Then I heard my own voice cry, as loud as the screams
of those black birds of ill-omen.

"Joisan!"

Joisan

I SQUEEZED CLOSER TO THE OPENING IN THE WINDOW, LEANED AS FAR forward as I could to view the ribbon of white road that ran along the lowlands. From my vantage point, which was, of course, well removed, that highway appeared untouched by time. I expected to see riders—travelers along it. Save that, for the stretch I was able to view, it was bare of any traffic at all. Still the road itself was, in a manner, reassuring. If—or when—surely, it was *when*—I decided to leave this refuge and take up my journey again (though I had no idea in which direction I would go) that would be a guide.

Now I strove to study the slope descending to the plain across which that road so boldly ran. There were a number of upstanding outcrops of stone, which I believed marked other ruins, even more decayed by the action of time than that in which I stood. I wondered if this had been a fortress of greater extent than it first appeared. The narrow windows on this outer wall suggested that those who had built it might have had reason to fear some attack from the north. However, for me now, the road was more important than piles of old stone blocks.

I made the rounds of the three other sides of the tower, attempting to view more of the keep itself and its surroundings here on the upper ridge. On the courtyard side the vines had

grown too thickly for me to break any peephole through. My
attempts to do so brought shrill cries from the birds, a wild
thrashing in the vines, so I left off such assault. To the east there
was merely another drop—though this lay farther away. What
lay below there showed a yellow patch, reminding me of the
desert through which we had made our way into the Waste. To
the west lay the long ridge, widening well out from the point on
which the keep had been built. There were the remains of
walled fields, more shells of buildings, a portion of the orchard.

Sight of that brought back both hunger and thirst. I abandoned
my exploration to seek out food and water. This morning, trac-
ing the water from the spring for a short distance I came upon a
stone walled pool. There I dared to slide out of mail and clothing, dipped myself, rubbing my body down with handfuls of
grass to scrub me clean, then undertook to wash my hair which
was still soil-clotted. Leaving it to hang free across my shoulders
and wind-dry, I did such brushing and cleansing of my clothing
as I could. The sun was caressingly warm on my bare body and I
found myself humming, even as our keep maids had sung when
they washed the linens along the water troughs.

I had drunk deeply. Now, pulling on, though I disliked their
fustiness against my clean body, my breeches and jerkin, I tried
to rebraid my hair, making sorry business of taming the still-
damp strands. Even the bronze clip, which held the coils in place
under my helm, was gone, and I tied it up as best I could with
twisted bits of long, tough grass.

Then, my mail shirt slung in folds across my shoulder, I went
hunting once more for the berry bushes. Only this time I had
another find to chew on. There was a kind of water plant, the
roots of which were crisp and sweet when washed clean. As I
crunched away at those, I remembered—though it was dim—a
part of a far different life, when such had been served in the
summer at our high table in Ithdale. My aunt had also had a
skillful hand in the making of sweets, and she had devised on her
own a recipe for preserving these thin stalks, cut small, in a
honey mixture for winter eating.

I looked down now at my berry-stained hands, at the mail,
which lay in a coil of brilliant folds under the sun. Ithdale was so
long ago, so far away, that my life there was more like the tale
of a songsmith, nothing that had really happened to the Joisan

who was here and now. Shrugging on the weight of mail, I went
exploring farther into the orchard-garden. But I found no ripe
tree fruit. There was a tangle of melon vines into which I dived
eagerly and came up with two which were golden ready, small
for lack of skillful cultivation—yet still to be prized. With those
in hand I started back to the courtyard, which I now looked upon
as my campsite.

There were furred things in the grass, which leaped or ran
ahead of my passing, but I had no knife nor dart gun with which
to hunt. In an odd way I could not bring myself to think of
killing here—even for food. This must be a rich hunting ground
for the cats—perhaps also for the bear—some of his kin were
noted as relishing flesh as well as berries and such.

Juggling the melons I climbed over fallen stones and so entered the courtyard once more, planning to use the sharp edge of
my belt buckle as a tool to slit the fruit. They might furnish both
food and drink. The sun now beat so hot that my mail was a
steadily irksome burden.

I had become so used to the loneliness of the keep since my
awakening that I gave a start when I saw that both cats had
returned, were lying lazily at their ease in the beam of a sun ray.
The female licked at her paws, her eyes slitted against the light.
Even as I came closer her mate rolled over, his paws in the air,
wriggling his body back and forth against the warm stone as if he
were relieving just such an itching as my own leather jerkin
brought in a portion of my back that I could not reach.

Seeing them thus taking their ease I paused, feeling very much
the intruder—an uninvited guest. The female blinked at me, took
no other notice, but continued to curl her tongue about a paw.
However, the male sat up and shook himself vigorously.

I stood there, melons in my hand, facing them both uncertain-
ly. Surely this was the strangest confrontation that could occur
even in this land. Then I rallied and found myself voicing the
guest greeting of my own people. These were not animals—but
much more . . .

"For the welcome of the gate"—I found myself speaking
aloud, and my gratitude did actually stir—"my thanks. For the
feasting on the board"—(though that was my own gleaning and
whether the cats could be thought to have ownership over the
garden was a point to be questioned, though I certainly would

not do so)—"my pleasure and my good wishes. To the Lord of this roof, fair fortune."

"Lord of this roof?" The repetition of my own words sprang into answer within my head. If such a manner of communication could express amusement that was what was plain to me now. "A pretty speech, woman of the Dales. So that is how you speak among your kind. Now let me but think a little . . . ah, yes. 'To the Farer on far roads the welcome of this roof, and may fortune favor your wandering.' "

That was one version of the Dale welcome for a guest unknown personally to any lord. That this cat would quote the exact formal words was again startling. How did an inhabitant of the Waste learn *our* polite courtesy? However, the cat was continuing.

"You did well to listen to us—and remain here." Now the light note had vanished from the mind-speech. Nor was I entirely surprised at the rest of what he said now.

"There has been a new stirring—"

When he added nothing to that, I moved forward to settle crosslegged on the heap of wilting grass that had been my bed (after all, he had given the guest greeting). Placing the melons on the stone before me (food was not my main interest now), I had a question ready.

"What manner of stirring? The Thas?" Since that or those had been the one menace I had met so far, my mind turned immediately in that direction. For a moment the fear that had been part of the dark and the stench awoke in me. My imagination painted a picture of tumbling walls (even such as these which had so long withstood the hammering of time), the ancient keep caught in a churning of the earth, all of it and us, too, sucked under.

"Perhaps Thas, among others." The cat did not shrug as might a man, but some inflection of his reply signaled such a gesture. "No, not as you think now—here. Old as are the protection spells laid on Carfallin, they still hold, and shall for perhaps many seasons yet. However, last night had its riders, its searchers, its seekers. Things are awake, watching, to prowl and sniff and hunt. Though as yet they are not sure of what they seek or how the hunt will begin."

"You believe that my coming has done this? But if the Thas had already burrowed their underground ways into the land—that

was surely done well before my arrival," I protested. I deemed it
certainly unfair to lay upon me the rousing up of Dark Forces,
when I had not called on any Power except to save my own life.
Nor had I used it, save only in the battle in the darkness, against
any inhabitant of the Waste.

The Thas had fled the light, yes but I did not think that they had
suffered any real hurt from its beams. No—I refused to have
such burden as this laid upon me.

However, even as a man might do, this time the cat shook his
sleek head from side to side.

"Even with that"—a lift of his muzzle indicated the gryphon
lying on my breast—"some stir now which could not be called
into action by such a talisman alone. Forces are on the move, we
do not know why—as yet. It is only that all that move are of the
Dark. Long ago boundaries were set, locks were made, spells
were cast. Within stated ways Light and Dark could come and
go, always apart. Now there is a straining of those containing
spells, a touch here, a thrust there—a testing to see if they still
hold. The reason for this . . . who can tell?"

"The Dales have been invaded." I seized upon that one
fact—though why the inhabitants of the Waste should take that
into account I did not understand. There was no doubt that they
had defenses that no such invaders could pierce. They need only
call upon perhaps the least of these, then return safely thereafter to their old ways of life. "I know nothing of how the
war there goes now, save that the fighting so far has not favored
my people. The Hounds of Alizon range far, they have more
men, better weapons. Could this war now have lapped into your
country?"

The female curled a scornful lip. "Men only—they hold or
call no Power. Our land would not stir awake for the likes of
them! The least of us could send them fleeing at will, or kill
without much effort. No, what stirs is rooted in the past, has
been long asleep, now it awakens. Those who rouse are not yet
fully awake, or you and every living thing, between the Mountains of Arvon and the sea would know it. However, they turn
and move in their sleep, and their enfolding dreams have come
to an end. It may well be that the cycle of slumber has finished.
We—those of our kind—never knew the appointed time of awakening. Such will cause a mighty change . . ."

She gave a last lick to her paw before folding it under her.

"It will not be well to be one such as you if and when the day of true awakening comes," she commented (with something of relish, I thought resentfully). "Unless, of course, you can learn a bit—and have not only courage, but also the will to survive."

I refused to give any ground to her. Though I had no intention of claiming any talent I did not possess, still I looked at her straightly as I answered.

"We all must learn many things during our lifetimes. If there is that which I must do—then I am ready to do it." (I thought of my plea to Elys and of how that had come to nothing in truth because the Thas trap had put an end to it. On the other hand I *had* learned through that. I remembered only too easily the burden of concentrating my will on the gryphon.) "As for courage and will—we cannot measure how much of each lies within us, we can only trust that there will be sufficient to carry through trials which may lie ahead."

I had suddenly a flash memory of my aunt—had that phrase sounded as if said in her very voice? A little so, I thought. Once the pronouncements of Dame Math had been the laws of the world to me. I brushed back the hair that I could only secure in such an untidy fashion and perhaps I sighed.

"There is another of your blood coming." The male broke through the silence that had fallen upon us. "He may even be the one you have sought. This one, at least, dares to ride the white road. No rune or spell set there has turned him back, though these forbade the way to others in his company. He comes now with one purpose in his mind—or so he believes. I think that he is to be fitted to another."

The melons rolled away as I got to my feet in an instant.

"Kerovan! But how do you know?" Then I had second thoughts. There could well be others of human kind in this land—scavengers, outlaws and the like. I could not count that this was indeed Kerovan.

My demand was met by a second silence. I waited for a painful moment or two, then was forced to accept the fact that these two furred ones would keep their own council. To strive to force any more information out of them, when they did not choose to give it, would lessen me in there opinion. It is very

odd to feel that one is an impulsive child in the sight of such as
these. My first reaction was anger. Still, I suspected that anger
itself, within the bonds of the Waste, might be a most dangerous
emotion unless controlled and used only at one's desire, as a
weapon—a feat I was certain I could not accomplish. Though the
control part—that I must learn.

If this promised traveler was Kerovan on his way here, what
mattered most was that I be prepared to meet him—to withstand
his anger. If, indeed, he felt enough within that shell he had built
about him to know hot human anger any longer. I must think
carefully, plan alternate moves, each depending upon his attitude
when we met. That we must resolve our difficulties—that was
far more important to me now than any waking sleepers or
stirring of long-dormant forces in the Waste.

I sat down on my heap of grass and worked to enwrap my
eagerness, control a heart that had begun to beat faster, to appear
as outwardly serene as the cats. Reaching for the nearest melon,
I began the awkward business of sawing away at its rind with the
sharpest edge of the belt buckle, thinking while I worked that it
would be well when I had eaten this piece of fruit (not because I
now really wanted or needed it, but because the very act of
leisurely feasting would be the beginning of my prized control)
that I search the rest of the ruins where I had not ventured
earlier. There might just be in that supposedly barren interior
something I could use as a weapon.

The melon was just at the proper stage of ripeness and I did
feast on its rosy, juicy interior, inelegantly, having to spit out
seeds into my hand and make a small heap of them to one side.
Shining black they were. When I had been very small I had been
given a coarse needle and a length of stout linen thread and had
spent the whole of an absorbed morning making myself a brave
necklace of just such seeds, which Harta the cook had saved for
me.

Harta—she had not been one of those who had come together
with us in the hills after the escape from Ithdale. So many had
been lost! I wondered if some intelligence somewhere decided
who would win through, who would never be seen again—or
were their lives a blind gamble of fate?

I went to wash my face and hands at the spring, wipe them on

sunwarmed grass, paying no attention—outwardly—to the cats
who had apparently both gone to sleep in the sun. With a little
more confidence than I had had to stiffen me during my first visit
to the keep, I once more entered the great hall with those strange
cat-shaped benches. This time I did not head for the corner
tower—rather I took the other direction.

There, in the deepest gloom of this chamber, I found a huge
fireplace, darkened on hearth and up the cavern of an interior
with the signs of smoke and soot. Its presence suggested that the
builders here had been at least human enough to need heat in the
chill of winter and that the Waste was no more hospitable at that
season than the seaward-reaching Dales.

On the wide and heavy overmantel, where a lord of the Dales
would have had carven the badge of his house, there was a
symbol deep wrought—one I had seen before. It was of the
circular body with widespread wings. Save that here it was dull
and time-stained, hardly to be distinguished in the poor light. On
either side of it was set, on guard, the figure of a cat.

There were drifts of dried leaves, powdering into dust, on the
hearth, but any remains a welcoming fire long gone. I remained there for a moment, then let my eyes range about the
room, trying to imagine how it had once been—who had held
high feast days here, if such were known to these people who
had drawn their stools and chairs closer to the flames in winter.
What stories had their songsmiths wrought to keep their minds
encased in wonder? *Had* they had songsmiths to take their
heroes' acts and make them live in song and tale?

I raised my hand high, striving to touch the symbol, and
discovered that even when I stood on tiptoe it was still above my
reach. At first I had thought it near invisible against the dull
stone in which it was carved. Now . . . I blinked, rubbed the
back of my hand across my eyes. The cats . . . they were far
more easy to study—there was a glint of fire in their wide-open,
staring eyes.

Was it some illusion of the dusk caught within this room, or
could it be that one of those heads was slightly larger, heavier of
jowl, than the other? I looked from left to right and back again,
began to believe that my guess was correct. The cat heads were
not in duplicate, but individual. Also I believed I had seen them

before, mounted on living, breathing bodies, lying at sleepy ease
out in the courtyard. Some worker in stone long ago had caught
both male and female; the same animals? Even with all the tricks
and talents of the Waste I could hardly accept that the two I saw
outside had been those whose portraits were sculptured here.
Time might stretch long for the Old Ones (and were any Old
Ones *animals?*), but surely not to that extent. If these were not
the portraits of the same cats, they must be distant forefather and
foremother and the strain had held true.

I stepped into the cavernous mouth of the fireplace, kicking at
the leaves, hoping against hope to turn up some piece of the
metal, the fire dogs that had once supported the burning wood,
some other fragment that would be promising. There was nothing left.

To my right a doorway in the inner wall led to whatever
survived at the other end of the building. Deserting the fireplace
with its knowing guard cats, I passed through that. The hall
beyond was wide enough to be a gallery and here lay the first
signs of furnishing I had seen, other than the stone cat benches.
All I wanted!

With a cry, I sped forward, to snatch at the black-tarnished
hilt of a sword. Only to find that what I held when I pulled it
from out the litter on the floor was a jagged stub. I tried it
against one finger, the metal flaked away thinly. There were
other weapons lying along the wall as if they had fallen from
stone pegs, which were still set there. Nothing had survived that
could be used. At last in my disappointment I sent the stuff
flying, with a kick that shattered it even more into a dust of rust.

There was another square room beyond, a second stair like
unto the one I had found in the outlook tower. I judged that this
must serve the second tower I had noted earlier—the one that
supported a living tree in place of the lord's banner. The steps
appeared secure enough, as long as one crowded against the wall
on the left, so I climbd.

On the second floor there was another doorway, as well as the
continuation of the steps leading upward, and I judged that the
doorless opening gave upon rooms that must have been built
above the arms gallery. I took that way now in turn.

Another hall here but a very much narrower one, hardly more

than a passage where perhaps two of my own girth could walk abreast, and, to my left, three doorways.

There had been doors here also—two of them, like the one in the courtyard, showed rotted bits of wood, the fallen debris, that had once formed barriers. But the one in the middle . . .

The wood of that looked firm and whole. I could detect no crack brought about by time, no skim of rust upon the metal fittings. There was a locking bar across it—from the outside! Had I come across such precaution on the lower floor, or in whatever cellars might be found in this place (I had no desire to go prying into such as those), I would have said this was a prison. It was perhaps a "safe" chamber such as some lords had for the protection of their more valuable belongings when they were from home, save that the bar lacked any of the ponderous locking devices usually in use on such.

I went forward very slowly to touch the wood above that bar, half expecting to have it crumble. Against the pressure of my hand as I applied more strength, it had a very solid feeling. There was no one to forbid me to draw that bar, and the shaft itself looked as if it lay lightly in the two loops through which it rested. At last, after some hesitation (I must not surrender to any fear), I knew I had to learn why one door in all the deep remained in the same condition it must have been when the building was at its most complete, the bar still sturdy, while elsewhere armor and weapons flaked away to the touch. There are many legends of how curiosity brought into peril those of the Dales who were unable to resist mysteries left by the Old Ones. At that moment I could understand the need that had driven those unfortunates, for I was under just such a compulsion to draw the bar that I could no longer fight it. Draw I did.

Perhaps it was the bar alone that, by some trick of its makers, had kept the door intact. For, as I pulled it to one side, and the door itself began to swing slowly toward me, cracks appeared in its surface, ran with a speed I could follow by my eyes, over the wood. There was a grating, a puff of stale air blown outward. The door slipped drunkenly on one hinge as the other snapped with sound sharp enough to make me start.

Half open, the door was fast falling into the same sorry condition as its two neighbors to the right and left. Pieces of the wood broke, crumbled in dusty puffs as they hit the stone pavement.

I shrank as that disintegration began, but now that it appeared to cease, with a last clatter, as the bar finally fell and snapped in two, I made myself edge forward to look into the room beyond.

I had only a moment or so to see—to look upon what had been sealed from time until I rashly had let in the years, and age itself wrecked, with fury, whatever the spell (I was sure I had broken a spell) had protected.

This room had not been bare. There were tapestries on the wall, and, though I saw their splendor only for two or three of the breaths I had drawn in wonder, they were so rich I could not believe that any human hand or hands had been able to stitch such. There was a bed, with a tall canopy, the posts of which were seated cats, each taller than myself. On the bed lay rich coverings of a tawny yellow like the fur of the cats, which grayed into ash brown, then were gone, as were the coverings on the floor. A table had stood against one wall and on it a mirror, its carved frame topped by a cat's head. On that table were boxes—whose richness I had very little time to see, other things gone fast to dust before I could identify them.

Were there chairs, stools, a tall, upright wardrobe chest such as might hold gowns any keep lady would find herself hot with desire even to hold? I am sure there were. I am certain I can remember having a hasty glimpse of such. I had not stepped across the threshold; I only stood and watched a glory that made me ache for its beauty become suddenly nothing. Windows were revealed now as the curtains that had been drawn across them withered away far faster even than a delicate flower can wither if it is left in the full light of the sun, having been idly plucked for no real purpose.

The light from those windows streamed in (there appeared to be no curtaining vine outside here). In its beans, the dust motes dance a thousand fold. Then . . . there was nothing—just nothing at all . . .

No, that was not true.

In the midst of one of those shining panels of sunlight there was a gleam, something that appeared to catch the sun and then reflect it forth again, not in a hard glitter but in a soft glow. I hesitated to cross that chamber. Only, just as I had been unable to resist opening the spell-locked door, so I could not now stop myself.

The dust was very thick. I coughed, waved my hands before my face, strove to clear the air that I might breathe long enough to reach what lay in the mote-clogged sunbeam. When my boot toe near-nudged it, I stooped to pick up a ring.

Unlike the rest of the metal in the room it had not flaked into nothingness. The band felt as firm as if it had been fashioned only yesterday. But the setting was unlike any stone I had ever seen in my life. We of the Dales are poor in precious things. We have a little gold, washed out of streams, we have amber, which is greatly prized. A few of the very wealthy lords may have for their wearing at high feast days some colored gems from overseas. But those are mainly small, polished but uncut. I held now something far different from those.

The stone (if stone it was) was near the size of my thumb, though the hoop which held it was small, clearly meant for a woman's wearing. This gem or stone had not been cut, nor did it need to be polished. For it had been fashioned by some freakish twist of nature herself into the semblance of a cat's head and the surface was neither pink, nor yellow, but a fusing of the two with an iridescent cast to the surface, over which rainbow lights slipped as I turned it this way and that. I slipped the band over my finger. It was as if it clung there, made for no other's wearing—also it felt as if it were in its rightful place at long last.

Moving closer to the window I turned my hand this way and that, marveling at such a thing showing against the brownness of my skin where the scratches of berry briars drew many rough lines. I did not know what it was but—it was mine! I was sure of that as if the ring had been slipped solemnly on that finger in some formal gifting. Once more I turned it again for the sun to catch it fair, then I heard . . .

A yowling arose, so sharp and clear it could have come from immediately below my window. I was looking out, down the slope toward the road. Both the cats were leaping from stone to stone, winding about bushes, disappearing, as they made their way through the jumble of ruins and stone that lay there below.

Beyond . . . there was a rider on the road! A rider! I saw sun flare in bluish gleam, small and far away—a mailed rider. He whom the cats had said would come? Kerovan?

Forgetting everything but what had drawn me for so many days, I turned and ran, dust rising up above me in a cloud that set me choking and gasping, but still I ran. I must know who rode the white highway. I could guess, I could hope—but I must know!

Kerovan

THAT JOISAN WAS HERE BESIDE THE WHITE HIGHWAY OF THE OLD ones—not trapped in dark and danger—was the only thought that filled my mind. Then she was in my arms, and I held her with such a grip as would keep her safe against the worst the Dark might send against us—so would I keep her as long as my strength lasted.

She was crying, her face wet with tears, as her hands closed on my shoulders in a grasp I could feel even through my mail. I forgot all the thoughts that had ridden me through long hard days, as I bent my head to find her lips, tasting the salt of her tears. A fire arose and raged through me as we so clung, forgetting all else but each other.

Only such moments cannot last. I loosed her a little, remembering who I was and why this great joy might not continue for me. This was a time when once more I must don inner armor, not for my protection, but hers.

If my hold loosened, hers did not. She only pushed back a fraction so that she might look directly into my face as her sobs came as ragged and uneven breaths.

"Kerovan—truly Kerovan . . ." Her voice was hardly more than a whisper.

Kerovan—my name completed the breaking of the spell. I

moved to put her away from me but she would not let me.
Rather she shook her head from side to side as might a child who
refuses to give up something upon which she has set her heart's
desire.

"No, you shall not leave me again! You were here—now you
try to go—but you shall not!"

I *was* here? What did she mean? Then the warmth still con-
suming me made that plain. The husk that had been Kerovan
now held life. All my good intentions, my knowing this was
wrong, that I was tainted—they were threatened by that warmth,
by her words . . .

Setting my teeth I raised my hands to her wrists. By main
strength I must break her hold, push her away from me. Still she
shook her head. Now she also writhed in my hold, fought me as
if she had been one of the tawny cats.

"No!" Her denial arose louder. "Do you not understand?
You shall never be free of me—you cannot. We—we must
be—"

Her voice faltered. I do not know what expression my face
wore, but hers became one of growing despair. Then her shoulders
slumped, her hands went limp in my grasp. It was she who
edged away.

"Let me go," she said in a low voice. "I shall not trouble you
so again. I thought that . . ." Her voice trailed off; she raised
one hand to smear it across her cheeks. Then she flung back her
head, tossing her disordered hair out of her eyes, away from her
face.

I could not answer, it took all my resolution to curb the
rebellious desire within me. I could only stand—alone. Her chin
lifted, strength of purpose shone from her eyes. There was that
in her carriage, her voice—such will and self-confidence—which
would provide a safeguard as strong as the armor and leather she
wore.

"I have no pride," she said, even when every inch of her taut,
straight body, proclaimed her right to that. "I listen to your
voice saying, 'You are not my lady, I have no wish to be your
lord'—but I cannot accept those words as a woman should. So I
come after you because—only with you, Kerovan, am I a person
in whom I can believe. Therefore, if you deny me again, and
ride on for whatever mission Imgry has set you—and how is it

that such as he dares say 'do this and do that' to *you*—I shall follow. Even if you are sworn to his service.''

As she studied me through slightly narrowed eyes, I could not even yet find the power of tongue to answer her. If I could not command my inner self, how then could I man my defenses against her? Not with this wild mutiny growing within me.

I shook my head, glad in a small way to be able to answer a lesser question.

"I swore no oath." I found *those* words easily enough. "I came at my own will. Had it not been my choice I would not have ridden forth."

Perhaps then, because I was so glad to find an excuse not to meet her personal challenge, I spoke of my mission—of what Imgry had learned about Alizon's search for a "power."

To my relief she listened with growing interest.

"And what success have you had in marshalling any of the Waste?"

I told her of the Wereriders.

"So—and now whom do you seek?" she asked.

I drew a ragged breath and shook my head. Instead I told her of my return to my camp, of the devastation I found there. At my mention of Elys and Jervon, she put out her hands, catching at my arm.

"Then they live—were left above ground! I thought—I hoped—that might be so."

I had a question of my own. "Where were you?"

She moved back a little, her hands busy now with her hair. For the first time I became aware of a rising wind, the fact that the sun had gone behind clouds. She frowned at the sky.

"There is a storm coming. You can feel it in the air. Up there"—she pointed to the rough, steep slope—"there is shelter—come!"

I could find no reason to refuse. Leading the mare and the pony, I followed her. For the first time I remembered the cats. There was no sign of them now.

The ascent was not an easy one, and above the clouds grew ever thicker and darker. As we rounded the side of a wall and entered into a courtyard the first drops of rain began to fall. Lashes of lightning cracked across the sky to the west. The roll of thunder was heavier than the rumble of Alizon war machines crowding through the throat of some narrow dale.

I loosed the pack pony and the mare from their burdens, Joisan stooped to catch up a share of the bags and packs, helping to draw these into a dark chilly hall. She caught at a smaller pack from the pony.

"Elys's thought—I am glad of this. But where is she? And Jervon? Did you send them away—or did they deem me dead and . . ."

"It was when we came to that road. Only this morning she said that they would travel no farther—for some reason that was forbidden. A Wisewoman who carries a sword is a thing I had never heard of. She cannot be of the Dales—"

"If it were meant that they should not come, she would know, of course. No, she is not of the Dales—nor the Waste either—her parents came from a wreck on the coast. And, though she was born here, her blood is strange."

Gloom of near-night darkness came quickly with the rush of rain outside. Her face was only a blur to me.

"She has power," Joisan was continuing. "And Jervon"—for a moment she paused, then continued in an even tone—"he accepts her for what she is. He is not the less in her eyes, nor she the greater in his. They are two halves well-fitted together to form something stronger than either. This may not happen easy or often, but when it does . . . Ah, then it is as if both have found a treasure—a treasure beyond dreams of other men!"

There was a ring of something close to defiance in her tone. I knew I must not confront her again on this subject, which lay heavy in both our minds. Instead I asked once more what had happened after the earth swallowed her.

So I heard the strange tale of her being caught in thick dark and hunted through that dark by the Thas. Also of how the gryphon had been her salvation.

"I do not know just how it was awakened to my aid. Somehow the strength of my will, my need, brought it to life. It was the light that showed me the door into a place—a very strange place."

She spoke then of a chamber wherein lay a maze of low walls, of how she had won to the center of that having perceived a pattern. In the middle she had taken refuge and fallen asleep—or into the web of another sorcery—and had awakened outside this keep.

"There was fruit and water here . . ." Before I could move she dashed out again into the courtyard, returned near as swiftly, laughing and shaking raindrops from her hair, bringing with her a melon, which she dumped on the floor between us.

"Give me your knife. Mine—all my weapons—were taken from me in the dark." Joisan plucked my knife from the belt sheath to slash open the melon. She pressed half of it into my hands.

The fruit was sweet, filled with juice—better than I could ever remember eating—bringing comfort to my mouth and throat. I produced in turn a cake of journey bread which we also shared— Joisan having gone to wash her hands in the fall of water beyond the door, shaking them as dry as she could.

"There are more of these—and berries, water plants—I did not go hungry once I reached here."

"And the cats?"

Joisan had settled herself cross-legged beside me, well within touching distance, only her hands lay loosely together on one knee. She made no move to reach out to me.

"Yes, the cats. You may not believe this, Kerovan, but those two are not animals as we know them. They understand one's thoughts and speech and mind-speak in return. There is—was, for I have not seen him since my first coming—also a small bear who can do likewise. The cats told me to wait, that one was coming. I climbed the tower and saw the road. But I wonder . . ." I saw her lift one hand now and regard it closely. Then she held out that hand to me and asked a question.

"Kerovan, you have been much more up and down the Dales than I. Have you seen the like of this before?"

I could see, even through the storm gloom, that there was a ring on one finger of the hand she had raised. Though I did not want—feared now—any touch contact with her, I did take that hand in mine and brought it closer that I might see the ring.

The stone was an irregularly shaped gem of some kind. And, oddly enough, once I had taken her hand in mine it became more visible, so that I could see the hue of the stone (if stone it truly was). It was unlike any color I had seen—both rose and yellow— the colors melting into one another.

"Kerovan!"

I did not need that alerting cry of my name. I had taken her hand in my right one. On my wrist, the band half-hidden by the drooping of the mail shirt was bright and clear, shining so that its light reached the strange ring and seemed to feed the gem. Thus its own glow grew the greater.

Joisan freed herself from the hold I had unintentionally tightened, brought her hand and the ring up breast high so that the gem near-touched the crystal gryphon. But there was no reaction from that talisman and Power-holder.

She put up the fingers of her other hand as if she would catch at the gem-set hoop, tear it off, and then she stopped.

"It contains no harm, I think . . ." she said slowly. "Perhaps you cannot see it clearly. But the stone itself is shaped in the form of a cat's head, though it was not cut so by men. The cats—"

"You are sure they are real?"

"Not hallucinations? You saw them for yourself—they are as real as this!" She held out her hand once again. "Did you believe them illusions when they stopped you on the road?"

"No." I was sure—whatever those two beasts might be, whomever they might serve (if servants they were)—I was certain they were real. I had been led to this place for a purpose even as Elys had suggested. I wanted to banish that conclusion, but I could not.

"Where did you get that?"

She told me of her explorations of the ruined keep in which we now sheltered, of a barred door—barred on the outside— where within until she had, as she said, "let the years in," there had existed a reminder of the past in furnishings. And of how all had vanished into dust before her eyes, leaving only the ring in a pool of sunlight.

It was such a tale as a songsmith might devise, but I believed every word of it.

"I have never seen its like . . ." I began slowly. "This"—I fingered the wrist band—"suggests it has some tie with Power."

"There are many things in the Waste—is that not what our legends always say? Somehow I think that this was meant—" She glanced at me—or at least she turned her head a fraction in my direction though it was too dark to see her expression. "Was

meant," she repeated, "to be found when the door was opened.
But why such a spell was ever laid and its meaning . . ."

"It is not of the Dark."

"I know," she agreed simply, her hand once more caressing
the gryphon at her breast. "This would have warned me. It is
very beautiful—and strange—and the way that it came . . . I
feel it is a gift."

There was a hint of defiance in her tone as if she believed that
I would urge her to throw the ring from her. But that was not in
my thoughts. There had been so little of beauty for Joisan since
she and her people had fled Ithdale—and perhaps even during
the years before. I had been able to give her no bride gift
except the gryphon—and that too had come by chance out of the
Waste. I wished for a moment of sorrow that the ring had been
my gift, also—a thing for her to cherish.

I had searched blindly for Joisan and I had found her—no
thanks to any real effort of my own. Such fortune was only
barely possible. That I had been helped, or guided, in the right
direction by some other intelligence—that explanation seemed to
me a little more credible. That was a bitter conclusion and one I
did not want to accept. I . . . perhaps we . . . were caught up
in—in whose web . . . and why?

That we must remain together from now on I must also
probably accept, for *I* was now without any guide to take us out
of the Waste and I could not let her go alone—in fact I knew she
would not.

Which meant I must speedily regain my inner armor, make
myself believe that any close feeling between us was wrong, that
if I yielded now—the easy choice—it would be worse for her.

I remained wary of even the smallest hint of surrender to that
other self. I had fought so hard to contain my desires, my
longings. Even now that struggle rose anew in me and I ached
throughout my body for Joisan to come into my arms once more.

By her own efforts, and with no help from me, she had
escaped worse danger than I had faced for a long time. I did not
want to think ahead—that we two might be led into new perils.
As my thoughts so twisted and curled, and I forced them into
hard conclusions, she spoke again.

"This is not a place of peace, such as one finds even in the
Dales. I was in one of those once, Kerovan—the night Toross

brought me out of the invaders' hands at the taking of Ithdale. That was a place of wonder . . . and he died there. So I have always known in my heart that he rests easy. This does not hold anything except many years of time's dust. Still we are safe here—as the cats promised. Do you not also feel that is so?''

Now her ringed hand reached, found mine. I could not help myself, but locked fingers with hers. This was Joisan, she was here with me—safe—while outside the storm rolled on and did not reach us. I felt nothing of old Power stirring here. In spite of her story of the long ensorcelled room, there was only a warmth that came from the two of us and was not born of any spell.

During that night, as Joisan and I shared shelter in the ruined keep, I dreamed again—as strong a dream as the one that had shown me the sleeper days earlier. But this was not a dream filled with any light for me to see by—rather total dark (or else I was blind)—for I could perceive nothing. I only felt—or heard.

"You labor to no purpose." A voice cut through that dark, the arrogance in it as sharp as any blow. "Our difference was settled long ago."

"Difference?" The wry amusement which colored that answer was plain. Though the first voice had been heavy with Power, this second speaker was not impressed. "That is an odd way to describe what passed between us then, Galkur."

I felt now a welling of anger warming fast to red rage, lapping about me in that sightless place as if to crisp me into ashes. The emotion swelled high—then vanished. I sensed that the being exuding that raw anger had it under control now, behind a wall that could not yield to any surprise assault.

"You play with words." This time he—or it—sounded possessed by icy contempt—or was that would-be contempt?

I discovered then that, in some way strange to me, I was not listening entirely to words, rather striving to weigh emotions—for those were of the greater importance here.

"I play with nothing," came again that lighter, amused voice, unruffled, betraying no more than surface interest in their exchange. "Most of all—not with men. They are very imperfect tools at the best. Have you not yet learned that, Galkur?"

"You name names!" The first voice snarled—like the snow cat I had seen Herrel become. Still I knew that these were not Weres, nor were they men.

"Why not? Do you now stoop to that small belief of men, that a name gives one Power over another? Ha, Galkur, I would not have believed you so diminished, even though the years have spun you far from what you were."

"Time has spun me nowhere!" Once more the heat of fury blazed, died, as the speaker rapidly checked it. "I am still what I have always been—and shall continue to be!"

"Now that interests me, Galkur." The second voice appeared to enjoy repeating the name. "What you are, and what you will continue to be, a statement you appear to take pride in making. What *were* you on the night when a certain female of the Dales used her puny talent to summon you? That plan was carefully thought out, guarded well, or so she believed. You were to pour yourself into her own lord, as water can be poured into a cup. Through him you would father the son he craved, while she saw (very poorly and ineptly, I must say) an eventual use for such a child, to her own purposes. You were never a fool, Galkur. Could you not foresee that a spell spun by such a one was not strong enough to hold even a fraction of Power, Dark or Light? Was a need for corporal life once more so strong in you? Having so poorly wrought, do you still say now that you are as you once were?"

A note of pity in that—enough to sting. Perhaps not real pity, I thought, rather a shadow of that, rooted in contempt.

"So," the second voice continued, "you willingly lent yourself (or tried to do so) to the fumbling incantations of a female whose pride and arrogance, among her own kind, were almost as great as yours have always been. And what came of it?"

There was no intelligible reply, but the control the other held broke. I heard a mighty cry, felt the blast of the smothering, fiery fury of his rage.

"You failed. *You*, Galkur, who in the past moved hills about as a player moves a counter on a game board—you could not mend a faulty spell. So what you deemed, in your pride, to be a small act became instead a large defeat. That game you began is not yet played out. Do you suppose that the sleeper does not sense what you move to do now? That you think once more to work through men to achieve your ends? He shall wake, and rest assured you shall not relish meeting him a second time, Galkur. Can you not understand? It was not his full essence that entered into the coupling, which was to serve you. Taking your place in that conception drew upon only a fraction of his Power. He did not even stir in his slumber as he launched a single shaft of will to defeat your plan.

"The Daleslord had his son, a little strange to be sure. But, when one petitions aid from our kind, there is apt to be a change in mind or body, which always discloses such bargain. Your female knew from the birth hour that what she had brought forth was not of her calling. She paid for that, did she not, Galkur? Now you shall have to reckon with the sleeper, since this time I think he will do more than just dream another life into being. You have meddled, and for that you must face the consequences. So do not look to your new pieces to be any more potent that that other was."

Once more the surge of anger scorched me with flames of hate.

"Our roads do not meet. What lies on mine you cannot begin to understand."

"I do not think that you understand either, Galkur. You were always too impulsive for your own good."

That calm second voice. I listened more closely, not only to catch the words, but for something else . . . Memory? I had heard it before, of that I was certain. There had been a ridge top—a man in gray who gave me a horse . . . A man whose eyes were so piercing that I felt them strike deep into my mind, read there every thought, good or ill, that I had ever harbored.

Neevor! He had said that that was his name for some people— he had—

Joisan—she had seen him, too. He had promised her—promised her—as I tried to catch that other shred of memory, I was suddenly aware of a new sensation. Hidden in the dark, as I was, with only those two voices to assure me I was not alone—when I had thought of Neevor there had come a change. They were now aware of—me!

"Sasssss!"

The dark broke with a lightning swift strike of light, so intense my sight was seared and a new dark enclosed me. I hung, I felt, in empty air, unsupported over a vast gulf into which I would drop—to fall on and on forever and ever! Fear tasted bitter in my mouth, I swayed back and forth in the midst of a vast whirlpool of force that struggled within itself—with me as the prize.

There was nothing I could do for my safety. I was helpless, at the mercy of whichever portion of those battled, intertwined powers won. In the meantime I endured such terror as I had never known. For if I hurtled into that gulf I knew well that all that I was—Kerovan—would be gone, without hope—an extinction worse than physical death.

Then . . .

As if a loop of cord I could not see shot through the dark to settle about me, I was aware of a firm support that drew me from where Power still strove with Power. The dark was no less at first. Then, far down below (though not in the gulf, that was safely behind me now) there came a glimmer. Weak with the aftermath of terror I hung in the embrace of this new force, watching that light grow larger and stronger.

Once more I was drawn into the hall of many pillars. This time I was very near the dais. That which had sustained and brought me here ebbed away.

I looked down at the body of the Sleeper. What might have been grotesque by human standards was, I now perceived, glory and power. I felt no shrinking. In this sleeper was embodied grace and majesty no human lord could aspire to.

Even as I stood there, still weak from my ordeal above that evil gulf of dark, I saw the eyelids twitch, arise slowly. I looked downward and our gaze locked . . .

Then—I could not remember! I could not remember! It became an ever-increasing ache, for my dream broke at that instant. There was left a need, a strong need, for me to learn— Learn what? Even *that* I did not understand, save that I was the less because I was not strong enough to hold and remember as I should have done.

I awoke into day and the ruined keep, with Joisan watching me—deep concern on her face. I did not want this—I wanted to be back there—to know . . .

Joisan—the desolation that had filled me when I thought she had been fatally caught in one of the evil traps of this land—the great burst of liberating joy that had been mine only yesterday as she had come running into my arms and I knew not only that she was safe, but was where I could hold her . . .

Where had those feelings now gone? They might stir feebly still—somewhere. I think that they did, now so hidden and overridden by a drive possessing me that I wished for nothing more than to have her gone.

So I actually urged her to go, out of my tormenting thirst for this other quest. Though I knew, even as I spoke, that not only would her determination keep her with me, but if she had chosen to return to the Dales I would be constricted to see her out of the Waste and into safety and I could not have forced myself to take the time for such a journey. This land held me now. I was sure I would never be free of its witchery—would be less than the half-man I already was if I attempted to leave it.

As we rode out of the keep, found our way down again to the highway, I could force no words, make no effort to explain. She must have thought me deranged—or ensorcelled. I was aware now and then that she was watching me with a frown of deep concern, that she made an effort to keep close beside me.

But Joisan was only a shadow now, moving through a shadow world. What was real were those two voices in the dark—Neevor and Galkur. That the latter was one of the to-be-dreaded Dark Lords I had no doubt at all. Then—the sleeper . . . What had I seen when his eyes opened and sought mine? What tie lay between us? A loose one, perhaps, but one that would tighten—must tighten—of that I was convinced.

We rode through the morning and there were no words between us—at least I remember none. Then we camped at the edge of a great cut the Old Ones had slashed through the heights so that their road of many symbols and signs remained smooth and level. I sensed, even on the safety of that starred ground, that there was peril nearby, closing in. It was true—the enemy I did not know was making his first move.

Joisan

WHAT I DESIRED MOST OF MY LORD WAS THAT HE UNDERSTAND ME. Understanding comes from within, it cannot be poured from another source. His greeting to me had been far warmer than I had dared to hope—even though he as speedily withdrew from the embrace. I would not make demands on him—I must approach him as warily as a scout spying on an enemy camp.

Rain curtained the keep when we reached it, making of Kerovan only a shadow among other shadows. I wished for light that I might see him better, but there was not even a fire. Because I must hear his voice I urged him to the telling of his adventure— of his meeting with the Wereriders.

The idea of shape-shifting was not new. We of the Dales knew from childhood strange legends and scraps of lore. Still one could never be sure such tales were true. This was the first time I heard one with a core of hard fact.

"They must be masters of illusion," I ventured after he told me of a stallion who had reared behind the high lord's table, a snow cat crouched snarling beside him. Illusions were the principal weapons of the Old Ones when dealing with men.

"I do not think so. Though they go armed and armoured, still their greatest weapon is their change. Even were that an illusion, it is a more potent one than I have ever heard tell of—enough to rock any man.''

''Do you think they will ride to join with the Dales?''

''I do not know. If they do, it will be the result of some bargain. They know that trouble is also rising in the Waste and they may fear battle nearer home. They did not like my story of the Thas—those creatures of the underground.

''Imgry is a planner of battles, a builder of armies—that is true. I think it is also true that he has learned those from overseas came not just to harry the Dales. What they seek is a thing we do not yet understand.''

''Some Power.'' I nodded in agreement. ''Also a Dark one, for the invaders, showing themselves to be what they are, could not treat with the Light.'' I felt my upper lip tighten as if to lift in a cat's snarl.

The cats! With the rain without they must have taken refuge somewhere but not with us. Where were they, I wondered fleetingly.

''A Dark Power,'' Kerovan mused. ''Could such a Power sense that it was being sought, gather in anticipation its own servants such as the Thas?''

''To what purpose? Any Dark Power would be to the Hounds as a Dale's lord to the outlaws,'' I pointed out. ''The invaders would soon discover that the evocation of the forbidden must make them slaves under such a master as they could not dream of—''

''Dream.'' Again he spoke as if for his own hearing. ''Yes—a dream—''

''What kind of a dream?''

That he spoke of something important to him, I sensed. I wanted to know, I needed so much to know, all I could of him, his ways, his thoughts, even his dreams. This need was a rising surge of desire in me. I had to use all my control to contain and subdue it lest I break out with a myriad questions and he turn from me again with even more coldness than he had shown. For until he opened gates, I could not enter—nor could I dare to try and force them.

''Just a dream.'' Now it was plain that he spoke to me in firm refusal to let me share some important part of his life. Instead he spoke swiftly, as if he would push all references to this from both my mind and his, asking of me an account of my own adventures.

I wished again for light—that I could see his face, read any emotion that might show there. Talking so in the dark was like lying under a hindering blindness.

We spoke also of Elys and Jervon whose escape from the Thas still lightened my inner gloom. However, I longed so much to ask my lord if he had noted how well they fared together—that they were two whom the Dales would say could not be joined in harmony yet still they were. Only that was another subject I knew, instinctively, I dare not speak of now.

So I made as plain a story as I could of my escape from the darkness through the strange spell of the winged globe. And we talked of the cats. Later I showed Kerovan the ring that was the only remaining treasure of what must once have been a room of treasures, before I let in Time itself to loot and pillage.

When I showed the ring to him, his wristlet blazed so we both knew that my find was in some way touched with Power. Yet I was certain that all it held about it was the shadow of the old spell, for it never warmed for me as did the gryphon, though it fitted itself to my finger as if that hoop had been fashioned to my size on purpose.

I dared greatly then to reach out my hand and clasp his. To my joy his fingers tightened around mine, did not repulse me.

"If there was only some way to get you out of the Waste." He spoke forcibly and his hand tightened on mine so that it brought pain. Still, the last thing I would do was try to free myself. "Imgry has his contact, that was all he desired. We could ride east . . ."

I did not try to argue with him. However, I knew, as well as if it had been shouted through the air of that dank, dark hall, that we would never ride back. The Waste had set its mark on both of us—neither of us could stray far from it again. I had nothing to return to—everything to lose if I went. Perhaps here I could also dream and find my dream was true . . .

We settled for the night, apart—always apart. I wept a little, silently, in the dark at another bit of hope that had come to nothing. It was not long before he slept. I could hear his even breathing—and I so longed to see his face, to watch over him as he slept . . . why I do not know, except that it then was a dear, deep wish—as if so I could keep all harm and sorrow from him, stand between him and ill dreams.

The gryphon at my breast glowed gently as I sat up again and laced my fingers about my knees, thinking things that hurt and made me despair. Then I saw a glow—eyes in the dark . . .

My hand twitched for the hilt of the knife my lord had given me. Still, almost at once, I guessed who came thus silently, and fearing to speak aloud that I might wake my lord, I strove to set up thought-speech of my own.

"What passes?"

"Nothing passes," returned to me swiftly, and I believed I could recognize the mind-speech of the male cat. "What do you wear on your finger, daughter of strangers?"

I held out my hand. The gem in the ring was also glowing a little, though less than the gryphon.

Once more I shaped mind-words: "That which I found—in the barred chamber," though it came to me that the cat somehow already knew of my exploration. Did he resent my prying into a secret I did not understand? I put out the fingers of my other hand ready to rid myself of the ring should he demand that I do so.

"She who wore that once was a great lady." His thought was born out of some memory I could never share. "If you found it remaining—then take it as her free gift. Through her will alone could it pass to another—"

"Who was she?" I dared to ask then.

"Names vanish with the years. She lived, she loved deeply, she had courage and drew to her others of great heart. She went from us by her own choosing, in the time that was right for her. Be content with that, daughter of strangers. But I think she has this day favored you beyond even your understanding."

The eyes were gone, just as he was gone out of my mind. I wanted—yes—just as I desired Kerovan's confidence, I wanted to learn more. But I knew that I never would. I lifted my ringed hand to my cheek, pressed the stone against my flesh. It was smooth, it was . . . I had no words for what flowed out of it to comfort me then—like a hand laid on a fever-hot forehead, a cool drink held to parched lips. I lay down once again and now I rested content, pushing away the future, knowing only that my lord rested within my reach and slept, and we were together so

that anything might come of that—and I did not think what
would follow from this hour would rend my heart.

I slept lightly so that, as the morning light found a thin way
inward, I sat up, grimacing as I stretched against the stiffness of
limbs. There had been no bed of grass this night and the saddlebag on which I had pillowed my head had not been the softest of
supports.

There was a sound. I looked quickly to Kerovan. His hair lay
dank on a sweated forehead, there was that in his face which
made me gasp. His eyes were shut—a dream? But what manner
of dream could bring such agony as now he showed?

Then that twisted expression smoothed away and his face held
a curious unalive look. His features might have been chiseled
from warm brown stone—lacking any spark of life. He was as a
monument raised to honor some hero long since gone.

I had not seen him lie so for a long time—stripped of the
defenses he used when he waked. He had been thus for the first
two or three days when we had traveled out of the Waste on our
way back from the battle with Rogear and that she-devil who
might have given birth to my lord but was no mother. Then he
had been weak and shaken from the ordeal of meeting those two
Power to Power.

Now for the first time I speculated about Neevor's words after
that struggle. He had called my lord "kinsman" and had said
that Kerovan had been someone else in part. Also I remembered
how my lord had tossed a name at his mother as one might hurl a
spear, and how she had been struck by the force of it.

What lay behind all this I could not know. Nor had Kerovan
after that action ever spoken of it. The Wereriders had told him
to find his kind. Perhaps that was what the two of us must now
do.

The Dales—I shook my head determinedly. We had done our
duty there. My people were as safe as I could make them,
Kerovan had carried out Imgry's orders. We were free of High
Hallack.

Then I realized the strangeness of that thought, for I am full
Dales blood. Yet—I cupped the gryphon globe, pressed it tightly
to me. All my life I had been told that it was a perilous thing for
one of my heritage to have any dealings with the things of the
Old Ones. I thought of my appeal to Elys—that she tutor me in

use of a talent like unto that which she controlled. I had been
wrong. She had known that and had evaded me. That was not
the way for me. One could learn some things, yes—the wording
of spells, the incantations necessary to build up within one's self
the strength of the Power. But Power itself did not come so—it
lay within.

The gryphon had served me in the dark when I needed it, only
I had discovered its value and use for myself. I had *willed* it.
What else might it do if I tried? I fingered it now and speculated.

I was not the same Joisan who had fled with her people out of
Ithdale. What was I then? That I must discover for myself. Even
as my lord must discover who he was and what he was. I
accepted at last that the quest was for him at that moment the
most important factor in his whole existence.

As this fell into place in my mind and I knew such understanding, Kerovan's eyes opened. However, that stony, locked-in
look did not fade.

"A good day." I summoned cheerfulness, making sure that I
would not be turned aside by any coldness from him. "A smooth
road lies yonder in the plains—and it will lead us . . ." I used
some of the old morning greeting then, adding to it such words
as favored our purposes.

He sat up, running fingers through his hair, so that the tumble
of it stood nearly as erect as a cock comb. His eyes slid away,
would not meet mine. I saw his lips thin and tighten, as if he
faced up to some duty he disliked but could not avoid.

I longed to ask what was the matter, knew the greater wisdom
lay in remaining silent, awaiting what he chose to tell me. Until
he opened a door for me, I must not strive to reach the inner
part, which I was sure was the real Kerovan—the one who hid
himself with such desperation.

He arose without a word. Turning his back on me, he strode to
the doorway, looked out into the courtyard, as if for some reason
he did not want me to see his face. Or was it that he did not want
to look upon mine?

"Will you take the mare, the pack pony, and ride? You need
only head due east." He said that with his back firmly to me.

Then he whirled about, as if he heard the scrape of an enemy's
boot, was prepared to front the foe. That locked-in look was

gone from his face. I read instead twisted pain there—a pain that brought me to my feet and a step or two toward him.

He flung out a hand to ward me off. In spite of my good resolution of holding to patience, I felt torment then.

"I—cannot—go." The pause came between each word as if those were forced out of him, that the very shaping of them hurt.

"By the heat of the True Flame!" His voice soared like a battle cry meant to rally a forlorn hope, "I must go—west!" His hands lifted to cover his face and, from behind that screen, came more words, muffled and with a chill of despair. "This may be a trap—I cannot save myself—but you—go you must!"

"Kerovan!" I used his name with authority, determined that he listen to me. "I, too, have a choice—" My control broke. I covered the distance between us and my fingers closed about his wrists. With a strength I did not know I possessed, I pulled his hands down, so I could look into his eyes.

His face was certainly alive now! There was a wry twist to his lips, his eyes blazed like pieces of amber in the full of the sun. I have seen flaming anger written on men's faces before, but this was a rage, controlled, still enough to shake me. However, I did not loose my hold on him. So we stood, linked by touch, though I knew at any moment he might fling me off.

"I ride with you." I said levelly. "As has always been my choice. You could leave me here bound and captive, and in some way I would free myself to follow."

"Don't you understand?" he demanded harshly. "I do not want you. You are nothing but a hindrance, I do not hold you by any duty. I have said that many times over. I want no lady! Also—I am done with the Dales! Wholly done with you!"

Now that I observed him closely, I could detect that there was an oddness about him. He would not meet my eyes, and as emphatically as he spoke, there was a note in his voice as if he were saying words that were put into his mouth. This was not any Kerovan whom I had seen. I remembered the anguish of his sleeping face—and I drew a deep breath.

He did not hurt me with words that came that way, though he acted now as if even my person disgusted him—so that I might never hope to find with him what Elys had found with Jervon. Yes—this was what he was meant to do—meant to do! What spell had been laid upon him in his sleep? Now that I looked at him keenly, I could see that, though his eyes were turned in my direction, there was an odd, unfocused look to them as if he did not see me, or perhaps even know where he was and what he did.

Only I was no maid soft from keep living. I had thrown aside all that when I rode forth from Norsdale. I had learned—a little. I felt that something dire lay ahead—a battle perhaps, a bitter one. Still I could face that when it came. He might not drive me away with words.

"Well enough." I spoke slowly now. "We are two people alone in a land that is not welcoming. Just as alone we shall go on to whatever lies ahead."

He blinked as one who was only just waking. At the change in his face I dropped my hold on him. He shook his head as one shaking away some tenuous thing fallen across one's face.

"The rain has stopped. It is not a bad day . . ."

I stood confounded by the change in him. He might only now have come to the doorway. All those wild hurting words he had uttered might never have been voiced. Because I must have some explanation for this I dared to ask, "Have you dreamed again?"

"Dreamed?" he repeated as might one who had never heard that word before, or did not understand it. "Perhaps. When one sleeps, dreams come. I—I think"—he spoke hesitatingly as one who is a little dazed—"I am under command again—and this time none of Imgry's. It is better you do not ride with me."

"You have often professed"—I pointed out carefully (I mistrusted his manner. Had the real Kerovan again been taken over by another in some fashion? I knew that I must be very alert now)—"that you care enough for me not to want me to come to harm. I cannot ride alone here." I stressed my helplessness—a helplessness I did not in the least feel. "Have I not already barely survived one of the Dark traps, and that by such good fortune as I may never hope to meet again?"

"You are free," he said dully, all the fire and life seeping out of him, the shut-away look back again, as if he were encased by a barrier I could not pierce.

"But you are not? Remember, Kerovan, once I did not go free either. I was taken to serve the Dark. What did you then?"

He swung away from me as if he did not hear my words any

more. Years of age might have settled on him. "You do not understand," he mumbled.

I wanted to shake him, to tear out of him somehow what made him this way. At the same time I knew that such action would be no use. He had dropped down beside the pack he had lifted from the pony last night, was fumbling out the packet of food.

"They do not suspect—" He was speaking in a monotone and I shivered, realizing that he did not talk to me—he was lost somewhere and I had no way of drawing him forth from the shadows where he now wandered. "No, they do not know *what* they would rouse—those fools from overseas. Their attack on the Dales—but a ruse. He has summoned them."

"Kerovan"—I knelt beside him to ask gently, "who is this *he? Is* he out of your dream?"

He shook his head. "I cannot tell. It is not 'will not' but *'cannot'.* I was— No, I do not know where I was. But there is one who waits—and I must go."

"So we ride," I answered with all the courage I could summon. I felt almost as if I companied now with a dying man, one who moved and spoke, but whose inner part might be extinguished—or near that. I tried to remember the name he had called in that battle of Powers—but I could not. Perhaps it was the kind of name lips such as mine might not even shape.

I found this loss of the Kerovan I knew far more fearsome than when he rode out of Norsdale. Had we shared more, had we known each other in a true uniting, perhaps he could not have been so easily enspelled. Yet I would not let him go. There must be some way I could bring to life again the real Kerovan.

Eating but little, I busied myself with the packets Elys had left among the pony's gear. I had fresh underlinen at last, and a comb to put my hair in order. I longed for the weapons I had lost to the Thas. Kerovan had not asked that I return his knife so I slipped it into my own belt sheath.

Before we left I took the chance of gathering some more of the melons, adding them to our food supply. There was no sign of the cats.

Kerovan kept silence, one I did not try to break. Sometimes his eyes crossed me, but it was as if I were invisible. So we went forth from the ruins, leading our animals down to the highway.

Kerovan insisted that I ride the mare, while he led the pony and walked beside me.

The wrack of the storm was visible in broken branches and sodden grass, but overhead the sun arose. While always the road bored on toward the heights, or as we discovered—*through* them!

The labor that had gone into the making of that cut, allowing forbidding walls to remain on either side, amazed me. This must have taken the work of years—or else was the result of potent magic, well beyond the comprehension of our breed. We stopped just before entering that cut to eat and drink, allowing the animals to graze.

Many times during our journey I had felt that, while Kerovan's body strode beside me, the real man was gone. I was chilled, my hopes dwindled. If he was in the grip of an adept of the Old Ones, how could *I* free him?

As I used the knife to cut a melon he suddenly spoke. "You have not chosen well."

"The choice was mine," I returned shortly.

"Therefore the results shall be on your own—"

What harsh or bitter prophecy he might have added was never voiced. I saw his eyes go wide; his gaze shifted from me to a point beyond my shoulder. There was a strong sensation of cold—as if a wind blew over numbing ice—striking my upper back.

Kerovan was on his feet, that trance-like state broken. I saw, under the shadow of his helm, the same face he must have shown to any Hounds he met steel to steel.

That cold bored into me. This was no tangible weapon—yet it could kill. I threw myself to one side, rolled, and then levered my body up again. Kerovan stood, a little crouched, as if ready to spring. He had not, however, drawn sword. While what waited there just beyond the border of the road . . .

A woman, dark of hair, slender of body, her face contorted in a mask of hatred and despair, a demon's countenance, was there. Though a breeze stirred the grass about her, her robe did not sway, nor did her veil move. I knew her . . . But she was dead! Consumed by her own foul magic.

The Lady Temphera, who had consorted with the Dark to produce a son, then failed when that son proved to be other than she had planned, stood watching us with the stark hatred of her last moments of life.

She was dead! I would not accept what I saw. This was some trickery.

Kerovan moved as I stumbled to my feet, held tightly to the gryphon. I refused to be frightened by a shadow out of the past.

There was no wand in her hand. No, that had been shattered with the core of her Power during that other meeting. Nor did she raise her hands in any gesture to summon forces. She only stood, staring at her repudiated son with those burning eyes. Not eyes—rather holes in a skull from which skin and flesh withered as I watched.

"Fool!" That was Kerovan who spoke. Once more his face was impassive. "Fool!" He held up his hand. On his wrist that band of blue blazed. A streamer of light shot toward the woman's death head. The ray appeared to strike a barrier, spread out horizontally across it.

"Show yourself!" Kerovan's lips drew back in a wolf's grin. He commanded as one very sure of himself and his own might.

The illusion (if it were that) moved. Swiftly the right arm swung up. She showed a clenched hand as the long sleeve fell away. Then she threw what she held. A flashing streak came through the air.

Straight for Kerovan's head spun that missile. He moved as swiftly, his arm across his face. I heard a noise as loud as a thunder clap—saw a burst of radiance, so that I blinked and blinked to clear my sight.

Through a watery haze I watched the woman sway. The bale-fire hate, which burned in the eyeholes, spread, consumed, until the head of the apparition was a horrible, blackened mass. The blaze ate on down her body. She seemed to be trying to raise her hands in futile defense, the fingers left trails of black in the air. I wanted to close my eyes, still I could not.

"Is this the best you can send against me?" Kerovan's voice swelled, carried, so that the walls of the cut ahead echoed it back to us. "To evoke the dead is a weakness."

"Weakness—weakness . . ." echoed back.

The horror shriveled, grew smaller, was gone. Kerovan stood, stone-faced, to watch it be so consumed. When the last blackened shred vanished he turned to me.

"This is only the first sending. Perhaps the least of such, merely to test us, or as a warning."

"It is—or was—a very impotent one." I found my voice.

Kerovan shook his head. "We cannot be sure. We can never be sure of any Power . . ." He stroked the band on his wrist with his other hand. "I think that we shall never again walk, or lie, or rest easy in this land—never until we have a final meeting—"

"With Temphera? But she is dead—"

"With another whose identity I do not know, who will use against me—and you because you are with me—all he can summon, perhaps to our ending."

Still he did not look hopeless or even troubled, as he said that. Nor was his face again closed or bleak. A new life had appeared there. I sensed he was excited, had been stirred fully awake rather than alarmed by what had been meant as a dire warning.

Kerovan

WHEN I FRONTED WHAT HAD ARISEN, BLACK AND SEAR, OUT OF THE past I felt that time had turned upon itself. This was she who had given me birth but had never been a mother. Only now she stood alone, lacking Rogear with all his ill-used, half-learned Power. Also, that symbol of her authority, the wand, was gone, having been shattered into nothingness when we had fought out our struggle in the past. Still, my hand arose, as if my arm was weighted with a shield and not with the wrist band that had served me so well.

Words came to me, not so much my own thoughts, as they were those of that other who was rousing now, once more within me, a presence—an essence—I feared. Still I could not wall out that intruder any more than all our struggles had served to keep Alizon's Hounds from baying across the Dales.

Even while I spoke those words, as if I were trained in sorcery, I turned my will upon the band, calling for a force that lay within it. I did not consciously understand what I said, what I did, only that this was the way I must meet this—this thing. For that it was a dead woman restored to malicious life—that I did not quite believe.

A spear of light answered my plea, struck at the head of the illusion, met a shield of such strength that it could not break it, ran across the shield seeking a way through, to consume the dead-alive.

I saw her turn into the specter of death. Her hands moved jerkily then as if cords were fastened to her wrists pulling them this way and that. To no purpose, for she had not been aided by any fear from me—she who was the embodiment (or meant to be) of horror and disgust. Without any emotion from us to strengthen her, she was burning away. Her old hate once more consumed her utterly. Who had striven to use her thus—and why?

Foul black trails in the air streamed from those hands. But they faltered, could not finish any symbol they so fought to form. I felt a contempt within me. If this was a show of Dark Power it was a paltry one. Surely no real adept had brought such a champion into our struggle.

Was the illusion then indeed Temphera herself, a long-lasting residue of evil once more provided with visible form because her strong hatred of me had survived even death itself? Perhaps in the Waste even so flawed a talent as hers could do this when signs and portents were right.

Only—she failed. Death ate her up a second time, perhaps firing her own hate to such a heat that it was able to consume her. She was gone. I watched for a long moment after her semblance had crumbled into ash, half expecting a second attempt. If this was some work of that Galkur—yet surely such as he could have provided a much stronger threat.

Joisan's voice startled me. During those moments when I had confronted hatred come alive I had forgotten her.

"She was an illusion—was she not an illusion, Kerovan? She—I know she is dead!"

Had I been quicker-witted, less still caught up in what had happened, I might have answered more prudently, rather than with what might well have been the truth.

"She hated me very much. Perhaps—in this country of Power—some portion of her did live on and when it gathered strength enough—"

"Can it be true that hate lives past death?" I saw Joisan shiver as she stared now at me.

The shell that had encased me since my dream of the night had cracked, fallen away when I had roused to do battle. I went to her and took her into my arms. They played with us, these holders of Power. Now I wanted nothing of them—neither aid nor attack. What I desired was to fight against them—all of them! There was only one way to do that, I now sensed. I must keep myself part of the real world—be Kerovan. Joisan was my anchor. My anchor? That sounded as if the poison of Power had already touched me, that I had begun to look upon her as an object to be used for my own purposes.

Joisan was real. She was love, not hate, though I could not release any answering emotion that I could believe was truly love. I was not using Joisan—I would not! But, even as I so argued and doubted within myself, I held her tighter.

Her body fitted itself to mine as if two halves had been joined to form—at last—a whole. I kissed her for the second time since I had known her, had come to realize the depth of her courage and spirit. She herself was the truest and finest thing a man might ever discover in a world full of deceit, mystery, and the darkness of evil.

We clung together, and now I was glad that my mother's rage had sought us out. For this joining was surely stronger than any intrigue of the Waste.

A lock of her hair fell free across her face and I kissed that also, gently, aware of a fragrance that clung to it as if she had worn a garland of sweet-scented flowers until their life had become a part of her. Her hands lay again on my shoulders, feather light, still I could feel the dear pressure of them through both mail and leather—and so I always would.

"Kerovan"—she was a little breathless—"if it takes foul illusion to so bring you to me, then may we be often so assailed!"

Once more I set my lips to hers, hoping that she could not read me. For only a few moments snatched out of time I had been a man—a whole man. Now that other compulsion—though I tried to fight it—settled about me once more, with an even tighter grip. I kissed her . . . but the feeling had gone.

She set her hands swiftly against my chest and pushed herself free for I had at once relinquished my hold. When she looked at me, there was desolation in her eyes and her hurt reached me even though I was fast losing the sense of feeling. I could no longer respond as I longed—yes!—as I longed, even under the spell, to do.

"You—you have left me again." Her voice was very low and

uneven as if she were close to tears, save that pride stiffened her. "Why do you so? What is there in me to which you cannot warm?" She wrung her scratched and sun-browned hands together with a gesture of one who is pushed close to the edge of endurance. The rosy hue of her ring—even it appeared to be touched with gray at this moment.

I swung around, no longer any more able to look upon her standing there—the brightness of her look, the beauty of her eyes, her face. That other inside me was fighting hard to stay alive—fighting with a strength that would have rocked my very body from side to side had I given way to it. Only for him there was no hope. I was bound to a future I did not understand or desire, into which perhaps not even Joisan, for all her greatness of heart, could follow me.

"The fault lies not in you—never in you," I got out harshly. "Never believe that it is *you* who have failed." To allow her to think that was a cruelty I could not bear. "It is mine—a curse laid upon me. Believe that, it is true, believe it!"

Once more I made myself face her. I wanted to lay hands upon her shoulders, to shake her until she promised me she would do as I asked. This was the stark truth—that I had nothing to give her, and I would not take and take until she was as ashy as the ring upon her hand—a love token I had not been able to give her. She *must* understand!

"I believe," she answered me then. Her hands fell to her sides. She stood straight, head up, her face sober, but with that heart-tearing look gone out of it. "I believe, yes. Only, I also believe that there is still my Lord Amber imprisoned somewhere inside of you, and he shall come to me again."

Lord Amber? For a moment I was puzzled—until the cords of memory tightened. That was the name she had given me when I first found her in the wilderness, leading her people—when she had accepted me as one of the Old Ones, who had somehow been moved to come to their aid.

"You are him, and you are Kerovan," she was continuing, "also you may be another. But in all of you I have found nothing that will send me from you. Nor can you do this— ever!"

There was no arguing with her. I must accept that her will was unbendable as the sword at my belt. I was afraid—for her. I wanted to ride—to run—but I must accept.

We prepared to spend the night at that campsite in spite of the evil thing that had materialized there. Before us lay the high-walled cut where the road ran on—already shadowed—and I had no desire to travel it in a time when the dusk was double thick. Once more, unable to really rest, I watched the footprints that appeared, clouded and then clear, as if many walked there, unseen, unheard in this world. Sleep was very far away. In fact I did not want to yield to it since dreams might lay in wait. I had had my fill of dreams.

Nor did it appear that Joisan wanted rest either. Instead, she sat beside me, also watching the road, one hand cupping the englobed gryphon tightly against her breast.

"They walk—" She broke the long silence between us in so soft a voice it was hardly above a whisper. "I wonder—are those unseen ones alive but ensorcelled, so that they must endlessly journey this road? Or are they but shadows out of the past whose memories linger so?"

I was surprised, though I should not have been, that she also was able to mark the slight dimming and brightening of those prints.

"I think," she added, "that they go upon some mission—yet their time, their world is no longer ours. Kerovan"—she changed the subject so quickly that she startled me into answering as I had not meant to—"what of your dream? Was *it* perhaps of another world or time?"

"I do not know. I—" A hand might then have been slapped hard across my mouth, silencing me. I could not, even if I would, tell her of that dream. If dream it was.

"Kerovan!" Joisan's hand caught now at my arm, though she had been careful not to touch me since I had closed my heart to her earlier. "Look!"

Farther along, within the walls of the cut, where the road lay like a white ribbon between two towering, blank walls—that was where she was pointing. Something else could be seen beside the night-induced shine of the symbols, the stars, and the flow of footprints.

Dark clots fell from the heights to strike upon the pavement, spread out in evil-appearing blots across its surface. I could think of nothing save the action of one of those war machines I had seen under construction in Imgry's camp, designed to hurl rocks into the heart of an enemy advance.

There was, in turn, a rising shimmer of light from the road itself. The fall of stones (the sharp impact of which we could hear) and the earth continued. Was this some effort to bury the highway, seal off what protection existed along that moon-bright length?

I was on my feet, reaching down to draw Joisan up beside me.

"We must go—now!" If the road was sealed we were lost! Again knowledge that was not mine came alive in my mind as if it had been planted there to await this very happening.

She looked at me steadily and then nodded. "If this must be done—then let us to it. Leave the packs. I can ride the pony—you take Bural."

We grabbed the closest of our supplies and water bottles, leaving the rest of the gear. As usual, neither animal showed any fear of the road—not at first. Ahead black masses heaped together, but they did not stay so for long. Rather the mounds melted, running off in besmirching rivulets. The very touch of the pavement appeared to transform solid into liquid and send it flowing.

"That smell—Thas!" Joisan cried.

I caught it, too, the same stench that had arisen from the churned earth back in the meadow trap, only stronger, more offensive. Now the mare threw up her head with a loud whinny, answered by the pony. They balked, so it was all I could do to force my mount forward. Joisan would not allow her smaller steed to hold back; I could hear her voice crooning encouragement.

The fallen earth *was* running in streams from the road's surface as rain might be channeled from stone, while that stomach-turning stench grew the worse. I saw movement higher above, far up the sides of the cut walls, though I could not make out clearly the form of the creatures laboring so frenziedly there, attempting to wall us away from the mountain land. They did grow more visible as they dropped farther down in their endeavor to start landslides. Perhaps, as they appeared to be failing in their struggle to barricade the road, they were now determined to launch a personal attack—to catch us as they had netted Joisan—using the earth as best they could, since that was *their* tool of power.

The mare's front hooves thudded into the first runnel of the black soil. She cried out as I had never heard one of her kind give voice before, gave á convulsive leap forward as if she had stepped into a mass of live coals. I heard a heavy sucking as her feet pulled free.

"Keep moving—fast!" I flung the order back at Joisan and drew my sword.

She did not need that command, for she was slappig the pony's rump with one hand, flogging the small beast on. The black flood was thick around the feet of both animals, seeming to circle about as if it was trying, like a bog, to suck us down. Then I saw that the globed gryphon was waxing brighter and brighter. From it came a beam of bright light. Around my own wrist the band awoke to life in a circle of cold flame.

Joisan lifted the chain from around her neck and began to swing the globe. As it passed thus through the air the light blazed even higher and brighter. I watched the sticky black tide on the road curl back from that radiance, as living flesh might shrink from a threat of pain or dissolution.

My companion kneed her pony on, and the animal quieted, as did the mare, once that blaze swept briefly across her head. Now my lady led, and the black earth not only melted from her path, but those masses of earth and stone that were still falling were deflected, providing us with a narrow path of safety.

I could hear our attackers. Where before they had moved in silence, scuttling through the dark which was their cover, now they uttered guttural cries from the heights on either hand. Their shadowy forms scrambled and shifted. I was sure they had sent parties down both walls to intercept us. Only they could not, dared not, venture on the road itself.

Our two mounts were sweating; the rank animal smell cut off some of the stench of the Thas. The beasts tossed their heads, but they kept steadily on until we reached the far side of the earth slides.

The scrambling along the cliffs intensified. I braced myself for an attack, which might well come if they were desperate enough at our escape. Joisan actually then tossed the globe in the air as if it were a ball. By the wide sweep of its light I saw clearly, for an instant, a creature that threw a stubby arm across its eyes, squealed, and fled, clinging to the wall as it climbed, after the

way of a lizard. Haired all over it was, and from the tangled
mass that covered the lump of its head, pale disks, marking eyes,
were turned in our direction before it gained the dark beyond the
light's reach.

Now safe beyond the bombardment of the avalanche, our
mounts broke into their fastest gait and we did not try to halt
their boneshaking run. Better to gain as much distance beyond
the present perches of the Thas as we could. I hoped that those
creatures could not keep up with us, though the form I had seen
had not suggested that its stunted body was meant for long-
distance running.

Straight as a sword blade, and now as bright as the moonlight
would lie on such a blade, the road lay open before us. We
needed that brightness, as the gleam of Joisan's ball torch waned
steadily, while the rise of the dark cliffs on either side increased
with every stride mare and pony covered. We might be riding at
the bottom of a deep gulf . . .

A deep gulf? I felt cold rise in me—the gulf of my dream!
Only here I was at the bottom, not riding through the sky—or the
space above. I turned my head up and back. Now I could see the
night sky—a sprinkling of pallid stars there, so far above . . . It
was as if I were caught, encased. I tried to breathe deeply, to fill
my lungs with air, which my body suddenly craved, as if I had
been indeed buried in the fluid earth that now lay behind.

I looked to Joisan, saw, to my alarm, that her body was
drooping. She gripped with both hands, not the rope hackmore
we had improvised for the pony, but the animal's mane.

"Joisan!"

I urged the mare closer. At my cry she raised her head a
fraction, turned a face that was hardly more than a white blur
toward me. Just in time I reached her side, caught and steadied
her body as she went limp, her eyes closed, ready to slide from
her perch on the pony's back.

"Joisan!"

I held her by an arm about her waist, though the pony snorted
as my mare nudged against it and strove to draw away. Somehow I managed to take my lady fully into my arms where she lay
unmoving, her head against my shoulder, face upward, her eyes
still closed.

"Joisan!" For the third time, and most urgently, I called her name.

The globe on her breast was dead, not even a small, wan light marked its power. Burned out? Had that valiant use of it to bring us safely through the Thas attack exhausted whatever energy could be summoned from it?

And Joisan—what had that drain of will done to her? I remembered her story of how she had willed the gryphon to lead her from the cavern underground and that its response had weakened her. Perhaps to use it again in such a short time had been too much for her. I raged at my own impotence. It had been Joisan alone who had brought us through this battle with the Dark—no credit to me. Now what could I do to bring her aid—or comfort . . .

"Joisan!"

At my fourth call I saw her eyelids flutter. She sighed, but neither looked at me nor spoke. I doubted that the mare could carry double for long. So I must push as far as I could, for it was plain that Joisan was in no condition to ride the pony now. To stay where these earth cliffs loomed above was folly. What the Thas had tried once they could easily assay again, and this time they might well be successful. We must win through this gorge— if it had any end—which, looking ahead, I began grimly to wonder.

I bound my lady to the mare's saddle—her lighter weight would be easier on the mount. The pony could not carry me, but I had those sturdy hooves—and I could put them to good use. The pavement was very smooth underfoot. I began to trot, discovering I could easily match my speed to that of the mare. The pony edged up beside me on the other side, for I kept close to Joisan, fearing that the lashings might slip and allow her to fall.

She was like one in a deep sleep, not moving except to the swing of the mare. I divided my attention between her and the heights on either side. Though I tried to listen for any sound above the clop of hooves from our two beasts, I heard nothing.

That stench was no longer in my nostrils. However, I knew that the earth itself obeyed the will of those hairy creatures and it might be they could still summon up some peril from it to strike at us. I dared not trust any surface beyond that of the road itself.

The rest of that night (it was not a dream, for my dreams had been more real than this—at least the dreams that had plagued me of late) finally passed. I moved as I had in the cold season when I had been on scout and caught in some storm wherein the misery of my body pulled at me until I might come to camp.

Pain shot up my stiffened legs as I footed on. After an interval I realized that the pace of the mare had fallen to a walk, that she breathed in great snorts, while the pony now plodded three or four lengths behind, its head drooping. Still it followed doggedly.

Dull-eyed, I looked about me. The heights had dropped somewhat. They no longer appeared to reach to the sky. I stood for a space, the mare blowing again. Fumbling at the saddle I brought out my water bottle, took a sip. which left me avid for more. Yet we had left our camp so quickly this was all we had and Joisan would need it, too.

She lay forward, stretched with one arm on either side of the mare's neck, her face half hidden in rough strands of mane. I made no effort to rouse her. Better that she sleep until we could reach some point of safety—if sleep she now did. I felt her dangling hand and it seemed warm to my touch—was she fevered? But I could not see to her yet, not as long as we remained within the least rise of those walls.

I urged the mare on, though she moved no faster than a walk, would stop now and then until I pulled at the reins, or slapped her rump. So intent was I on keeping her moving that I had not realized we had worn out the night until I saw the gray gleams of predawn lighting the mounds of earth on either side, the paling of the road.

It was a matter of the stumbler leading the stumbling when we came at last to the end of that cut, crossed a valley and—

The road came to an end!

I wavered on my feet staring up at the rockwall of what was a mountain, a mountain planted directly before our faces. Straight into that the road ran—and stopped as if the mountain had been raised from its stone roots somewhere else and dumped to cut off our path.

Somehow I got Joisan down. There was no going farther. We were enough in the open so that we could not be attacked here without seeing the enemy well in advance of any rush. I was done out, and both mounts exhausted. The valley had a trickling stream, which flowed not too far away and there was grass growing. I laid Joisan down, to be supported by the pack which I rolled from its straps, making her as comfortable as I could.

Her face was pale, she lay limp under my hands. If she still slept, the rest was very deep. Unsaddled, the mare sought water, to dip muzzle deep into the stream beside the pony. I dropped down beside Joisan, took her beringed hand in both of mine, my own head nodded, in spite of the need I knew to be on guard.

I was too tired now to think of what lay ahead—save that the rise of that mountain drew the heart out of me. That we should win up its stark sides with no supplies, no sustenance, in this grim land—no, that was beyond any power.

My head must have fallen forward . . .

Then . . .

The need—the burning need—which seized upon me filled me so it drove out all I had clung to—that part of Kerovan who was a man—the part that reached to Joisan and a life he understood. I was—another . . .

Joisan

I AWOKE IN THE LIGHT OF DAY, ROUSING OUT OF CONFUSED DREAMS
and fear. There had been a great darkness, and, veiled by it,
evil had moved. Even faint memories of that made me shudder.
The specter of the Lady Temphera might not have been potent,
but worse had faced us in our flight up the road. That the Dark
had not raised power enough to engulf us wholly puzzled me, for
I did not see in what manner we could have withstood such an
attack. I had once more used my will upon the globe and—

Now I raised my head to look about. I lay on the surface of
the road, half supported by a small pack. There was no lingering
stench of Thas here. Turning very slowly, for action was, I
discovered, a great effort to which I had to bend all my will and
energy, I saw that the heights of the cut no longer loomed over
us. We must have somehow won through though I had no
memory of the latter part of that flight. Before us now was the
wall of a true mountain, its crest so wreathed by mist or clouds
that one could not tell how high it reached into the sky.

The road ran straight into the first upward slope and then . . .
At that point it was as cleanly cut as if some Power had moved
the mountain here as an insurmountable barrier. There was only
rock—cracked, stained—bearing signs, I believed, of having
stood a heavy assault by some fierce force.

191

Directly before this stood Kerovan, his back to me, his arms hanging by his sides. His fingers continually wrapped into fists, only to loosen again. His body was taut, tense, as if he were half devoured by the need to gain what he wanted.

Somehow I got to my feet, took an unsteady step. My body was again as weak as if I had but crawled out of a bed wherein fever had sapped my strength. Yet, when I moved, there came a slow inflow of energy. Kerovan remained oblivious, as if only the mountain now mattered.

I staggered to where I could see his face. His features were grimly set in a mask of determination. Suddenly he drew his sword, took a quick step forward, and tried to force the tip of the blade into a crack that ran jaggedly down the stone.

When I looked more closely at the wall, in this full light, I could see that once there must have existed an opening there, which had been sealed by force, for the stone was fire darkened, and, in some places, looked as congealed as the lumps of metal scavengers brought out of the Waste. Though what could possibly melt *rock*?

He thrust fruitlessly at the crack, prying until his steel rang in warning and I half expected to see the blade break off short. With a gesture born of anger and frustration, Kerovan threw the sword from him, to clatter across the roadway, while he strode forward, to stand with his hands pressed palm flat on the rock, his head a little forward until his helm clashed against the mountain barrier.

I had half raised my hands. Then it caught at me. The gryphon—I clutched at it quickly—a protective talisman. Kerovan—could it be Kerovan who sent forth such waves of energy as left me trembling?

His shoulders tensed the stiffer. Outward spread that aura of power, now holding me where I was. I even believed that I saw a haze of light outline his body. My skin prickled and the short hairs about my forehead stirred of themselves. Between my hands the globe began to glow.

He was using his will—all the inner strength he could call upon, even as I had done. That backwash of force caught me, held me prisoner, immobile now, unable even to speak.

His body became slowly tenuous, as if solid flesh and bone thinned, was only a vessel holding something else. I found that sight so frightening I strove to close my eyes—yet I could do nothing else but watch that titanic battle; for battle it was—a man's strength pitted against ancient, unmovable stone.

Thinner grew Kerovan's form, he was only a shadow of a man now. My own fear made me draw once more on what lay within me. If Kerovan was to vanish, then I must still seek him—he must not leave me so! I had thought, upon awakening, that my strength of will was exhausted. I discovered now that there are reserves within us all that are not known to exist unless some great task must be faced.

The globe—I had only that. I lifted it in both hands, held it above the level of Kerovan's hunched shoulders. If he must, for some reason, win through this rock, then I would do what I could to aid.

This time it was not the globe that took on life and fire—but the gryphon itself! I saw its small figure move and that was not just my fancy. The globe shattered—fragments as thin as powder shifted through my fingers. A prisoner long confined was at last free! Not only free, but growing. For a moment its weight rested between my palms. Then those wings fanned the air . . .

The gryphon trumpeted, voicing such a note of triumph and exultation that my heart leaped in answer. Then the creature spiraled up, beating wings against the air so long denied it. For the space of a breath or two it circled about our heads, always growing—first as large as a mountain eagle, then so huge that the very shadow of its outstretching wings shut out the sun.

Those red eyes were aglow with fierce fire, its hooked beak opened, and once more it sounded its cry. Having tried its wings, it wheeled, to fly straight at the barrier against which Kerovan, seemingly unaware of it, still labored uselessly to force an entrance.

I caught my breath. The great flying thing (it might have topped Kerovan had it alighted on the road) did not swerve, rather hurtled like a bolt at the wall. And—just as Kerovan had earlier appeared to grow tenuous, so now did the wall become smoke. Into that winged the gryphon, vanishing from sight. Behind, Kerovan stumbled ahead, as well he might when the solid barrier against which he had leaned was suddenly withdrawn. Able to move once again I threw myself after him, fearing that the two of them might be lost to me.

There followed a fear-filled sensation of deep dark and cold, of being hurtled through a space in which my kind had no life. I could not breathe, yet I willed myself on.

Then I was in another place. Those are the only words I can find to describe it—another place. For I will always believe that I went out of the world meant to nourish my people, entering into one so different, so answerable to other laws and customs that I was or would be forever lost. For, in my folly, I had gone unprepared and alone.

No, I was *not* alone. I saw Kerovan rise from his knees. He must have sprawled on his face as the barrier gave way. Ahead, fast vanishing into a misty cloud, the gryphon beat wide-stretching wings.

Kerovan stood, his face dull and lifeless, showing, I believed, the countenance of some man caught in a sorcerous dream. I knew I could not reach him, that if I screamed aloud, even beat upon his body, he would not hear or feel. He glanced from side to side, and I sensed that what he saw was not altogether strange to him. Now he strode on, following the gryphon, at the fast pace of one obeying a summons. I would not be left behind so I broke into a short run to keep up with him.

From time to time (I was afraid to take my eyes long from Kerovan lest he vanish in some way peculiar to this otherwhere place) I glanced around. There was light, though it came from neither torch nor lamp. We traveled down a long aisle between huge pillars, so large I do not think that two men standing, holding their arms full length, could have touched fingers about that girth.

Those pillars were carved with lines of a long-forgotten tongue— if the language had ever been known in my own world (which I doubted). There was a cloud of mist hanging above us that drifted—as real clouds might—while ahead shone a core of stronger light, which I believed was Kerovan's goal.

He moved ever faster, until at last he ran. Gasping, I tried to keep up with him, but that fatigue with which I had awakened, the draining of the globe, slowed me. A sharp pain struck beneath my ribs, making me gasp and slow even more.

I was afraid. If Kerovan got beyond my sight I might lose him forever. Still there was no way I could break the spell that held him, of that I was sure.

On and on—that brighter light grew larger. I could see more details of the pillar carvings. Not that they meant anything, save that the message they must record was of greater import than I could know or guess. The Waste was a place of wonders, both of good and evil. Here, I knew, was a place of great Power—yet I could sense neither evil nor good. Was there a third way, neither of the Light nor Dark, that had laws of its own?

Then came a sound rising above the clatter of our boots, a crooning, a singing. From deep notes, which were akin to the rumble of drums, the song rose to the freedom of trumpets proclaiming victory—only to fall again.

The light flared brighter still. Had it risen so in answer to that song? I saw, in the heart of it, a dais from which a point projected in the direction from which we had come. On that platform rested a long case of some transparent substance. At the head of that the gryphon reared, its bird foreclaws resting upon the case, its beast hind paws firm set on the dais. The wings of silver white fanned the air gently, while from its beak issued that song.

Kerovan halted at the foot of the dais, stood swaying. One hand rose to his head as if he were so mazed he did not know where he was or what he did. The gryphon did not turn those glowing eyes on either of us. It held its own head high, still giving voice. I thought I heard a pleading note growing stronger in that song.

Slowly Kerovan stepped upon the dais, fell rather than leaned forward, so that both his outflung arms rested across the case as he knelt there, his head drooping between his arms. He remained as if he had come to the end of all striving, could make no further effort. The gryphon bent its crested head in turn, its cruelly pointed beak aimed—

I tried to cry out a warning, but there was a barrier in my throat, a sealing on my lips. Using my will as a lash upon my falling body, I staggered on toward Kerovan. If he could not defend himself against that rapacious beak, perhaps there was something I could do. Englobed, the gryphon had served me. Free . . .? I did not know—I could only hope.

Before I reached my lord's side I saw that it was not at his head or shoulders that beak was aimed. The winged creature now pecked determinedly at the covering of the box. As I came to lay

hands on my lord, attempting to draw him out of danger, I saw
what lay within and it froze me for a long moment.

Man? No! Monster? Again no. There was nothing evil about
that sleeper, strangely shaped though his body might be. Here
was the gryphon fused with what was partly man. But this
encoffined one was far greater than both in his own way—yes, I
knew that also.

I found myself on my knees. My hold on Kerovan's shoulders
tightened so I was able to draw him a little toward me, away
from where that great beak strove to break the surface of the
sleeper's coffin. Thus we were clinging together when there was
a crackle—lines of splintered transparency ran swiftly outward,
even as earlier the globe had broken in my hands.

My lord tried to rise, half fell back against me, so I steadied
him once more against my own body. Our eyes were not for
each other now, rather for what was happening to the case.
Those cracks grew wider. Fragments flew outward as the gryphon, seemingly heartened by its success, struck faster and deeper.

Then all the substance of that encoffining fell away, became
powdery dust. Once more the gryphon reared above the sleeper
and opened its beak. Only this time it did not sing, instead it
gave a shout, perhaps an alarm.

The eyes of the sleeper opened. They shone red, as fiery as
those of the bird-beast towering above. One hand was lifted from
its grasp on a sword still resting on the stranger's breast. The
beast bent its crested head and I saw the man's fingers move in a
caress, scratching among the feathers as one gentles a favorite
hound.

Now he, who had been so freed and awakened, looked around
at my lord. After a long moment his eyes met mine in turn.
There was awesome wisdom in those eyes, other emotions I did
not know nor could I name—which no one of human birth might
understand. I could not turn away, though I winced, for it
seemed that this other invaded my mind, learned more from that
single glance than any of my own kind could in a full lifetime.

Then he turned again to Kerovan as he drew himself up, the
sword loosely held in one hand, the other arms resting across the
gryphon's neck as the creature squatted closer, offering to lend
him its support. With that wicked-looking beak it was smoothing
its master's own feather-crested head.

There was no change in the blankness of Kerovan's expression, no sign of the fear and awe that were mingled in me. The gryphon-man leaned forward, laid the sword aside, set his hand, which was more like the taloned foot of a bird, under my lord's chin, raising his head, to peer more intently into those blind eyes.

Fear overcame awe in me. As I had earlier sought to protect Kerovan from the beak of the gryphon, so now did I fling out a hand to strike at that hold. Once more those fiery eyes swung on me. I sensed a feeling of surprise, a questioning—then again that mind invasion which I could not understand.

He reached back and picked up the sword with his other hand, to use it, as a Wisewoman uses her wand, drawing lazy smoke curls in the air. I was forced to my feet, pushed back. The gryphon uttered another sharp cry, bobbed its head in my direction. Its newly awakened master lowered the blade to point at my breast.

There came a weight, a force I could not withstand, urging me away from the dais, putting me against the nearest pillar. Then the sword point shifted, but I discovered that I could not move so much as a finger. The gryphon-man, having so disposed of me, gave Kerovan once more his full attention.

He stretched even as might a human awakening from a deep sleep. Though he wore no clothing his silver-white body was robed with power which flooded about him. I felt that I might easily become what Kerovan now appeared to be—a mindless servant.

Though I sensed no evil, I knew a growing anger that my lord had been so reduced to another's will—be that one of the great Old Ones or not. So I struggled within for my freedom—or if not, to project to Kerovan the knowledge that he was the equal of any—should he choose to be. My dear Lord Amber should not bow or serve . . .

The gryphon-man leaped lightly from the dais and approached me. If there was an expression on his alien face the strangeness of his features hid it from me.

There shot into my mind, burning enough that I might have cried out with the pain, speech—so strong that it was a shout in my head.

"Why do you fear for him so? Do blood-kin war?"

This was far more powerful mind-talk than the cats had used but having met with that I was ready.

"What have you done to him then? And who are you?" Old One or not, I would grant no courtesy as long as I saw Kerovan so.

"I do nothing with him, save lead him to his true heritage."

The gryphon roared—such a sound as I would not have believed could rip from that bird beak. It reared on its hind paws, presented its talons as it might for defense. The beast was facing away from us, staring down an aisle beyond.

Its master whirled about, leaped back and caught at the sword. He gestured. Kerovan moved toward me, still as one who walks in sleep. Then the Old One joined us as the gryphon took wing, flew in the direction it had been watching.

The gryphon-man's arm moved like a flash of light through the air. With the point of the sword he drew a circle around the three of us—for I had found I could move forward again, in fact I was urged so. The circle glowed, flaring up from it a radiance through which we could see, yet it sent streamers far above our heads.

From the direction the gryphon had taken there appeared a whirl of dark shadow—advancing jerkily, as if it found difficulty in its path. It puffed forward, retreated, and then puffed again. Though we could no longer see the beast, which had gone to confront it, we could hear its continued roars of challenge.

I clutched at Kerovan. Under my feet the floor shifted. Near the shadow the pavement buckled upward, to let a black stream spew outward. The gryphon-man set his sword between his knees; both of his hands moved in a series of signs. Around us the haze wall thickened and blazed at the same time. Kerovan's arms came about me, his face was alive again.

There followed the sensation of being lifted by a whirlwind. I dared not look down lest I see nothing below. We were sealed in by the light, and now the gryphon-man laid one taloned hand on Kerovan's shoulder, the other on mine.

That light touch brought warmth, drove out my fear. No matter, however, if this stranger so sought to comfort me, what counted most was that my lord held me in his arms.

The streams of light whirled enough to make me giddy. I closed my eyes, but the sensation of flying was not lost. I no longer heard the gryphon's roars. Had the creature been overwhelmed? I hoped passionately that was not so.

"Telpher is in no danger."

The stranger had reassured me then. Who *was* he? Then— we swooped downward with such speed that I held even more tightly to my lord, felt his grasp also stiffen.

Fresh air . . . I opened my eyes. We stood in sunlight. Here were flowers—a feeling we had returned to our own time and world. Again came a trumpet call as a winged body passed over us. The gryphon flew to perch above the wide arch of a gate.

Though we stood in the open there were still four walls boxing us about. Each was pierced by a wide arched gate, three of which showed hard usage from time by fallen stone, but the fourth, where the gryphon had landed, was intact. Flowers grew in drifts of soil that spread in from the ruined gateways. There was even a tree or two that had taken root here.

The gryphon-man stood a little apart from us now. Even in the full light of the sun there remained that glow clothing him. He turned slowly, facing each of those doorways in turn. I do not think he meant us to hear him, but perhaps his earlier invasions of our minds may have linked us, for I caught thoughts carrying overtones of grief.

"Matr, Yoer, Rllene! Has it then been so long, and you gone so far?"

To each door he made a small gesture of the head as one uses in bidding farewell to a companion-friend. It was only then that he turned his attention once more to the two of us.

"We have but little time. If Galkur dared to invade the hall, he will follow swiftly . . ." He once more studied Kerovan with the same searching intensity he had used before. This time my lord, now awake, looked as straightly back.

"Yes," the Old One continued. "I can well understand now what moves Galkur. Only his power appears somewhat lessened, perhaps by time. Now . . .!"

He flung up his head and, from his beaklike mouth, there sounded a roar not unlike that which the gryphon had uttered before it flew into the dark. The sound was oddly magnified; it filled, I thought, both heaven and earth. There was an answer.

A man who appeared as human as a Dalesman walked toward us under the arch where the gryphon crouched. His gray clothing was that of any wandering merchant. Only I knew him and spoke his name—with relief.

"Neevor!"

His answering smile was as kindly as that of my uncle when, as a small child, I had sought him out over some matter of unhappiness or doubt. A human smile, surely, and a warm one. From him flowed reassurance like a warm cloak placed about my shoulders in the chill of winter.

My naming of him came only moments before my lord did likewise. Kerovan took a step away from me. I believe that at that moment he reached for the same assurance that had comforted me.

"So—Neevor—your hand is in this matter also?" The gryphon lord thought-spoke.

"Was it not from the beginning, Landisl? I come now to take my part in the ending. When Galkur made mischief did not the dream of it enter *your* slumber? He thought then to shape a man-tool"—Neevor nodded toward Kerovan—"to his patterning and his purpose, taking advantage of a fool. But then, whose power essence interfered? Now what have you to say concerning the result of your dreaming, Landisl?"

The gryphon-man's beak-mouth opened on a sound that was not human laughter but carried the same note.

"Yes, it was I who spoiled Galkur's plot—even in my sleep. As to this one"—talons touched Kerovan's shoulder gently, then gripped tight—"I have yet to prove him. You know the Law, Neevor—the future depends upon—"

Neevor interrupted him. "Just now it may depend upon Galkur. And you stand alone of the Sky-Ones. It took four of you to defeat him once."

Landisl's eyes glittered like sun-touched rubies. "Some powers wax with time, some wane. I believe that Galkur has lost somewhat. Or surely he would not have played games with the aid of a self-taught fool of a sorceress to foster a plot so easily overturned. What are his new plans, Neevor? It was your choice to spend years wandering, what have you learned during that restless travel to and fro?"

"Never to underestimate such as Galkur. His game has new elements, Landisl. There is a race of flawed and evil men overseas who entered this world through one of the gates. They

are of the Dark, doubly so, though their learning is of another
kind that does not answer to our Law. Therefore it is twice
dangerous. They are embattled now and they need a new force
for aid.

"Through their own ways of detection—and some reaching
out on Galkur's part—they have learned of Arvon and what may
be tapped here. Though their conception of Power is distorted,
and they do not understand our usage, they come seeking. They
sent war into the Dales, endeavoring so to clear a path to us.
And they are of a kind who can always provide a rallying point
for many who have nourished the Dark here.

"Galkur ponders now on giving them more aid. So many of
our Great Ones have gone, seeking gates of their own—new
worlds beyond. Of those who remain, very few are full adepts—
only a handful as learned as Galkur. So . . ."

"So you use your spells to send these two to awaken me?"

"Send, no. It is by your doing that even one stands here, that
you have already acknowledged." He nodded toward Kerovan.
"It is by their own will and courage that they have won here."
There was a sharpness in that. "Those qualities they have in
plenty. Kerovan's birthright none may take from him. Daughter"
—now he looked directly at me, once more smiled with such
sweet gentleness that I longed to throw myself into his arms—"I
told you once that you had a Key—to be used in the right time
and place. You have done well with it. Now it remains for us to
do as well with what will follow."

Above the arch the gryphon roared.

Neevor half turned to look behind him through the gate.

"It seems that our time for doing so is now," he observed.

Kerovan

ONCE I HAD PACED A CERTAIN HALL IN A DREAM, THEN I DID IT waking—or was all a dream? What is illusion and what is truth when the Old Ones choose to weave patterns beyond the understanding of men? Was I more than one of strange blood? What part weighs in me the strongest?

This time I watched the sleeper wake; then came the first trial of strength between old, long-opposed Powers. Now we stood again in the world that the human half of me knew and welcomed. Struggle lay before us, though four was now five—a small army indeed. This would be such a battle as once before I had known when, to save my dear lady, I went up against the Dark.

There was a reason, going back to my birth—or before that even—which bound me to this course, and, through it, bound Joisan. Perhaps I was even first fashioned to play a part here—but that was not so for my lady.

Had I been able at that moment I would have caught her up, hurled her from us into safety. As I gazed at her that part of the inner self, which I had kept under such tight restraint and tried to banish, awakened as had the sleeper. I knew then, for all my fears, I could never set her apart. We were indeed bound together for good or ill.

Not because we had once been used by our elders to insure an alliance of the Dales. There was something far stronger to unite us. Her eyes met mine with level courage. The spirit that burned in her fought that cold within me, warming my best part back to life. I lost the icy touch forever.

My sword sheath hung empty. I had no bow, not even a knife. Also I believed that what we awaited could not be harmed by any weapon forged by men. Neevor carried only a staff of rough wood such as might be cut from any sapling, bits of bark still clinging to it. The sleeper—he held a sword, yes, but in some way I dimly understood it was not made for thrust or parry, cut and slash, in crude open warfare. The gryphon on the gate perch moved a fraction, its beak a little open so its serpent tongue lolled out, its wings slowly fanned the air.

I do not know why or how at that moment my hand sought my belt pouch—my left hand. Fingers fumbled with the clasp and then groped within. What I drew forth was that bit of blue metal I had found in the noisome nest of the Waste.

It was a broken piece of metal, about which my fingers now curled tight—surely of no use in any battle. But, weaponless as I was, I stood shoulder to shoulder with Joisan. I saw her fingers go to her breast, fall away empty, as she remembered the globe was now gone.

A tongue of thick dark such as we had seen in the aisle of the sleeper's hall burst from out the ground just beyond the gate. The very earth might be vomiting forth evil it could not stomach. This was an offense against the light of day, the air, the place where we stood.

Once more the gryphon roared a challenge. This time, however, it did not fly forth to meet what came. I looked to Neevor, to Landisl. Neither showed any surprise, certainly no hint of dismay. Still I sensed in them a wariness, in spite of their outward appearance of ease.

Joisan's hand sought mine. She closed her fingers slowly as if she half expected I would shake off her touch. The warmth of her flesh against mine was what I needed most—again she was giving fully, openly, all I lacked.

Echoes of the gryphon's roar died slowly. Beyond the gate the black mass whirled, grew smaller, thicker, more solid. In an eye's blink there was no dark—only a man. Or . . . could one name him *man?*

He was tall and, like Landisl, bare of body. To the waist he was well proportioned, fully human-seeming. His head was crested with a thick growth of curling dark hair and his face sternly handsome. Those features might have formed the countenance of some ancient hero-king.

Only—that half-heroic body with its noble head, was belied by what lay below. From the waist down he was clothed by a wiry pelt much coarser than any hair or fur, and his thick legs ended in—

I glanced quickly away. Hooves! Hyron had suggested that I seek kin. Was this one of my own blood—the other half of me?

The mixture of noble and worse than bestial which he presented raised in me such a feeling of loathing as made me want to kill him. Or else run to hide myself from the eyes of those among whom I stood because I carried that same stamp upon my own body. There awoke in me once more that cold loneliness with which I had lived for so long. I shared blood with . . . Perhaps this beast-man could even claim my kin allegiance.

"No!"

It was not I who cried that denial aloud, nor had it come from either Neevor or Landisl. Joisan! She did not eye that monster, coming ever nearer the gryphon-shrouded gate, her eyes were for me, demandingly, even as her hold on me tightened.

"No—you are no part of him!" I saw her lips shape the words, but I heard them in my mind. That thought-send was rich, filled with what was needed to soothe the bleakness about my heart.

"A new day; another meeting . . ." Galkur (if this was Galkur) broke through that short moment of oneness with my lady. His voice was also deep, rich, and was meant, I thought, to be beguiling. He spoke aloud, not using the mind-speech.

Neither Neevor nor Landisl replied. The half-man smiled. This was a smile which, if one did not look below the face, might have charmed even a prudent doubter.

Did I stir then, or had he already considered that there might be some cord between us which he could draw upon?

"You stand in strange company, my son." He used the last two words with deliberation, emphasizing them.

His stamp was on my body, perhaps had always been my bane. I carried a taint of the Dark—was such truth coming to light at long last? My self-doubts returned in hard array.

Neevor raised his staff. The rod of wood made a barrier before me. I strove to shake free of Joisan's hold. This *was* the truth! I was kin-bound to the Dark. Could they not see it? My mother's ambition, the will of this Dark Lord, had made me tainted stock. If I remained with them I would bring down in defeat those about me. As an unwilling enemy in their midst, I would be a key by which he could enter their stronghold.

"Only if you believe—accept—the lie. The choice lies with you, Kerovan."

Joisan! She would not release my hand, holding it and me prisoner as she cupped it against her breast, even as I had so many times seen her cup the gryphon.

"Keep your lady, if you so desire, my son." Again that warm enticing smile. "Who wishes to part devoted lovers?"

Mockery in that. My other hand clenched. But, may all Powers forgive me, a part of me answered to him. What did I want with this girl out of the Dales, I, who could summon, could have, any female I wished?

Pictures trailed languishingly through my mind, clear, detailed. I was reduced to a slavering dog trailing a bitch in heat. This was foul, and I was invited to wallow in the filth. Joisan was no part of me.

I tore my hand free with strength enough to send her staggering backward. Inwardly I faced that seeping foulness, which spread until I longed to sear the flesh from my bones to rid myself of such stinking evil.

"Come." He beckoned to me. The sorcery he put into that single word set my whole body trembling. Where else could such as I go? It was only fit that kin should go to kin . . .

I bit my lower lip, feeling no pain, though my own blood dribbled down my chin, clenched both fists. I was a part of this monster, so I must withdraw from those who were clean in body and mind.

"Kerovan!"

I shook my head—I must withdraw from her most of all. I was of the Dark—evil and foul. These others had tried to save me—or they had deceived and used me for some purpose of their own. They could keep me no longer.

Joisan had fallen to her knees, I stooped and tore from her belt the knife I had given her. Good clean steel, very sharp, ready for what I must do. I could not attack that thing waiting out there—calling me so. But I could do the next best thing—remove his key, make sure I could not be a traitor!

My hand moved with the practiced ease I had learned long ago as a boy sweating under the tutelage of a master fighting man. The sharp edge neared my throat. Fire blazed, burned at the wrist of my knife hand—thrust up into my eyes. My arm fell as if dragged back by a great weight. Fire burned in my other hand—the pain reaching deep into me. Only there it found nothing to feed upon—to slay . . .

I looked down dazedly at my hands. The blade lay on the pavement at my feet, but the fire still ran about my wrist, shown between the fingers that grasped that metal fragment from the nest.

"Kerovan!" Joisan once more flung herself at me, catching that weighted arm as if she feared I might again raise it. There followed swift on her cry a thought.

"Only those of the Light can hold or wear quan-iron, boy. Trust yourself first."

Landisl? Yes! I was not, I could never be kin to Galkur. I thought his name with the same savagery that I would have shouted a battle slogan. I was drained, weak, but afire now with anger. My fate lay in my own two hands. I had just had material proof of that. Had any here the right to decide for me what my future would be? I had walked, ridden, slept and awakened again, for so long seeking the truth. Now I knew it.

Save that this was not the matter of my own awakening; it was a matter of the age-old confrontation of Light with Dark—in which I bore only a part, perhaps a small part. I stared at that beast-man. Though he still smiled, the deep warmth had vanished—in its place was a sly contempt.

Anger burned higher in me. I had no Power as these reckoned it. My anger was of human kind. Perhaps the Old Ones could play upon the inner core of a man, shaping him for their use. But there comes a time when even a slave may break for freedom.

Though I wore the mark of the Dark One—he did not possess me. Nor was I of the Light. I was myself.

Will—will is the core of some kinds of Power. I had wrought with my will before. Slowly I fought that weakness in me, raised my left hand. Remember, I told myself fiercely, what Landisl reminded you of—the wristlet, the broken piece of metal. They were of the Light, as you always guessed. You are Kerovan. It does not matter whose seed, whose sorcery, brought your life, in whose womb you grew—you are you alone. What you make of life lies within you.

Silence held us. Joisan stood with her arms crossed on her breast watching me now, as if what she saw was not one she knew, but neither was he a monster. I was me. I was not to be pushed, used, possessed. *I* was free to make such choices as I deemed best, and from this moment I had no past, nor kin, only myself—and Joisan! Always Joisan!

We were allied, I had chosen to be allied—Neevor, Landisl, the gryphon, Joisan, and I.

"Galkur . . ." I found satisfaction in naming the enemy. Meager as any strength of mine might be, I needed that fraction of support that his naming might bring; thus I called his name aloud.

There was no smile on his face now. The shadow of nobility that had masked it vanished. These were the features of one of the Dark Ones swollen with awful pride.

"Son . . ." he returned. His voice was still honeyed, but he leered crookedly.

"No son of yours!" I returned, welcoming the heat of metal about my wrist, balanced by that piece near-piercing my other palm.

"You bear my seal." He gestured to my hooves.

"A man may have yellow hair and still not be Sulcar." I did not know from whence came that ease of speech.

"My son—come to me!"

He snapped that as an order. A stir toward him answered in me, faint now, was still in me. I clenched my left hand tighter about the fire I held. I was Kerovan!

His hand came up to draw symbols in the air. I watched them form like smears of greasy oil dribbled across cleanliness, fouling the sunlight.

Again the tug within me—stronger. I planted my hooves, stood straight. I was Kerovan.

"I am no running hound for you, Galkur." I did not raise my voice, rather used it as if I spoke of unimportant things. "You needed a servant, you strove to fashion one. But you have neither son nor servant."

His face grew hard, cold, with very little of the human remaining in it.

"Hound you are, slave you are, mine you are."

I heard then a harsh crow, not human laughter, but carrying with it the ghost of that.

"Galkur, when will you admit that your sorcery failed? Surely you must have known that from its very inception. You did not used to be a fool."

The cold mask tore; underneath was seething hate.

"What matter is this of yours?" he spat at Landisl. "There are Laws—"

"Laws? Do *you* take refuge in such now? Did you believe you would weave with Power and I would not know it, even though I lay in the Long Rest, and you thought me safely caged so? You sought out the Lord of Ulmsdale even as his lady desired—you strove to fill him with your inner force—then . . . Tell me now, Galkur, what did happen. What really happened?"

The Dark One turned his head from side to side, his face was that of a demon out of a night's worst dream.

"Look at his body! He bears my mark upon him for all men to see. You cannot deny that. I shall yet prove him mine!"

His eyes caught my gaze—held. They grew larger, were pits of fire, dark depths preparing to swallow me. All else vanished, narrowed to those waiting pits. I would be swallowed . . .

I was Kerovan! I was myself. That fire, the dark, the stench was not mine. Belief in myself was my shield. I was no Dark One's spawn.

"Do you still claim him, Galkur?"

Beyond the fire pits the voice rang clear.

"Do I, or Neevor, lend him aid now to stand against you? He fights his own battle because he is what he himself has made—and that is not one of your line. Indeed his birth came not from your desires—nor from his mother's wish—though that set upon his body your mark because she wanted a claim upon you. But in the very moment of his birth *she* knew she had failed! My doing, Galkur—mine!''

"You could not—'' The fire pits shrank, flames no longer sought to lick me down. They were only eyes in a beastly face. "You could not—under the Law—''

"That Law you broke, Galkur, when you so meddled. And, in the breaking released me. He is Uric's true son—in part—a fraction of his mother's . . . but there is something more. In time he shall choose, if he will, another path. Do not seek to hide behind the Law now. Face us all!''

Energy poured out of me, fusing with other sources of Power— that from Landisl, from Neevor, whose staff once more rested point down—yes, and from Joisan. The gryphon voiced its roar. Joisan's face grew pale and strained. I wanted to hold her close—but this was a time when all our strength must be turned elsewhere.

Forms congealed in the air behind Galkur, ready to feed into him energy in the same way we combined our own forces. There were horrors among them from which any sane man must avert his gaze, others which might have passed for Dalesmen and women. I half expected to see Temphera among them.

The drain of energy became stronger. Above my head a snake of flame lashed, would have sunk its fangs into my eyes. I was Kerovan—these were illusions of the enemy. He had failed to entice me—he would fail again. Neevor's staff cracked, broke into two pieces. The jagged end of one flew into his face. It was met by a band of blue flame. I had flung out my wrist without thinking, instinct had willed that.

Joisan swung halfway around, fell to her knees, her arms flung up above her head to ward off invisible blows. I saw blood start out on her cheek.

Rage, as fiery as those eyes had been, filled me. I turned my wrist; a blue beam shot toward Galkur. One of his misshapen followers darted between, exploded, leaving behind only a stench.

At last the gryphon took wing, planed down from its arch perch to stand over Joisan's body where she had sunk, face down, on the pavement. It covered her, its beak open in an enraged hiss. The broken ends of Neevor's staff took on life, rising, darting through the gate at the Dark forces. They did not

touch the Dark Lord, but they struck like well-aimed spears at
the figures capering about him.

I moved forward, step by step, no longer trying to bring down
Galkur himself, but aiming the ray at his band. Each one of
those taken out of this struggle would drain him of strength.

The Dark Lord caught up one of his own monstrous servants,
rolled the creature into a ball that he hurled at me. Then behind
that attack, he himself leaped forward.

There was another beside me as I swept that balled thing out
of existence. Landisl, his sword high, stood between me and the
hoofed one.

Galkur skidded to a quick stop. His body began to swell. I
saw some of his followers fade as he absorbed their substance.
The bristly hair on his lower body fluffed, its ends giving off
yellowish light.

Landisl's silver body shone as bright as the sword he now held
with both hands. Waves of force burst from its sky-pointing tip,
rippled down the length of the blade to encircle his body. He
became a pillar of light.

The Dark Lord changed, also. Black flame burst from him,
swirled and thickened again into something giant high, which
reached out a huge appendage to slap at the burning torch
Landisl had become—slap and flinch, without landing a blow.

For a long moment it seemed that both were so equally
matched neither could move. The point of the white light fell
forward as if it were a swift sword. It touched the swelling Dark.
A black stain from that spread up the light, dimming the glory of
the white. I staggered as the pull upon my energy grew heavier.
Through a mist of weakness I saw Neevor hunch far over, his
face as gray as his clothing, his eyes closed. The gryphon and
Joisan were now behind me; I *felt* their united energy pass me on
its way to Landisl.

That stain spread no farther, the white held. Then there came a
great upward flare of light, blinding me. Almost too late I flung
my arm over my eyes. I fell to my knees, sprawled forward—
there was no strength left in me.

Joisan

I THOUGHT THAT NEVER AGAIN WOULD I SEE SUCH STRIFE AS THAT IN which my lord had faced his own kin in the Waste on that other day of torment. But that was only a skirmish with outlaws on a border raid compared to the battle with the Dark Lord Galkur.

Though I did not even see the end clearly, my whole life force near drawn out of me, I knew when it came for I had roused a little into a warmth. The gryphon crouched between me and all evil, curving its claws about my shoulders, holding me to its breast, even as it had once rested against mine. I knew then such a feeling of peace and safety, in spite of my weakness, that I think I whimpered a little, as might a child begging for comfort, finding it at long last.

I saw only a great upward surge of light and then it struck down upon the foul darkness that threatened us. The black thinned, drew in upon itself. Once more that white blade lifted—now it was like a great pointing finger. Down it jabbed in turn.

A sound rent the air. It tore through my body, not my ears—that scream of defeat, of death and defiance still, mingled altogether. I slid then into shadows which welcomed me but were not of any evil sending.

"Joisan!"

There was no longer the softness of the gryphon's silvery

mane against my cheek, rather the hardness of mail. I opened my eyes and saw what I had longed for. Perhaps all my life I had desired this without realizing what my full lack had been until it was at last mine.

My dear lord—not looking down at me with his face closed, his lips straight, his eyes hooded, so disciplined by his will that he could chill my heart. Rather this was my lord as I had always dreamed he could and would be some day.

I raised my hand, though that was difficult, for my own flesh was like a heavy weight. Still I persevered until I could draw fingertips down his cheek, make sure by touch that this was he indeed, no illusion born out of my lonely longing. On my finger the gem from the past pulsed and grew redder as if it held heart's blood full within it.

It was a lover's ring, I knew, and now it was a lamp leading me into another heart, wide open, ready to receive me.

"Kerovan . . ."

He had called my name loudly to summon me back to life. But I said his softly because it was so dear to me.

"It is done," he told me.

What was done—the battle? That no longer mattered. It lay in the past and the past no longer held us. It was what lay ahead that I yearned toward.

"So . . ."

Beyond Kerovan's shoulder I saw Neevor, the gray man. His face was thin, older. When he spoke my lord looked up and around. For a moment I was afraid again, for a shadow of his old stern self—the one I had fought against for so long—crossed his face.

"It is done!" He said that to Neevor defiantly.

"The gryphon-man?" I tried to raise myself higher to look about. "My gryphon . . .?"

It was Neevor who answered, while my lord's arms were so tightly about me that his mail bruised one. But I cherished that small pain because of its cause.

"They have completed their pattern," Neevor answered me.

I did not miss Landisl—he was so alien a being that he awoke in me only awe and some fear. But my hand strayed to my breast where the gryphon had once hung, and I remembered how it had come to shelter me during the last of that battle. I felt an emptiness of sadness and loss.

"Kerovan." Neevor again addressed my lord with a sharpness I had not heard from him before. "Remember this, their plotting went awry. Though he tried to make you, Galkur had no part of it."

My lord smiled oddly. There was a ruefulness in his expression, yet such peace as I had never seen in his face before.

"No hand in my making, only in my marring, is that what you wish to impress on me, Lord? Well enough. And Landisl—what was he?"

The age I had seen in Neevor appeared to be fading.

"*He* had a part in you—so that in time you may—"

"No!" my lord interrupted, shaking his head. "No, Neevor. I will follow no road to the holding of Power—that one you would like for me to choose. I may have some small right to claim such, but I want not to be the master of any force. I am myself, Kerovan. I want nothing to make me more—or less."

"You agree, in truth." Neevor had been watching us both closely. He made a small gesture with his hand as if he tossed something to the wind, to be borne away. "This is then your free choice? There may never be another time to choose otherwise, you understand." The gray-clad man did not draw back, still suddenly there seemed to be a growing distance between us.

"My choice is to be Kerovan, lord of nothing, *man* of no great talent," but my lord spoke more to me than to Neevor, as if it were very necessary that I understand. "I am only myself."

"Which is the one important thing," I found words easily. "You are my dear lord, what else you desire shall come through your own efforts always. I think you are to fashion a fine new fortune for us both."

Neevor laughed.

"Well done, children. Enter into the world of your choice. I foretell you shall find it in no way lacking, and perhaps you shall encounter a surprise or two along the way."

Then, as one can puff out a candle flame, he was gone. I settled back into my lord's arms with a sigh of content.

"Our world." I caught his head and drew him down until our lips met with a warmth which became pure flame—to light us both—forever.

About the Author

Andre Norton is an outstanding science fiction/fantasy writer who is best known for the strange, memorable, wholly believable worlds she creates.

She has received the coveted Gandalf and Balrog Awards, and her works have been translated throughout the world.

She lives in Florida.

From DEL REY, the brightest science-fiction stars in the galaxy...

Dear Reader,

Your opinions are very important to us so please take a few moments to tell us your thoughts. It will help us give you more enjoyable DEL REY Books in the future.

1. Where did you obtain this book?

Bookstore	☐1	Department Store	☐4	Airport	☐7	5
Supermarket	☐2	Drug Store	☐5	From A Friend	☐8	
Variety/Discount Store	☐3	Newsstand	☐6	Other_____		

(Write In)

2. On an overall basis, how would you rate this book?

Excellent ☐1   Very Good ☐2   Good ☐3   Fair ☐4   Poor ☐5   6

3. What is the main reason that you purchased this book?

Author	☐1	It Was Recommended To Me ☐3	7
Like The Cover	☐2	Other_____	

(Write In)

4. In the same subject category as this book, who are your *two* favorite authors?

_____ 8
_____ 9
_____ 10
_____ 11

5. Which of the following categories of paperback books have you purchased in the past 3 months?

Adventure/		Biography	☐4	Horror/		Science	
Suspense	☐12-1	Classics	☐5	Terror	☐8	Fiction	☐x
Bestselling		Fantasy	☐6	Mystery	☐9	Self-Help	☐y
Fiction	☐2	Historical		Romance	☐0	War	☐13
Bestselling		Romance	☐7			Westerns	☐2
Non-Fiction	☐3						

6. What magazines do you subscribe to, or read regularly, that is, 3 out of every 4 issues?

_____ 14
_____ 15
_____ 16
_____ 17

7. Are you: Male ☐1   Female ☐2   18

8. Please indicate your age group.

Under 18	☐1	25-34	☐3	50 or older	☐5	19
18-24	☐2	35-49	☐4			

9. What is the highest level of education that you have completed?

Post Graduate Degree	☐1	College Graduate	☐3	Some High	20
Some Post Graduate		1-3 Years College	☐4	School	
Schooling	☐2	High School		or Less	☐6
		Graduate	☐5		

(Optional)

If you would like to learn about future publications and participate in future surveys, please fill in your name and address.

NAME_____

ADDRESS_____

CITY _____ STATE_____ ZIP_____ 21

Please mail to: Ballantine Books
DEL REY Research, Dept.
516 Fifth Avenue – Suite 606
New York, N.Y. 10036

F-4